PASSING

Amanda MacAndrew was born in 1947 and now lives in Buckinghamshire on her farm. She has three children and her husband is a photographer.

... ...

PASSING PLACES

Amanda MacAndrew

ARROW

First published 1994

1 3 5 7 9 10 8 6 4 2

The right of Amanda MacAndrew to be identified as the
author of this work has been asserted by her in accordance
with the Copyright, Designs and Patents Act 1988

This book is sold subject to the condition that it shall not,
by way of trade or otherwise, be lent, resold, hired out, or
otherwise circulated without the publisher's prior consent in
any form of binding or cover other than that in which it is
published and without a similar condition including this
condition being imposed on the subsequent purchaser

First published by Arrow in 1994
Random House UK Limited, 20 Vauxhall Bridge Road, London
SW1V 2SA

Random House Australia (Pty) Limited
20 Alfred Street, Milsons Point, Sydney, New South Wales 2061,
Australia

Random House New Zealand Limited
18 Poland Road, Glenfield
Auckland 10, New Zealand

Random House South Africa (Pty) Limited
PO Box 337, Bergvlei, South Africa

Random House UK Limited Reg. No. 954009

ISBN 0 09 938001 3

Typeset by Deltatype Ltd, Ellesmere Port, Cheshire
Printed in Great Britain by Cox & Wyman Ltd, Reading, Berkshire

For Hilary Johnson,
with thanks

1

Edinburgh, December 1962

'You will be a leader when you grow up.' Her mother had said this to the ten-year-old Andrea. Her father had told her that she would be a great beauty, and that was all that mattered.

Andrea remembered and believed these prophecies till circumstances forced her to admit that something of her charmed future was awry.

Sometime, probably about two years later, things had begun to founder. Maybe it was the tumultuous hormones or perhaps it was just the realization that parents were not God. Anyway, Andrea became ugly and where she led no one cared to follow. Parents would like to be God, but it is not in their gift. If the Infant Samuel receives a message from On High, all is well and it comes about that he is great. There is no argument. God, however, does not suffer from ambition. It would be contrary to His nature. Andrea's parents had hopes; they demanded rewards.

Spots sprouted, as did the bosom. The former were large and abundant, the latter was not. Her shape became thicker at the bottom like an old pane of glass. Her thighs, knees, calves and ankles terminated in large round feet without graceful undulations on the way.

At rising fifteen, Andrea was invited – or rather her mother had contrived that she be invited – to go to a party. Although she harboured suspicions, Andrea had not fully realized the extent of her deterioration. She was no longer a beautiful child. Her fair hair had darkened and become greasy, and her nose shone. But her short-sighted eyes behind the glasses were still a mystifying green and perhaps the teeth concealed by the brace may have been pearly white and would, one day, be straight.

In those days, frocks were worn to parties. Andrea's was pink and did its best. She wore satin shoes with heels and felt

1

tremendously grown-up, and beneath her stockings she had removed the hair from her sturdy legs with a sandpaper glove. She had done the same to her forearms, which was a grave error, for though they were smooth and pink like raw sausage links at first, they would soon become bristled with pricking hairs of a greater strength than before. Her hair had been set and her mother pounced on her face with a concealing stick called Erace. This meant that instead of being red, the spots were now beige, but not the same beige as her natural colour. This was a shame, but it was dim December and artificial light might be kind. Her father had a whisky or two. 'You look beautiful,' he said. Andrea believed him.

The dance was in aid of deprived and handicapped babies. Before the actual dancing in the Assembly Rooms, the MacInlays gave a dinner party.

The MacInlays lived in Edinburgh's New Town in conspicuous splendour and central heating. Andrea's parents, James and Ishbel Innes, were higher up Edinburgh's social scale because James was in the law, a Writer to the Signet, but their house, overlooking the playing fields of Donaldson's Hospital, was chilly and austere despite the immaculate and discreet taste with which it was furnished. The MacInlays were in soft drinks and showed no shame when it came to an exuberant display of wealth, and gave extravagant little parties, despite the snide asides from those who sneered at the vulgarity but accepted their hospitality. The MacInlays were fizzy and lurid like their famous product, Macpop, and clearly enjoyed their wealth. 'They get up my nose!' Ishbel Innes confided to her husband more than once, because she was gratified by her witticism. Ostentation was a social catastrophe whereas draughts and discomfort were the hallmarks of good breeding and commendable stoicism.

Kirsty MacInlay was at school with Andrea and had much of everything, including an older brother. Kirsty also had knowledge, shapely legs, no acne, and received Valentine cards from outside her family. Andrea admired Kirsty and had not yet learnt to be jealous.

'Come ye in. Come ye in!' Hector MacInlay was loud in mouth, complexion and dress, and wore the kilt, much embellished with jabot, sporran and silver-buttoned jacket. Moira, his wife, was wearing something shiny and expensive that had not been got 'off the peg' at Jenners but had come from the boutique at Gleneagles.

James Innes suppressed a shudder and was pleased to be able to abandon Andrea and return to the restraint of his own home in his sober Rover. Andrea would be run home in the Jag at the end of the evening, or the 'wee small hours' as Mr MacInlay put it, while placing a hot hand on her back and shoving her in to the room where Mrs MacInlay was topping up her drink. No one else of Andrea's age had arrived. Punctuality was the politeness of kings, and the Innes family.

Fingering a mysterious glass of something called 'cup' that smelt slightly of mince pies and tasted of nothing recognizable despite the profusion of fruity bits floating in it, Andrea was interrogated.

Yes, she liked school. Yes, her parents were well. Yes, her little brother was too. No, she wasn't sure what she wanted to do when she grew up. Was she clever? No, not really. Did she enjoy the summer holidays? Yes.

Truthfulness can be tedious and Andrea was a slave to absolute truth tempered with politeness. She had not got the imagination to entertain her hosts with lurid gossip, intriguing symptoms and the ungrateful revelation that she found North Berwick very dull in August. However, the speed with which Moira MacInlay was downing the martinis probably eclipsed all other forms of concentration and Andrea could have blethered on about her ambition to become an embalmer, her brother's kleptomania and Ishbel's mid-life pregnancy without causing one of the expertly plucked eyebrows to be raised.

The Blair brothers arrived. They had been to dancing classes with Andrea about ten years previously and since then had grown a lot. They were at school in England and did not wear kilts or drink cup but requested, and got, gins and tonics. They drawled and had plenty of conversation. Moira adored them.

The hateful cup was difficult to drink, the fruit got in the way and Andrea was not sure whether one gulped and hoped, or filtered the stuff through the teeth. Her brace was no help at all, and when Moira tried to include her in the badinage between herself and the Blair brothers a beastly slice got stuck in her gullet and she exploded all over the stiff and shiny number, splattering Moira's bust with sticky drink.

'Dear me! Dear me!' She was thumped on the back by Hector's gammon steak of a hand, while Moira mopped her rigid bosom and the Blairs sneered. Moira said something most ungracious about the obnoxious qualities of the cup's base, which was Macpop, the very substance that had enabled her to spend so lavishly.

Kirsty had appeared successfully dressed in royal blue with matching shoes. 'Hello, Clootie. You sick already?' She smiled condescendingly at Andrea and kissed both Blairs with total self-assurance.

'Why Clootie?' Hector asked, pouring another calming martini.

'I don't know,' Andrea replied, scarlet beneath the Erace, which made her spots even more conspicuous. She feigned interest in a framed escutcheon backed with the MacInlays' tartan, which hung above the Royal Copenhagen goose girls on the mantelpiece.

'Like clootie dumpling, of course,' said Kirsty. 'In other words, spotted dick.' The Blairs sniggered.

'Now, Kirsty, that is not kind,' her mother whispered for all to hear.

Fiona and Marion Brown, similar but not identical twins of fifteen, the robust, plain sisters of a delicately beautiful brother called Angus who was rising seventeen, and their embarrassed older cousin called Malcolm, who had surprised everyone by kissing Moira's hand, completed the party. Moira shrieked with delight at the continental gesture, but that was the conclusion of Malcolm's gallantry. (He had done it for a bet with Angus and stood to gain the almighty sum of ten shillings.)

The dining room was sort of sumptuous, and the large round table was laid with much Venetian glass. Electric coals glowed and flickered from a wrought-iron basket in the fireplace. The table centre was dominated by a healthy silver nymph poised on a pitcher, a trophy that Hector MacInlay's firm had been awarded by a temperance organization for services to sobriety. Andrea was seated next to a Blair and the Brown brother, known as Wee Angus. Even Fiona and Marion, who were gauche and clumsy, managed to look as if they were having a good time, seemingly unperturbed by the silence round the table, as they shovelled grilled grapefruit, chicken with rice and trifle into their eager mouths. Andrea hated the food and was horribly aware of Mrs MacInlay's splattered dress. The eldest Blair addressed all his conversation to his left where Kirsty sat between him and Blair the younger. Andrea never did learn their names, though they referred to her all evening as Clootie. Wee Angus didn't speak at all so no one knew whether his voice was yet to break even though this was not his first visit to Kirsty's house. She often invited boys to impromptu parties, though she had found Angus to be a dead loss as he was apt to slope off quietly, presumably with a good book.

Hector MacInlay kept up a hearty monologue while his wife picked at her food and swallowed a lot of pink wine.

Andrea felt sick and found the wine, which she had never tasted before, to be surprisingly sour despite its strawberry colour and pretty bottle. The sauce on the chicken had settled and a film had formed on its surface, but it was not as horrifying as the thick skin of the trifle's custard. Andrea and her brother, Neil, were allowed to leave custard at home if it had become 'Kirkcaldied' (a private joke concerning linoleum). Surely at a dinner party you could do what you liked. After all, her mother had told her to enjoy herself and that she had not yet done. So she left the quivering mass all sprinkled with hundreds and thousands on her plate and took a determined gulp at the wine.

'Don't tell me you are on a diet, Clootie!' Kirsty exclaimed.

'Of course she isn't,' Hector roared in reply. 'I can't stand skinny girls. Give me something to get hold of. A man needs to be kept warm of a night.'

Andrea felt the rising blush as she crammed the revolting pudding into her mouth.

'That's my girl! Have some more.'

'No, thank you! No . . . really. Please, I don't want any more.'

5

But Hector would not hear her as he dumped another quaking dollop on her plate.

'Never mind,' said Marion. 'Fiona and I will eat it, we know you hate custard.' The Brown girls were plain-speaking and would become splendid doers of necessary things when they grew up. They were the sort that went a-colonizing or ran hostels for the wayward, whereas Wee Angus rather liked poetry.

The girls all went upstairs to titivate, as Hector winkingly put it, while he and the boys lingered in the dining room and the Blairs hoped in vain for port. Wee Angus wondered what exactly was a 'maiden loth'. He had asked his sisters but they had misheard him and insisted that it was a type of bread like a cottage loaf or a sliced pan. Wee Angus felt destined to loiter through life, alone and pale . . . This cheered him. Malcolm hoped the bet about kissing Mrs MacInlay's hand would be honoured; he needed the ten bob badly.

Andrea was delighted to have a chance to chat to the Browns, who seemed utterly at ease and accepting everything with equanimity. Kirsty showed them her photographs and made much play with her lipstick and mascara. The Erace had quite worn off and Andrea had nothing with which to replace it. In the bathroom she found some talcum powder, which she rubbed into her skin without satisfactory result.

Kirsty's brother, Mungo, was in disgrace. He had failed his Highers and was now at a crammer, which cost a lot, where he did very little work. Most of his days were spent sitting in coffee bars in the company of his girlfriend whose reputation was lurid. She was known as the Bicycle of Bruntsfield. Kirsty told her friends of the awful atmosphere between Mungo and her parents. The Brown girls were intrigued and giggled a lot. Andrea was baffled.

'Why is she called Bicycle?'

'Because everyone rides her, silly!' Kirsty was painting her nails a sugary pink that was meant to match her lips but didn't. 'Blast!'

The varnish had smudged. Another layer went on, the effect was tatty, so she abandoned the project and removed the lot.

'Here, let me have a sniff!' Marion pretended to be in ecstasy as

6

she smelt the nail varnish remover. 'That is my favourite perfume, just like pear drops.'

'I like the cream you put on your feet when you have athlete's foot,' said Fiona.

'Mungo says you-know-what smells of kippers!' Kirsty volunteered, which caused the Browns to fall about like playful walruses while Andrea sat awkwardly on the edge of the bed. She could not imagine what it was that smelt of kippers, and preferred not to speculate about that sort of thing. Her curiosity about sex and birth and the improbability of it all had once greatly entertained her and her best friend. She had a rough idea of the mechanics – after all, these were the sixties – but recently she had chosen to shut the whole issue out of her mind.

Her mother was pregnant. At first the prospect was rather thrilling since she already had a little brother so there was no fear of being usurped by a newcomer. All that had been got over ten years ago. It was when she realized what her parents must have done for this to come about that Andrea began to fear that she would die of embarrassment, humiliation and disgust. She had tried to keep the secret for as long as possible but Ishbel showed no shame and was delighted with her news.

'When is the baby due?' Kirsty asked Andrea.

'I don't know,' she lied.

'Fancy having parents that still do it!' said Marion, not meaning to be unkind. Evidently Mr and Mrs Brown were quite past passion, Mrs Brown having developed a deep voice following an operation ten years ago and Mr Brown's spare time being filled with golf.

'Do they have a double bed or twins like my parents?' Kirsty enquired.

'Double.'

'There you are!' Kirsty sounded knowing. 'Some men can't be trusted at any age, given the opportunity. They are like wild animals. Mungo can't resist the temptation. It's like a primal urge, he says.'

'But Mungo is young,' Marion said. 'Not like Mr and Mrs Innes, who are really old.'

'Do they do it a lot?' Fiona asked Andrea.

7

'Of course not! Only when they want to make a baby, and there have only been two of us so far.' Andrea was getting defensive. She hated this conversation, and could feel the sweat, or as her mother insisted, perspiration, making damp patches on the pink material under her arms. 'It happened while they were asleep.'

'You won't catch me sharing sheets with a fellow in that case,' said Fiona.

'You want to watch lav seats too,' Marion added.

'Don't be ridiculous,' Kirsty sneered. 'You can't get pregnant just like that. You have to do a lot of puffing and heaving and kissing . . . Babies don't get made while people sleep.'

'Yoo-hoo!' a cheerful voice, a little slurred, called from the foot of the stairs. 'You must come now or you will be late and you won't get your programmes filled.'

'Och, don't fuss, Mum,' Kirsty shouted.

Andrea fled downstairs. She was delighted to escape from the conclave in Kirsty's frilly bedroom, which seemed so sophisticated compared to Andrea's own room where bald bears and old toys still lived on shelves painted with the Flopsy Bunnies. Kirsty's ceiling had blue wallpaper on it sprinkled with stars. Andrea had stared at these silver heavens whilst trying not to cry. Now her sensible coat was on over her sticking out dress and even the prospect of a programme that needed to be filled seemed preferable to the curiosity of the other girls about the night-time cavortings of the senior Inneses. Once she had found out about birds, bees and babies, Andrea had longed to grow up and be a nun, but she was uncertain whether such a thing was possible with her father being an elder of the Kirk.

The Assembly Rooms were aglow with festivity and glittered in the slightly tawdry manner of public merriments. The band was playing a reel with relentless rhythm, while the more unruly young Scots whooped curdling cries. This practice was considered abhorrent by Miss Cairns, who taught dancing at school. Andrea had only ever danced to the sound of the piano with the relaxed pedals that stood in the Memorial Hall. She danced well but was too lumbering to be included in any team, but at least she knew the steps.

The programmes were tiny but the list of dances was long. Even if all the boys of their party did what their mothers had instructed and gave each of the girls a dance, there would be many blanks.

'What you want to do is to fill it in yourself with lots of made-up names,' Fiona suggested. 'Then no one will start feeling they've got to do something about you. Also it makes your parents happy. Only don't make it too readable or you will find that you get asked lots of awkward questions. Marion had an awful time stopping Mum from asking Lyle Nile and Keith Kincardine to come and play tennis.'

The Browns were veterans of the teenage dancing circuit. They were always asked with the convenient Blairs despite them all hating each other.

A Blair had block booked Kirsty, whose programme was full, which was a reprieve for Wee Angus. Had Andrea worn her glasses she would have seen that it included the dance he had grudgingly requested with her. The Blair said he couldn't bear tribal dancing and promised to take Kirsty to the adjoining nightclub to smooch once she had enjoyed the triumph of dancing with both brothers in the Dashing White Sergeant. She looked with pity on Fiona and Marion who flanked Wee Angus. They had equipped Wee Angus's programme with all the Shakespearean women they could remember except Goneril and Regan to whom their brother objected.

Someone had got hold of some brandy with which they laced another, yet more vile cup, and Andrea began to feel much better. She danced the Hamilton House with Wee Angus and fairly bounced about as she had been taught, pointing her toe and putting her hands on her hips. Being large she had always danced the man at school. After a while she realized that no one jumped up and down. They shuffled and glided and the women who really knew their way about clasped their hands behind their backs. She started to enjoy herself, the music was captivating and thrilled her in a way that the floppy piano would never achieve.

Reeling is such joy in that conversation is impossible, and you meet so many people on your way down the set. She even saw Mungo MacInlay, but their encounter was so brief that she could not detect the aroma of kippers. He had brought his girlfriend, who wore false eyelashes and whose stilettoes were pockmarking the floor in a wicked way.

Eventually the music stopped and then there was another glass of laced drink. This was heaven.

Bored Cousin Malcolm had undertaken to do the eightsome with Andrea. Their set was hampered by some silly people from England who got the wheel all wrong, but the foursome to follow gave her a glimpse of the bliss of adulthood. The subtle twisting of the figure, the setting and circling, and then the change from strathspey to reel time was bewitching. Maybe she would forgo the nunnery. When it was over, Malcolm disappeared and she sat on a gilt chair chatting to the Browns, who were perfectly used to having no partners and bore no grudges, for grudge-bearing had been excluded from their manufacture. They giggled and screeched but did not really include Andrea, who was impervious due to another drink and sat watching the swirling dancers in a glazed haze of rapture.

Andrea was alone when, bluffer than ever, Mr MacInlay came up and asked her to dance. She had to accept as she knew Hector would realize that her programme was fanciful and that Adam Adamant was unlikely to have booked her for a turn. To refuse would have been rude and rudeness was the most awful crime according to the Innes family. The children had been taught to do a please or a thank you for everything. James Innes raised his hat so often it seldom covered his balding head, and he spent much of his time letting others through doors. Ishbel would have been proud of the way her daughter smiled with pretended pleasure at Hector MacInlay and allowed herself to be led off into the Gay Gordons. It was not such fun dancing with just one person, and the Gay Gordons is such a sweaty process with all the twirling, promenading and clutching polkas. Still, the band were playing with enthusiasm and Hector, for all his bulk, had a fine sense of time. Dancing with Kirsty's father wasn't so bad and anyway, it would not last long and she could sidle off to the ladies on some pretext. The Browns were probably in there. (She had not noticed them leave with their father, who had fetched them because late nights were unwholesome for the young, even in aid of deprived children.)

The dance was nearly over and Cam Robbie's second team would soon be playing the gallop.

'Do you like dancing, Andrea?'

'I love it,' she answered enthusiastically, which did not sound much like her. Normally she would just have said, 'Yes, thank you.'

'You are a good dancer . . . do you know what that means?' Hector squeezed her hand and she looked at him bemused. 'You do know what it means!' he continued. 'Come along, pet, let's you and I go and have a proper dance. You are a canny one. Behind that shy exterior and that contraption on your teeth I reckon there lurks a tigress.'

Andrea did not think she had heard him properly and told him that she hoped to be rid of the brace by Easter.

'My, there'll be no stopping you then!'

Perhaps Mr MacInlay had overdone the 'cup' too. He ushered her from the main dance floor and took her along to the nightclub where it was murky dark and a juke box was playing 'Stranger on the Shore'.

He held her firmly and brought his stubbled cheek down and laid it against her ear. The movements they made were not exactly dancing. The waltz and the quickstep had been taught at school but this shuffle to music was not on the curriculum. Andrea began to feel uneasy.

'Relax, wee one,' Hector whispered down her ear. He must have bitten the lobe by mistake – such things might happen, she assumed, especially in the dark. With her nose pressed to his jacket she had only one eye working and once it had got used to the gloom it saw that Kirsty was doing much the same thing with a Blair's cheek pressed against her ear. Each girl's working eye saw what was afoot. For an instant they understood each other.

'What was that, sweetie?'

'Kirsty is over there,' Andrea seemed to shout.

Hector sprang back, rearranged his sporran, and suggested they go and find some breakfast.

'That,' said Andrea, 'would be lovely.' She meant it.

A boney kedgeree and burnt sausages were being served in a brightly lit anteroom. Shiny-faced and weary dancers were being

11

silly with bread rolls. Mrs MacInlay was crying into a cup of black coffee beside bored Cousin Malcolm. Evidently Mungo had suggested that his mother should away and boil her head. Her head would not need boiling, it was pickled already. Somehow, the evening seemed over.

'I live towards Haymarket,' Andrea said as she noticed the Jag was heading past Holyrood.

'I thought you and I might have a look at Auld Reekie from Arthur's seat. You would like that, wouldn't you?'

'Won't they be expecting you at home?' Andrea asked, hoping that this jaunt would abort. She had never enjoyed scenery and Edinburgh by night seemed scarcely worth the bother of going up a hill for. She longed to be at home, her head ached, the shoes pinched and she was bothered by the stains in her armpits, as well as suffering an overwhelming urge to go to sleep.

'Don't worry, no one will notice if I am away for a while. They will just think that I am having a nightcap with your father.'

'My parents will be in bed by now,' said Andrea. 'I have a key. They said they would trust me to let myself in. But I must not be long. I have to get Petunia his milk, no one else remembers.'

'You are the perfect daughter . . . and a great wee girl.'

The car stopped beside Duddingston Loch. There was not much of a view and all Andrea could see was an overflowing litter bin. She wondered where those vicious swans went at night. She had always hated the loch since a particularly greedy bird had pursued her, hissing with outstretched neck, when she tried to reserve some of her stock of stale bread for the ducks. At least it did not seem that Hector had a walk in mind.

Suddenly he lunged at her and held her firmly while his mouth came down over hers. She struggled as she felt his hands unfasten the back of her dress. He forced his tongue between her teeth. Then she bit him. The brace snapped.

Hector roared with pain, and Andrea managed to remove the broken plate from her mouth, leaving him with a hunk of pink plastic impaled in his tongue by a snapped wire spring.

'You bitch!'

She began to cry.

He extricated his tongue and flung the plate out of the window to perish abandoned amongst the empty Macpops beside the municipal bin.

'You little bitch. You did that deliberately. You led me on. You knew what was up. You're a cock teaser.'

'I didn't mean to hurt you, Mr MacInlay. It's just that I didn't understand.'

'Now I suppose you are trying to be innocent . . . You can't get away with that, gaol bait.'

'Please take me home.'

'I will that, and right away.'

Blood dribbled on to his jabot as he drove down into the city and through to the house overlooking Donaldson's Hospital. Lights were on outside and in the hall. Andrea noticed that her parents' light was extinguished just as the car stopped but was not old enough to realize that they would have stayed awake to worry about her. She was, after all, only fourteen and had never been to a late party before. They had not wanted her to know that they would fret; she must be allowed to grow up.

Petunia was looking out of the dining room window. Did he miss her or was it just that he missed his milk?

Hector also noticed the light. Andrea jumped out of the car and began to run towards the door but he was too fast for her.

He caught her by the wrist, and zipped up the back of her dress as he marched her up the path and rang the bell.

'Don't do that, I have a key,' said Andrea in desperation.

'We have some explaining to do and I want to tell your parents before they get any silly ideas from you.'

Andrea was dumbfounded. Surely stopping your friends' fathers from unzipping your dress and putting their tongues in your mouth couldn't come under the heading of being rude? Maybe she should offer to pay for the laundering of the bloodied jabot. She hoped that she would not be made to pay for a new plate with her Post Office Savings.

It did not take long for James Innes to come to the door in his camel dressing-gown, feigning to appear newly awoken.

'Hello, lovey; did you have a nice time? Have you forgotten the key? Hector! How kind of you to see her home. What do you say, Andrea?'

When, oh when, thought Andrea, will they let me speak for myself?

Hector handed James Andrea's coat, which she had left in the car in her haste to escape.

'I am afraid, James, that I am returning your daughter rather the worse for wear. I am sorry that I didn't realize that she and her cronies had got hold of some booze and contrived to get themselves drunk, and now, if you will pardon the expression, your wee girl is greetin fou.'

Indeed, the tears were trailing down her face but not, as Hector was implying, with maudlin drunkenness.

'This can't be true, Andrea!' James sounded horrified and made to usher them inside. One did not want neighbours to hear of such a thing on the doorstep of a Writer to the Signet.

'I'm not drunk,' she attempted to defend herself, but the tears, sweat and tiredness, plus the ache in her mouth left by the absent plate, defeated her. She was even forbidden to take Petunia with her as she was banished up to her bedroom with threats of retribution to be meted out to her come the morning.

Retreating, she endured the ignominy of hearing her father apologize to Hector, who in turn replied that we were all young once, that James must not be too hard on her and that the inevitable 'sair heid' would probably be grief enough to prevent her from being so foolish in the future. He added that he had hoped to spare James and Ishbel this mortification and had tried to get their daughter to sober up by taking her for a walk in the fresh air after the party, but she had been beyond such simple remedies. He did not explain the blood on his jabot but implied that some of the young had been rather obstreperous.

Loudly refusing a drink, he left, but not before he had implored James not to punish her too severely, though he wondered whether the Innes family would ever hear much of what really had happened at the party as doubtless Andrea would have trouble with the memory! He made it into a joke.

James made it perfectly clear that neither he nor Ishbel would

14

treat the night's antics as a joke and he would deal with her in the morning.

Andrea couldn't sleep for misery. Not the misery of finding herself to be less than perfect, but of not being believed by those she trusted most. What was more, had that awful incident been 'Love'? Was that what there was to look forward to?

2

'I am utterly scandalized and mortified! How could you behave like that with the MacInlays, of all people? What do you imagine they must think? You, with a family of such standing, your father in the law and an elder, you should set an example to others. Especially those from the more vulgar echelons of society.'

'Calm yourself, Ishbel. Let me talk to Andrea.' James had delayed his kirkgoing to add his weight to Andrea's castigation. 'You are a wicked girl to subject your mother to this disgrace, especially now, when she must not be distressed. Something like this might cause her to be taken ill and then you would have to carry that guilt as well.'

A spot of porridge was stuck to James's tie. He had excelled at St Andrews University and wore his triumphs round his neck. It would be black affronting to face the congregation in grubby neckwear.

'What have you got on your tie, Dad?' Neil had sidled in to see the fun. It was not often that Andrea was the subject of parental wrath; it made a change.

'Porridge . . . That's nothing! I heard your father say that Mr MacInlay's jabot was dripping with gore. What in heaven's name were you up to? You are meant to be a correctly reared young lady, not a brawling tripper or a teddy girl.'

'I'm sorry. It wasn't like that.'

'Like what, pray?' James sometimes felt he should have become an advocate. 'Are you denying that you had been drinking strong liquor?'

'No, only it wasn't much, and I wasn't drunk.'

'You, my dear girl, were evidently paralytic. Why else would poor Mr MacInlay endeavour to get you sober before delivering you home? What about his injury? Explain that!'

'It was an accident.'

'The whole episode sounds like one large catastrophe. Where is your brace?'

16

'I don't know,' Andrea lied.

'Well, as a punishment for your appalling behaviour and ingratitude you will not be getting a replacement. You will go through life with crooked teeth and every time you look at yourself in the mirror you will be reminded of the ruin you brought on yourself by drink.'

'But Andrea's teeth are straight,' Neil protested.

James ignored this remark. 'Furthermore, you will not be allowed to go to any other parties till you are fifteen, and instead of going with your mother and brother to Auntie Mary you will spend the end of the holidays in Glasgow with your grandmother.'

Andrea tried to appear chastened. In reality all her dearest wishes, except perhaps to visit the mummies in the British Museum, had been granted. No more brace, no more parties . . . what bliss. As for the proposed stay with Aunt Mary, well, that was something she had been trying to dodge for ages. What made people imagine that children enjoyed the seaside, especially the east coast in winter, when the height of excitement was a walk on the links and a go at putting while the fierce waves buffeted the Bass Rock and the gulls flew backwards?

'Can I go to Grannie's too?' Neil begged.

'No, certainly not, you are not being punished.'

Sometimes the world seemed most contrary to the Innes son and heir. Auntie Mary was a pill.

Writing a letter of apology and delivering it to the MacInlays was the remaining issue. Once that was done the incident would be closed, James told Andrea, as she was dismissed with several sheets of thick headed paper, discreetly engraved.

Andrea had her doubts about that. Her parents were inclined to regurgitate misdemeanours. The roller towel incident was still live even after two years.

Dear Mrs MacInlay,
  Thank you for having me to dinner and taking me to the dance. I had a lovely time. I enjoyed the dance and the dinner.
  I am sorry I behaved so badly. I am sorry I was drunk. I am sorry about the accident. It won't happen again. I am not

17

allowed to go to any more parties. Please will you thank Mr MacInlay for bringing me home.

Yours sincerely,

Andrea Innes.

This took a while to write but eventually Ishbel considered it adequate and Andrea was sent to walk to the New Town. The fresh air would do her good.

Ishbel was concerned that her daughter seemed to suffer no physical remorse. Another cause for worry. James always said that those who got hangovers never became alcoholics. Andrea would need rescuing from the gutter of Rose Street unless she mended her ways, her mother predicted.

Hector had ambitions. With such a name one required to be knighted. Nothing improves a Hector like the prefix of a sir, and Scotland is peppered with dubbed worthies called Hector.

Moira would appreciate a title, she would open fêtes with relish, dressed in enviable chic at a cost that would have rendered the sum raised by the event rather paltry.

To achieve his aim, Councillor MacInlay was a bastion of local government and a significant benefactor of worthy causes. His generosity was always conspicuous, left and right hands were both in the know. He hoped to gain recognition through much grafting on behalf of the Conservative and Unionist Party, and held high office in the constituency as well as in Scotland as a whole. Their funds were enhanced.

That Sunday morning he awoke to realize that his conduct the night before might be misinterpreted. Would Andrea's parents believe his story? Yes, probably. Had the child really been too drunk to remember? That was doubtful, as was her continued silence on the subject. She didn't seem to be the sort who was expected to make up vicious tales. Her truthfulness was probably steadfast. She lacked imagination. Something must be done to keep her quiet, or what was to have been Sir Hector would remain Mr MacInlay and have to resign from all office and live in ignominious obscurity.

Having considered and dismissed all forms of physical

18

violence, and pondered on bribery without success, he decided that she would be silenced only by guilt. Hers had been the fault. She must be led to think that she was the siren, the temptress, the nymphomaniac and man-eater. Hector began to believe that he had lacerated his tongue in self-defence. He had been shamelessly pounced upon.

Unlike James Innes, Hector observed his Sabbath on the golf course. Juanita, the maid, had cooked a kipper to fortify him, which succeeded only in stinking throughout the house. Moira, who was in bed with a vile headache, sniffed the waft of fishiness and felt sick. Kirsty slept on regardless, her crumpled dress thrown in a corner for Juanita to rescue later.

Outside, Andrea prayed that she could deliver her letter and escape without being detected. She had loitered down Drumsheugh Gardens and over Queensferry Road in the hope that all the MacInlays would be out and doing by the time she arrived. She doubted whether they would be at church, but she hadn't expected them to be asleep. Kirk and church were not essential every Sunday but, according to the Innes philosophy, Hell awaited those who lingered in bed till noon.

Juanita answered the door and Andrea gave her the note. Thank God she could escape an interview. She turned to run down the steps, but just as she reached the pavement she bumped into Hector, who had returned, infuriated because in his distraction he had forgotten his golf clubs. The aroma of kipper still hung about him.

At first he didn't recognize the miserable podgy girl with spots and glasses who tried to dodge past him. Then with a pang of disgust he realized that this barely pubescent lump was last night's temptress. The man-crazed nymphomaniac became a very unlikely concept, as indeed did his participation as either pouncer or pouncee.

Already enraged by his self-enforced lateness, he grasped her roughly by the elbow and forced her to stand facing him.

'What the hell are you doing here? Come back for more, have you?'

'No. I was bringing a letter. My father said I was to write to Mrs MacInlay about last night.'

'What does it say?'

'Just thank you for the party, and sorry for behaving badly.'

'Is that all?'

'Yes.'

'I'll take it. Give it here at once and then go home.' He held out his hand; it had orange hairs all over the back. As a child, he had resembled an orang-utan.

'I have just given it to the foreign lady.'

'What foreign lady?' He hoped ardently that it had not got into the inquisitive grasp of Gerda Gillespie, Moira's great friend, who had a teutonic appetite for facts.

'The lady who answered the door.'

'That is not a foreign lady, that is a Spanish maid,' he sneered. 'Well, I had better get hold of it before anyone gets some more silly ideas. You don't want everyone to know about that disgraceful carry on last night. I wonder what would happen if your dad, the pillar of the Kirk, got to hear of how his wee girl throws herself at men. I hope you didn't tell your parents about your dreadful conduct in my car?'

Andrea shook her head, firmly negative, and then boldly but very quietly she replied that she had not thrown herself at anyone on purpose.

'So now you are pretending that you are not responsible for your actions, because you had been made drunk or been drugged? Come away, you can't fool anyone with such a tale. Now, I want you to swear that you will never tell a soul about what you did last night. It's for your own good, because if anyone – anyone at all – found out what you are really like, it would ruin you and your family for ever. Do you understand?'

'Yes, Mr MacInlay. Can I go now? They'll be expecting me home.'

'Not till you have sworn never to tell.'

'I swear.'

'You had better do it on the Bible, like in court. Do you know what happens to people who tell lies after they have been sworn in court?'

'No, Mr MacInlay.'

'They get hanged!'

She thought he might be mistaken. Only murderers like Hanratty, or traitors, got hanged, but she was sufficiently frightened to let herself get taken into the house and sat in Hector's study while he looked for a Bible and gave Juanita half a crown for the letter, which he pocketed without reading.

Finding a Bible was not easy. It was not something you could ask for without arousing curiosity. In the end he found a Church of Scotland combined psalter and prayer book that Mungo had won at Sunday school, and made her swear silence as she held it aloft in her right hand.

'Stop crying, for goodness' sake. What will folks think if you walk home in tears? Dry your eyes.' He reached for his handkerchief but drew the letter from his pocket instead.

'You will give the letter to Mrs MacInlay?' she implored.

'Of course. Now run along. Here, perhaps this will stop your tears.' He offered her a five-pound note.

She was confused. Of course she wanted the money but she thought that accepting it was probably wrong.

'No, thank you. I can't.'

'Yes you can!'

She recalled a notice in the paper shop to the effect that refusal often offended. She thanked him quietly as she took the money. It worried her. It did not feel right, but a fiver was a real wonder. It would mean The Beatles' new record, Evelyn Waugh's *The Loved One*, a black polo neck sweater, but she would probably have to wait to see *Psycho*. Some scent called Gin Fizz would be heavenly.

'Now that is to remind you to keep the secret. Do you understand?'

All the way home she was troubled by the money, and she was almost resolved to turn back and post it through the MacInlay letter box when she met her father walking back from morning service.

'Did you deliver your apology to Mrs MacInlay?'

'I gave it to Mr MacInlay. He said he would give it to her.'

Hector burnt the letter on the golf clubhouse fire. He could not bring himself to read it.

Meanwhile Andrea stuffed the fiver under the elastic of her

21

winter knickers where it crackled reproachfully until she managed to hide it more discreetly.

Christmas Day passed and was celebrated according to custom without much spontaneity. In view of Ishbel's fragility, the Innes family stayed at home and ate a modest turkey and a total abstainer of a pudding. There were no extra visitors.

Andrea went to church with her mother and the Episcopalians, while Neil accompanied his father to the Presbyterians. The mixture of religions was about the only exotic element in this conventional marriage. To irritate her mother, Ishbel had at one point contemplated joining the Kirk, but she preferred to ask God to forgive her trespasses rather than her debts which sounded so much more shameful. Besides, the singing was better and the sermons generally shorter at the English church. Neil said he was happy to be made to go to the Church of Scotland, as merely leaning forward in prayer was much kinder on his boney bare knees.

Christmas always involved the Queen's speech, loyalty to one's sovereign being essential. Effie Lammont, Ishbel's mother, rang to wish everyone a Happy Christmas just as they had all sat down and tuned in. Ishbel rightly suspected malice.

Everyone thanked Effie for her presents which were, as usual, untidily wrapped books, well thumbed and grubby. This year, a calico bag full of wooden jigsaw pieces, all small and dark with no picture for guidance, had also been sent. *I expect it will bring you hours of fun*, she had scrawled on the back of a snowy scene that had formed the front of a card last year. It seemed likely that many bits would be missing, indeed it was doubtful whether they all belonged to the same puzzle. Andrea, however, was really thrilled with her present, a gruesome encyclopaedia of mysterious rituals including a large selection on mummifying and a vivid account of the ways of the Aztecs.

'A most unsuitable gift', according to Ishbel, who was trying to concentrate on what the monarch and her man wished for their subjects. On the whole it appeared to be peace, goodwill and harmony amongst all at home and in one's larger family beyond the seas. It was all thoroughly encouraging, observed James, who insisted on continuing the custom of taking Andrea and Neil for a damp cold walk before tea.

Ishbel and James were as happy together as any couple could be. They had enjoyed no peaks of rapture nor sloughs of despond. Their aims were at one: to live a decent life and provide a decent upbringing and home life for their decent children. A deviation from the norm would put them about. They were a popular couple who would provide cheerful non-challenging company, and they were often invited to dine with the best. Ishbel was not shy, she just lacked flair when it came to returning hospitality, and so her pregnancy was a wonderful excuse to call a moratorium on entertainment. James did not mind; he was anxious for her welfare and loved her because she was his wife and he never shirked his obligations or commitments. She had once been very pretty, but the perpetual pursuit of propriety had restrained her from achieving a generous attractiveness often found in mothers verging on middle life.

James had met the MacInlays outside St Cuthbert's on Christmas Day morning. As an elder it was his duty to welcome them. Since he never undertook hopeless causes, he did not express a hope to see them on other occasions during the year. Hector was prominently jovial while anxious to be back with their new hi-fi, Mungo and Kirsty stood in sullen impatience, Moira, looking far more appealing than Harold Macmillan in her Russian hat, was charm itself.

'And where is Kirsty's wee friend Andrea? We did so enjoy having her at the dance. I hope she enjoyed herself?'

James said he knew she had enjoyed herself more than usual and hoped that the unfortunate incident was forgiven. He explained about Andrea being of her mother's Church and then became flustered in case Moira thought that her bad behaviour had been a result of being reared as an Episcopalian. While drunkenness might be widespread amongst Anglicans, it was scarcely ecumenical to make such implications.

'Be sure and tell Andrea not to bother to write. Christmas is such a busy time,' Moira smiled. 'We must be away. Hector will be anxious to get at the bubbly.' She waved a gloved hand and tottered off on immaculate chisel-toed stilettoes.

Though it was not as sophisticated as Kirsty's record player, Andrea was overjoyed to have been given a Dansette. She could play heaps of singles on it, one after the other, but kept her new Beatles record hidden till she could devise a way of explaining its acquisition. The rest of the fiver had gone on presents in an attempt to salve her conscience – Gin Fizz for Ishbel, who feigned delight but retched at the smell, and two books for Neil: *The Guinness Book of Records*, all wrapped and official, and a surreptitious comic annual because Neil, as well as being a devotee of the Broons and Oor Wullie, was a profound fan of Desperate Dan and longed to join his pie eating club. Comics, apart from *Eagle* and *Girl*, were forbidden, and they were only permitted because the adventures were noble, the characters virtuous and the editor was rumoured to be in holy orders. James got a handsome clothes brush to join the legions of such brushes already in his possession. It was very expensive. No one thought to ask where the funds had come from. It was assumed that Andrea had saved.

'Maybe we have been rather hard on her,' Ishbel suggested to James. 'Maybe it is a bit mean to force her to go to Mother in Glasgow when she could be having a grand time at the coast with us.'

James was inclined to agree till he remembered how Moira MacInlay (that hat was so becoming) appeared to be in ignorance of Andrea's apologetic letter. While he did not feel much would be gained by pursuing the matter, he was resolved that the punishment should continue. He was not a man to change his mind.

Andrea was mightily relieved.

The ban on parties, however, was lifted when the whole family was invited to see in the New Year with the Browns. It was to be a happy Hogmanay with supper and games, with all uproarious behaviour caused by excessive high, rather than strong, spirits.

Mrs Brown was hearty and organizing, and the house was almost in the country and full of shedding dogs. Marion and Fiona had woolly ponies but, much to their mother's

24

disappointment, had never become enthusiastic. They had fallen off everywhere without the slightest sign of remorse or thwarted competitive spirit. Wee Angus was allergic to horses so he was allowed to pretend a preference for golf. He had to put up with the dogs and tolerate the sneezing and streaming eyes caused by their fur. When he grew up he was going to live in a cloister or on a peak in Darien, whichever was less hairy.

Andrea knew that Kirsty had refused to go to the Browns. The Blairs likewise would have died rather than be forced to play charades. They were to Twist the Night Away at the MacInlays' house where the hi-fi system was well stocked – also the cellar.

Ishbel felt sick and inclined to be idle. *The White Heather Club* was enough excitement for her. Thus James and the children went alone, promising to return promptly in the New Year to be her first foot.

For once the Brown heating system seemed to be working and there was unlimited Coca-Cola to drink, while the adults and bored Cousin Malcolm had champagne. Mr Brown was in the wine business, an entirely acceptable calling.

Neil and Andrea were all set to enjoy themselves. Andrea loved being with Fiona and Marion, who were almost as nice as her best friend, Susie, had been before she had been sent to boarding school. Since her plaits had been chopped off and she had been kissed by an Etonian, Susie was thoroughly bored by Edinburgh. She and Andrea no longer enjoyed the old private jokes and speculations, or giggled till they were breathless.

About twenty people of all ages were at the party. Malcolm did not participate at all except to smoke a great many cigarettes. The Browns had charge of their nephew while his parents were stationed abroad and did not feel it was their place to stop him. He was a tedious youth and complained a lot, but at least he appeared contented while he puffed at his Passing Clouds.

'What has happened to your plate?' Marion asked.

'I lost it.'

'Well done, you look much better without it. Did you see that photograph in the paper yesterday of the swan with its beak stuck in a brace beside Duddingston Loch? I bet it was just a stunt to launch the Provost's antilitter campaign.'

There was a great pot of somewhat dire kedgeree made exotic by a hint of curry powder and some slippery beetroot that bled into the rice, but not much else to eat, though the girls had contrived for pudding several alarming jellies and a fruit salad made jolly with glacé cherries. People were already prodding at the kedgeree when Hector and Moira arrived, full of apologies for their lateness and obviously fresh from another, more generous party. They disguised the quarrel that they had been having in the car beneath a veneer of enthusiasm.

'Kedgeree . . . my favourite!' announced Moira, while accepting a large glass of champagne and serving herself with a minute quantity of food.

Hector pretended not to notice Andrea, but she was not so self-possessed and fled, followed by Fiona.

'I can't, I won't come down. Please leave me here, I'm perfectly happy.' Andrea fell on Fiona's bed and pretended interest in a book. 'Is this good?' It was *Angelique, Marquise des Anges*, and had a lurid cover. She wondered whether she would ever look like that if she were given a miracle spot cure and an ebullient head of blonde hair. (The bosom would probably be all right, hers was getting bigger every day.)

Fiona was not to be put off. 'Come on, Andrea, do come down. Who are you afraid of?'

'No one.'

'Well then, you don't need to hide up here.'

Marion came in with a trayload of food. 'If there is one person I can't stand it's that gross Hector MacInlay. He is so boastful and his breath smells.'

'Let's get rid of him,' Fiona said.

'Oh yes, very easy. What shall I do, just go up to him and say, "Someone here isn't using Amplex," and wait for him to disappear in embarrassment? Very simple. I'll just nip down and do that.'

'No, we'll get Malcolm to do it.'

'Malcolm won't do anything, he's sulking because he couldn't go to Kirsty's party.'

'Oh yes he will. He will do anything for money. He is on his last packet of fags. How much have you got?'

'Nothing,' said Marion. 'I spent all my Christmas money on The Beatles' record and these beatniks.' She lifted her skirt to show off a pair of red and black knee-length pants whose horizontal stripes did not flatter her thighs.

'Me neither. Have you got any money, Andrea?'

'Only a ten-bob book token from my aunt.'

'That will do.'

'But Malcolm can't buy cigs with a book token,' Marion protested.

'No matter, we'll get Angus to swap it. He's got pots of cash.'

Wee Angus agreed to give Malcolm ten shillings in exchange for Andrea's book token, provided no one kissed him at midnight.

Malcolm fancied himself as a mimic – he had ambitions to appear on *That Was the Week that Was* – and the bribe was accepted eagerly.

Angus and Marion rejoined the party and made themselves enormously pleasant, while Malcolm, Fiona and Andrea let themselves into Mr Brown's office and rang the house number.

While Radio Luxembourg blared, Andrea clinked glasses and blew a party whistle. Fiona did her impression of a cork popping and drink being gluggingly poured as Malcolm spoke to Mr Brown in a high foreign voice.

'Pleece, pleece, you give message to Mr MacInlay. You say him to come home. Party no good. People very bad.'

'Is that Juanita?'

'Pleece tell Mr and Mrs MacInlay to come home now.'

Andrea blew up a balloon and let it go so it skittered farting round the office and came to rest on a golfing trophy.

Despite the girls being practically hysterical Malcolm managed to keep up the act. He had learnt the trick of maintaining a straight face by deep breathing. However, he hung up immediately when Mr Brown began to talk to him in Spanish.

'Christ! You didn't tell me your father could speak Spanish.'

'Are you sure it wasn't French?'

'French, Spanish – what does it matter? It is all bloody foreign. Now where's my money?'

'You get your money when we see them go. Cash on results here.'

Andrea had never done anything so subversive before and it made her feel wonderful. Throughout her childhood she had been convinced that adults were faultless. All parents were perfect and only the young were flawed. Now it transpired she had been wrong. It was quite in order not to like and respect everyone who was grown-up. Who knew, maybe it was possible even to criticize the Queen's choice of hat. She had been severely upbraided for doing this last year when a photograph of the royal party at the Braemar Games showed her in a hideous bonnet plus quaintly perched feather.

'Of course Dad can speak Spanish,' Marion said when they had all met again. 'He fought in their civil war when he was young and had fire in his belly.'

'Which side was he on?' asked Malcolm.

'Ours, of course!'

Though Moira didn't leave with her husband, the ten-shilling note belonged to Malcolm. Hector, had he not been anxious about the state of his house, was delighted to have an excuse to leave. That wretched Innes child seemed to haunt him. It had been Moira who insisted on going out. He had never been keen about leaving Kirsty and Mungo to have their party with only Juanita in charge.

At Moray Place the house was gloomily dark and silent except for Elvis crooning something soulful. Kirsty sat smoking beside the record player while the second best Blair tried to pick the lock of Hector's cocktail cabinet. Mungo and his girlfriend had disappeared to a better party with the rest of his mates, and Juanita, far from being distressed, was entertaining the very best Blair in one of the MacInlays' twin beds.

The success of the Browns' party may not have been entirely due to the absence of two of the guests but certainly Ishbel's chilly propriety and Hector's loud bonhomie were not missed. Even James became an asset; his broody hen imitation nearly gave Bunty Brown a seizure. It was while they were acting *Dr Finlay's Casebook* that this talent was discovered. Moira had squirmed about in a hopefully fishy way whilst opening and shutting her mouth and flapping a couple of copies of the *Scottish Field* to imitate fins. 'No props! No props!' everyone shrieked in vain, and then James pretended to lay an egg.

Such was the triumph that his team went on to do *Lay Down Your Arms*, with James clucking fit to burst, and *The Road to Manderlay*, but only Wee Angus guessed *The Lay of the Last Minstrel*. The other team did *Champion the Wonder Horse* because Mrs Brown was first class at neighing, and *There Are Fairies At The Bottom Of My Garden*, which was quite rude, and *The Wind in the Willows*, which was hilarious and would have caused Ishbel to have miscarried with shock.

Then it was midnight, everyone stood in a ring and sang 'Auld Lang Syne' and drank in the New Year. Malcolm came in with a piece of coal and a prehistoric black bun that had been in the Brown family since Nannie died. True to their word the twins flanked Wee Angus like Gog and Magog and deterred all swooping kissers. Andrea kissed everyone without a flicker of self-consciousness. It was wonderful. When Malcolm came and kissed her, he smelt deliciously of tobacco. That was heaven.

James took them home. He had offered to give Moira a lift back to Moray Place. As they drove through the streets they saw revellers spilling out of the pubs and staggering home to an uncertain welcome and the certainty of a hangover on Ne'erday morning.

'You go in and first foot your mother, Neil, and take Andrea with you while I just nip Mrs MacInlay back to Moray Place,' said James as they approached Magdala Crescent. He and Moira had been chatting all the way home. Andrea had never imagined that either could be so animated.

But Ishbel and her baby that would be born in 1963 were already asleep – as were Andrea and Neil when James got home.

3

Being a late developer was a conundrum. One day Andrea was being told that she was a big girl and should behave accordingly, the next that she was only young and should do what she was told. Maturity was elusive. There was everything to grow out of and in to, there was very little of the present that was lasting. She was floating between conditions. Any attempt she made to be independent or express an individual opinion was greeted with derision or worse, sarcasm.

'I suppose you think you look With It.'

She hated it when adults used the language of youth. She felt patronized.

'So now we are going to be treated to the latest smart ideas from your little school friends, I suppose?'

This hurt because often it was true. Her original ideas were few, and she admired her bolder friends who expressed opinions and defied or ignored disparaging remarks and snide comments.

Normally she was embarrassed beyond reason when the older generation made fools of themselves because she felt it was done purely to entertain those of lesser intelligence like herself. She cringed to see them debase themselves. However, she had been delighted and proud of James when he had revelled in his chicken imitation. James had not always been a lawyer; once he had been young and had enjoyed amateur theatricals and been greatly stimulated making people laugh. Andrea was gratified by this discovery, and felt an affection for him that had been absent for many years. Neither parents nor children would ever admit to a lack of love one for the other, and yet it was true, especially between mother and daughter.

Andrea had been a perfect baby. Perfect to her parents, especially to Ishbel, who was so delighted at her own brilliant achievement of giving birth that all the unpleasant side of marriage became, for a time, worthwhile. Slowly, slowly Andrea had slipped from being the embodiment of perfection to the level at which she found herself at the age of fourteen, somewhere near the midden. Ishbel's conflict was within herself. One part longed for her daughter to be brilliant, witty, the idol and envy of all, and the rest of her hoped she would be able to keep her daughter suppressed and incapable of being her rival. There had been a time when Ishbel enjoyed being young and pursued by admirers, including witty and talented James Innes.

With Neil, their son, it was different. Being neither clever, nor particularly sporting, but merely a moderately pleasant, quite good-looking eleven-year-old boy with all the normal flaws and faults, he was no threat, only a disappointment.

Ishbel was already busy with plans for the accommodation and care of her baby that was due in the summer. Third time lucky! On that child her hopes were fixed.

Andrea had found her mother in the future nursery. The adjoining room was called the night nursery, which sounded mighty grand and the sort of suite to be found in a ducal household. The truth was not so impressive, but nevertheless, Ishbel believed in doing things properly. Nurse Glasgow, who had been engaged for both Andrea and Neil, would come out of semi-retirement for the baby's first month. Thereafter they would see. Ishbel felt that a proper nannie might not be necessary and maybe some nice inexpensive foreign girl might fill the bill provided she was of good family.

Andrea had assumed that she would move to another room on a lower floor once the baby arrived, and Neil, being younger, would remain on the nursery floor. There were sensible bars on the windows to stop silly children dropping out and braining themselves. Andrea was beyond such foolishness, unless of course she wanted to do it seriously, in which case the Scott Monument would make a far more dramatic site for suicide than hurling herself into the variegated laurels that flourished in both back and front gardens.

'I have been thinking,' said Ishbel, as she rummaged through a chest of baby bits and pieces, searching for a cobweb shawl that she appeared to have lost. 'I've been thinking, and Daddy agrees with me, that you should keep your room and that Neil, being the boy, should move downstairs.'

'But you promised me I should have the second spare. I had it all planned. I wanted to put stars on the ceiling.'

'Well, that settles it. I'm not having stars put on any ceiling in our part of the house. If you are keen on such excruciating tastelessness you are best staying up here where no one else will be affected.'

'But Neil will want to stick pictures of cars and footballers all over the walls downstairs.'

'Well,' she said indulgently, 'he is a boy, after all.'

Andrea thought she would cry. 'If I do have to stay up here – '

'There is no *if* about it.'

'Well then, please can I have my room painted, and could I have a bedside lamp?'

'What is wrong with your lamp? Have you broken it?'

'It is a toadstool, and it plays a tune.'

'Don't be difficult, darling. I'll see what we can do.' Ishbel made it sound as if Andrea had asked for John the Baptist's head.

'And it will be repainted, won't it?' She was determined to persist. She could stand the simpering bunnies that frolicked round her walls no longer.

'Yes, all right,' Ishbel sighed. 'The painters are coming in to do the nurseries next week, they can do yours at the same time provided you leave it tidy.'

Andrea brightened. 'Can I choose the colour? I would like it to be a sort of sunset orange, or maybe navy blue?'

'Certainly not!' said Ishbel. 'There is nothing wrong with magnolia.' Holding her hand in the small of her back, she straightened herself up and was aware that Andrea was near to tears. 'Maybe we'll get you a carpet – those rugs on the lino are a bit childish – and then you will be able to play your gramophone without the rest of the house having to listen to that awful pop stuff, though of course you will have to be very considerate when the baby comes. We don't want it waking up screaming. You do understand, don't you?'

Andrea didn't, but she knew argument was pointless. She was

quite fond of her room and it would be lovely to be rid of the Mickey Mouse mats. A really shaggy wool carpet would be heaven, but she expected it would be hair cord instead.

'You see, darling, you are such a big and responsible girl now that it would be far better for you to be near the baby rather than Neil. Boys are so . . . well, you know, so sort of unsuitable when it comes to that sort of thing.' Ishbel meant buckets of nappies and filthy bottoms but she hoped Andrea would take it as a compliment that she was considered responsible enough to live next to such a precious newcomer.

Ishbel seemed to brace herself as she gave her daughter a kiss. 'Thank you, darling, for being so kind and reasonable.' She knew she had won and felt she could afford to be magnanimous. 'You really are very grown-up these days.'

Andrea looked quite pleased. She could recall a time when her mother's approval had been the centre of her universe.

'It is odd,' said Ishbel, who was never one to ignore a potential pitfall, 'it is odd, however, that a great girl like you has not started to have periods. Still, I don't suppose that it is anything to worry about, yet.'

Andrea worried about it at once. Was her mother saying that she was likely to grow up to have a deep voice and a beard like Miss Tron, an alarmingly aggressive fund raiser for ill-used animals?

'I have arranged for you to have your hair cut before you go to stay in Glasgow. I think you ought to have a perm. Your hair is so lank, unlike those lucky Browns with their curls.'

Andrea shuddered at the horror of it. This perm had been mooted before. Only the most ghastly girls at school ever had it done, the sort who wore plastic jewellery that had to be confiscated and who carried umbrellas and wore bathing caps covered with rubber flowers.

'No thank you, I don't want curls. Marion and Fiona hate being born with curls. Sometimes they try to get rid of them by ironing their hair. I want to grow it long and have a fringe.'

'And a right sight you would look. You are no model girl, you know. You would look half-witted with a fringe, like that poor creature who works in the laundry.'

'Please, Mum, I really do want to grow it long. I promise I will keep it out of my eyes.'

'You can have long hair when you have learnt not to chew it.' Andrea always sucked her hair when she was agitated, and she spat it out now and draped it behind her ear. Ishbel continued, 'Anyway, it will never grow if you don't get the split ends cut off.'

In fact Andrea's hair, though somewhat greasy, was not that bad. When it was clean, and not in her mouth, it had quite a pleasant bounce and sheen. Ishbel had inherited her thin hair and fine features from her mother; Andrea's thick hair came from the Innes family, as did her large, round face. Of the two children Neil had inherited the best of both his parents, which was not entirely just, as he would go through life indifferent to his own good looks except to curse them when he was pursued at school by certain prefects.

Andrea was still condemned to go to Glasgow when Ishbel and Neil went to North Berwick, but the fact that her banishment to her grandmother was meant as a punishment seemed to have diminished. Ishbel relished the idea of being alone with her son. She preferred to be going without Andrea whose crime, while not forgiven, seemed to be temporarily forgotten. Both outings would start in a couple of days' time.

Petunia would have to be fed by James or the cleaning lady, Jessie MacBryde. Petunia, when young, had gone to the vet to be spayed and had come back castrated. Though James had tried to convince Andrea that Petunius might, in view of the recent discovery, be a more suitable name, she had refused to change it and so the name remained, which was more than could be said for the cat's brief tom-hood. He, or it, had grown enormous like some pneumatic eunuch whose carnal desires had become centred on the stomach as opposed to the loins. Petunia was not a cat to let anyone forget to feed him. Andrea liked to think that he loved her most of all. She may have been right, but it is hard to tell with cats.

'When the baby comes, you must be very careful to keep that cat away from the nurseries.' Ishbel did not explain why. Andrea was beginning to share her brother's opinion that this new baby was going to be a bloody nuisance as well as a blasted embarrassment.

Mr Michael had disappeared into oblivion several years before, but his deserted wife, Miss Fay, continued to call the hairdressing salon after him. Hairdressers, chefs and dress designers, when male, always carried greater cachet, she would confide in her clients, who were all extraordinarily refined and loyal but scarcely the first amongst the fashionable. (Moira MacInlay would have declared it hopelessly out of date.) Ishbel went there weekly to have her fine hair sensibly set and to get her nails painted an unobtrusive pink. The whole shop was pink and smelt of synthetic roses and ammonia. There had been consternation amongst the elderly clientele when the individual booths had been removed and now everyone could see everybody else having all manner of artifices applied to their fading locks. Now all Haymarket knew who was blonde and whose waves came from God.

The only good thing about going to Mr Michael, according to Andrea, was being able to read lots of copies of *Woman* and *Woman's Own*. Not that she was interested in what makes a good light sponge, nor did she care for crochet or endless love stories. What she loved to devour were the problem pages. Sometimes the problem was so horrific that Evelyn Home merely gave the answer and one had to guess the question. It certainly stretched the imagination. A jolly clergyman gave sound advice on how to be good and happy and a doctor also answered anguished letters.

Having had her hair washed while she gazed into Susan's armpit, Andrea had been shown to a pink seat and swathed in pink wrappings to wait to be trimmed. She was so absorbed in the trouble a reader was having with her inverted nipples and the astounding advice that she should wear shells in her brassiere that she didn't notice what was happening until a dribble of foul-smelling chemical plopped onto the page she was reading. She looked up and saw that Miss Nancy was busy winding her hair on thin rubber rollers.

'What are you doing?' she asked.

'I'm just starting the perm, dear,' said Nancy, dabbing her with more chemical and twisting more of her lovely straight hair into hateful sausages.

Andrea jumped out of the seat and tore the curlers from her hair.

'No,' she said. 'I don't want a perm, I've come to have it trimmed. I don't want to be all covered with frizz, I want to look like that.' She pointed at a large photograph of a model in the window. She had a helmet of straight hair framing her high cheek-boned face, with a fringe just brushing her enormous eyes heavy with mascara.

'Wait while Susan checks the booking,' said Miss Nancy. 'I'm sure your mum booked you in for a perm. I've set aside the whole morning for you.'

'Aye,' said Susan, 'it is a perm right enough.'

'Well, I'm not having one!'

'Sit down, dear. You are disturbing the other ladies.' Various flushed heads peered out from under dryers. They could not hear anything but gathered there was a kerfuffle.

Having persuaded Andrea to sit down, Miss Nancy started combing her damp hair and Susan passed another roller.

'Don't do it! I won't have it.'

'Now listen, dear. Your mum wants you to have a perm, and you are very lucky. After all, these other ladies don't have kind mums who pay for them to have smart hair. Now the sooner we start the sooner I'll get you finished. Look, Mrs Gilchrist here isn't making a fuss, and she had to book weeks ago. You were lucky we could fit you in.' Mrs Gilchrist appeared to be covered in hundreds of the small rollers and looked quite benign as her pungent head was covered with more chemicals, a paper bag and a pink plastic cap before the whole concoction disappeared beneath the dryer to be cooked. 'You'll see, Mrs Gilchrist will look just lovely in an hour and a half from now.'

'But she is really old. I don't want to look like that!'

Miss Fay herself now appeared. This was not the kind of scene suited to the serenity of her beauty parlour.

'What's the trouble?'

Susan, Miss Nancy and Andrea all spoke at once. Susan, being the newest junior and not much older than Andrea, was on her side. Miss Nancy wanted the tip that went with three hours of manoeuvres, and Miss Fay wanted to be paid for the perm and to keep in with a regular, if not particularly extravagant, client.

'I am not going to be turned into a frizzy idiot.'

'Hush, dear, you will look lovely with wavy hair, and it always looks better after the first few sets.' Miss Fay was trying to be conciliatory. Quite a few of the red-faced ones had poked their heads out to catch the argument.

'I want straight hair. I want hair like that picture over there, but if I have to have it cut I want to look like Helen Shapiro.'

'That would look really great,' said Susan. 'They waves are awful square.'

'Be quiet, Susan. No one asked your opinion,' Miss Fay snapped. 'One more interruption and you will have to serve your apprenticeship elsewhere.'

'But that is not fair.' Andrea tried to stand up but was held down by Miss Fay, who put both hands on her shoulders and looked at her with a daunting determination in her azure-lidded eyes. Andrea noticed that her puce lipstick was running into the small cracks round her mouth and her breath was strongly minted.

'You, young lady, are going to have a perm, like it or not!'

This was more than Andrea could stand. What business was it of this painted harridan what she did with her hair?

'I will not let you touch me!'

'Whatever is going on?' a quavery voice asked. Its owner, who was fairly ancient, appeared to have her grey hair in many tubes attached to a machine by wires. One hoped that she could be extracted in event of fire.

'It is all right, your ladyship,' Miss Fay replied. 'Nothing to worry about. Just a wee girl being a little difficult.' For once, Miss Fay regretted her decision to adopt the open plan.

'I am not being difficult. I am just telling you what I want.' As she turned in the chair, her hand struck a trolley. The wheels lodged beneath the dryer, which started to topple, just as Susan tried to save it from falling and Andrea jumped up and the whole lot went flying. Curlers, papers, chemicals and all the accoutrements of hairdressing cascaded on the floor and rolled, spilled and scattered themselves in all directions over the pink

37

linoleum and amongst the feet of all Mr Michael's scandalized customers.

'I'm really sorry,' Andrea gasped when she saw what she had done. 'That was really clumsy.' She stooped down to retrieve some of the spillage and in so doing capsized the manicurist's tray. Several of the more stridently coloured nail varnish bottles cracked as they hit the floor and mingled with the rest of the mess.

'Get out!' shrieked Miss Fay.

Andrea had never imagined that she could cause such devastation.

By this time the whole shop was buzzing, not with machinery, but with the outraged chatter of the customers. Only the ancient noble woman held herself aloof, or as much as she could with her head in such an awkward spot.

'Quick,' said Susan, 'come with me.'

She pushed Andrea through a door at the back of the shop and they found themselves in a sort of broom cupboard-cum-kitchen. There was a decidedly squalid sink in the corner quite unlike the pink porcelain at the front of the shop. 'We've got to get this gunge off your head.' Susan turned on the tap and rubbed Andrea's hair with some Sunlight soap. 'Wait there while I get some shampoo.' She returned with a bottle of pink liquid and put the snib across the door. 'My, what a carry-on! You'd think the place had been hit by a bomb!'

'Shouldn't you be out there? I don't want to get you into trouble.'

'Och, I'm through with this place. I canna' bide yon Miss Fay. I'm away to London to get a job in a boutique. Scotland is dead.'

'What about your apprenticeship?'

'Is that what they call it? It's more like being a skivvy, just washing hair and passing things and sweeping up. I'm that fed up with asking old women about their holidays. I wanted to be a real hairdresser and get to do great haircuts, not all this crimping and curling they snooty women and their grey hair.'

'You could cut my hair,' said Andrea.

'Really?'

'Yes, only you had better be quick, and I can't pay you.'

38

'Sod that! Just wait while I find some scissors. Helen Shapiro was it to be?'

'Can you do that?'

'Of course! I'll just make sure the door is locked and I can't do much about a mirror. You'll have to make do with the reflection in the window.'

Once Susan had made a few tentative snips she became bolder, and Andrea's hair fell all over the floor as she was transformed into a Helen Shapiro doppelganger. Susan sang, 'Don't treat me . . .'

'Bom bi bom!' went Andrea.

'. . . Like a child,' Susan concluded, as another lock got chopped.

They laughed and the hair settled on the butter with which Miss Fay devised baps filled with sandwich spread for her lunch.

'Here, look at this!' Susan opened the cupboard beneath the sink which housed, not only Ronuk and Rinso but several bottles of Gordon's Gin.

'Now you know why that woman smells of mint!'

That woman, meaning Miss Fay, was beside herself with fury outside the door of her glory hole. She battered at the locked door and demanded to be let in at once.

'Away and take a running jump at yourself!' Susan shouted back. 'Would madam care for some refreshment?' she asked Andrea who was now very lopsided about the head. 'Maybe a wee snifter to steady your nerves?'

'Susan, come on,' Andrea implored. 'You'll get the sack.'

'I sincerely hope I do!'

Her wish was granted almost immediately by Miss Fay, who shouted her dismissal through the door.

'Great!' Susan replied. 'I was going anyway. I'm going to set up on my own! I've got my first client already.'

'You are forbidden to poach my clientele.' Miss Fay's accent was deteriorating down the social scale as her rage increased. 'Come out at once!'

'Just a few more minutes while I get madam sorted.'

Andrea's hair did not really grow in the same pattern as the immaculate Helen but the length was about the same. Susan had

39

cut it very short at the back, quite short on the top and the fringe, and left long chewable fronds to wave seductively in front of her ears. The shape was decidedly unusual. Both girls were delighted.

'If you don't come out of there at once, I'll call the police and get them to break the door down.' Miss Fay sounded as if she originated from the seedier bits of Leith docks, which was, in fact, the case.

'Ready?' Susan tweaked at her masterpiece. 'Now, when I open the door you come with me and we will show these dafties what is what. We'll walk straight through with our chins up just like Mata Hari in yon film.'

Arm in arm they walked through the astounded shop full of women in various stages of indignity and mortification about the head. At the pink curtained glass door Susan and Andrea turned and took a bow.

'My, what a load of ninnies!' was Susan's Parthian shot.

There was, predictably enough, one hell of a scene when Ishbel learned the truth. Andrea was defiant – there was no point in any other behaviour. No one, however devious, could conceal the fact that most of their hair had been cut off and that where once a conventional schoolgirl style had existed with its side parting and kirby grip, a novel interpretation of the avant-garde was now to be seen. Susan had been bold with her scissors. If Andrea had been less stout and maybe without her National Health glasses and possibly with fewer spots, the effect might have been striking. As it was, despite Susan's naturally skilful technique, Andrea looked rather alarming.

'What in the name of goodness do you think you look like?'

'Helen Shapiro.'

'Don't be ridiculous. No one, not even this Shapiro person, could look like that, not unless they were trying to be funny. Why have you disobeyed me?'

'Because I don't want to look like the Little Princesses in that awful book by that governess Crawfie.'

'Andrea, will you please stop insulting your sovereign!'

'Nor do I want to look like Mrs MacBryde's little Christine.

She has a perm and she wears luminous socks and used to have a doll that wet its nappy. You said that was common.'

'There is no call for snobbishness!'

'Well then, can I go to the pictures with Susan this afternoon?' *Psycho* was on in Costorphine and Andrea longed to see the stuffed corpse.

'But Susie is away skiing.'

'Not Susie. Susan from Mr Michael.'

'Certainly not! No daughter of mine goes gallivanting with shop girls. You are forbidden ever to see this Susan again, or her friend Helen Shapiro for that matter. Do you understand?'

Reinforced with several doses of Gordon's and half a tube of Polos, Miss Fay shut her salon, donned her plastic mac, overshoes and rain mate and set off, crammed with indignation, for Magdala Crescent. She rang the bell and shook the rain drops from her floral umbrella like a porcupine preparing to be peeved.

'I wish to see madam,' she announced in her grandest Morningside accent to Jessie MacBryde who had stayed late.

'Yoo-hoo! Mrs Innes, there's a woman to see you!'

Ishbel found this familiarity awfully jarring but put up with it on account of Mrs MacBryde's commendable enthusiasm for polishing brass.

Miss Fay refused to take her mac off, because what she had to say would not take long. Then she sat down and made a wet mark on the brocade, so she stood up and did remove the coat, and her overshoes because she was proud of her ankles and placed the lot, plus her rain mate, on the floor near the electric fire where the heat caused a nasty smell to permeate the room and stifle the Christmas hyacinths.

She was extremely cross, and however much she apologized, Ishbel got nowhere. Reputations and flooring were ruined, clients were defecting and profits dwindling and all because of Ishbel's dreadful daughter.

It is one thing to admonish one's own child, but quite another to have that child disparaged by others. Ishbel said she was sure the accident had been a mistake, but Miss Fay was adamant. It was malice and wanton destruction and she wanted paying, not

41

only for the damage but for the loss of reputation and clientele, not to mention her staff's time and, furthermore, the perm. She would waive the cost of the haircut as she did not want the hitherto good name of her establishment to be associated with such an abomination.

Andrea was asked to apologize, which she did most sincerely and offered to help clear up the mess. Miss Fay said that fine words cut no parsnips nor buttered any ice with her. All pretence at remorse was insufficient, she added, swallowing her prominent Rs with ever increasing outraged refinement. It was pecuniary recompense she was after.

Ishbel was at a loss. She felt sick and went off hopefully to be it, and left Andrea alone facing her accuser. The fact that her fury had unsettled a pregnant woman was all grist to Miss Fay. Small wonder Mr Michael had decamped.

James, unaware of the drama, returned from the office like a *deus ex machina* and soon had Miss Fay in a state of fawning adoration. He had acquired a cunning skill and was a renowned pacifier. He dealt with Miss Fay with ploys similar to those he used when convincing his clients of the reasonableness of his fees and the imprudence of their testamentary schemes. It involved quite a bit of gin but nevertheless Miss Fay tottered off in her overshoes convinced of her victory and clutching a cheque that covered but a fraction of her original demands.

Ishbel had felt so unsettled that she had gone to bed. She received the news of her rescue with great relief but was daunted by the thought that her continued patronage and promotion of Mr Michael's was a condition of the settlement, provided Andrea never went near the place again.

That suited Andrea well. She was trying to find something stylish to go with her new image. The Fair Isle sweater and kilt that she had been told to wear for her visit to Glasgow lacked impact. Maybe if she got her pocket money in advance she could get a black polo neck sweater in the sales.

'You are a selfish girl to cause your mother such anguish,' James said. He insisted that she should forfeit her pocket money to repay him for pacifying Miss Fay. But he was glad that Andrea was forbidden to return to that establishment – her hair looked dreadful. He told his wife that he couldn't help feeling sorry for the child.

'But she thinks it is marvellous!'

'Well then, she must be deranged.'

4

It was with enormous relief that James deposited his disgraced daughter at the Kelvin Club, where his mother-in-law was a member, while he went to mingle with his Glasgow associates at the Western Club across Royal Exchange Square. The Kelvin Club was founded for the use of a most refined class of womanhood, and employed an austere group of female staff who wore white caps like brow bands and black dresses with small pleated and starched aprons. Andrea sat on the prickly horsehair sofa and felt spare. There was nothing interesting to read so she studied the print of Queen Victoria's coronation, which appeared to have been a most disorganized affair, quite unlike the coronation of 1953, which Andrea recalled chiefly for being the event that caused the acquisition of the Innes television.

The club secretary, in neatest grey and reeking of propriety, answered a telephone that stood on a stalk. James Innes had rung to say that Andrea was to take lunch at the club and wait to be collected by her grandmother in the afternoon. This was most irregular, but rules could be waived once in a while, the secretary supposed, especially to oblige a Writer to the Signet.

The cheerless dining room was gloomily furnished with small polished tables and severe chairs. A convex mirror like a leviathan's eye rimmed in gilt hung above a fireplace containing a paper fan, despite the chilly season. Sensible overcooked food was served in polite portions from an abundance of electroplated dishes. Food at the club was for fuelling purposes only. Ladies who wished to be frivolous after shopping at MacDonalds or Pettigrew and Stevens would have to go to Fullers for indulgent walnut cake.

Various examples of gentility were lunching discreetly and conversing at the murmur with their identical cronies. Lips were pursed as they glanced with distaste at a party who were going to the pantomime, which was still on at the Alhambra.

A mother, a robust grandmother, a taciturn old man and three raucous children seemed impervious to the acid looks their loudness caused.

Andrea, though at least three years older than the eldest of the girls, was dressed in precisely the same clothes of kilt, sweater, and knee socks whose garters made itchy corrugations on her stout calves. She felt miserable, overgrown and horribly conscious of the unsuitability of the shrunken Fair Isle pattern stretched over the dreadful bulges of adolescence.

The children were rowdily excited and the disapproving ladies were delighted to inform each other, hats nodding, that such uproarious behaviour would surely end with tears before bedtime. At intervals throughout the meal, one or other of the girls would disappear to the lavatory. It seemed that fizzy drinks could not be kept in their body cavities for more than five minutes.

'Look, Mummie!' The eight-year-old rushed in delightedly waving a bunch of paper bags. 'I found these in the loo. We could use them for our elevenses!'

The mother and grandmother screeched with embarrassed mirth, while the old man, who was either deaf or simple, looked quietly puzzled.

'You can't have those. Go and put them back. They belong to the club. They are for ladies that need them.'

'What do they need them for?'

'I'll tell you later.'

'Tell me now!' the child demanded.

Her mother tried to confide in her in a low whisper but the child would have none of it and wished to know all the details then and there. She had questions that she must ask in her loudest voice.

'Do you get this curse?' she asked her mother.

'Yes . . . Now shush.'

'Does everyone who has got bosoms?'

'Yes . . . Now please be quiet.'

'What about Grannie? She's got huge bosoms.'

'Well no, dear, she's a bit old,' the mother whispered audibly.

45

'That girl over there, she's got bosoms – does she get the curse?'

'Why don't you ask her?' her older sister suggested.

'Sit down at once!'

'Those ladies in the corner,' she pointed to a pair dressed overall in Jaeger, 'do they get the curse?'

'Why don't you go and ask them too,' her sister piped in again as her grandmother gave her a sharp slap.

'Mother! How dare you! You know I don't believe in hitting children.'

'More's the pity, dear! Now run along all of you and get ready while Uncle Jock goes to find a taxi . . . No, I think we will walk, the fresh air will do us good.' The children looked morosely at the curling fog.

'Does Uncle Jock get the curse?' The youngest child was eyeing his plump front inquisitively.

'Shut up!' her mother shouted. 'You know I believe in answering all your questions but I can't just now.'

'What are they talking about?' Uncle Jock asked.

'Menstruation, dear,' the grandmother, his sister, boomed.

'Good grief. Bless my soul!' Uncle Jock then retreated into a brooding silence. Evidently his ears had deceived him yet again.

Effie Lammont was sitting, or rather posing, on the horsehair sofa when Andrea came downstairs after lunch. She offered her cheek to her granddaughter and kissed the air behind in a most continental manner. An ancient beret was pulled down on her head and the rest of her clothes were drooping and greenish black with age. Her feet, still neat, were laced into well-polished, pre-war, bespoke shoes. Her lisle stockings had to be ordered from Forsyths. Once a flamboyant dresser, Effie now clothed herself in the manner that befitted a twice widowed grandmother with a mysterious past and artistic proclivities. She swooped on Uncle Jock, descending the stairs with his party, and insisted that he had partnered her at the Junior Bachelors' Ball in 1923, and he, dotty and disheartened, pretended to agree. His sister recalled no such liaison and looked with distaste on this weird interloper.

During this conversation the younger girl was able to ask Andrea whether she got the curse.

'No, not yet,' Andrea answered, quite unaware that later on in the day she would discover this to have been a lie.

It was left to Effie's housekeeper, Milroy, to sort this problem, and produce the necessities.

'This is what comes of too many late nights at an early age, Miss Andrea,' she chided, 'and too much of that government orange juice.'

Though Andrea knew that being sent to stay with Grannie Lammont was not to be interpreted as a treat, neither Effie nor Milroy imagined for one minute that this visitation was of a penal nature. Effie distrusted everything that came from Edinburgh, including the east coast weather, and assumed that Andrea, who did look a trifle odd, had been sent to stay for a change of air, a sure remedy for any kind of dyspepsia or low spirits. Ishbel had told her mother that Andrea was being difficult. This, Effie treated as a cheerful indication that her granddaughter was not entirely submerged by the Edinburgh ethos. Little more than forty miles separated the two cities but far more than that divides their souls.

In her youth Effie had been somewhat Bohemian and quite beautiful in a chiselled way, and had been fêted by artistic Glasgow once it had begun to sicken of rounded marshmallow models. Indeed, she had been painted by a 'Boy' or two, and had spent some fairly idyllic times in Galloway. Her first husband had been an artist too, though never the first to adopt a trend. His style was rather lugubrious and he made quite a bit of money by painting cattle and sheep doing nothing in misty glens. His conventional style hid a lively imagination and it had been felt that one day he would be able to release his brush from heathery burns and do something innovative. He was contemplating becoming a colourist when he was done for by a tram.

Effie remarried quite promptly and, surprisingly, chose an Episcopalian priest called Douglas Lammont. He was kind, pious and mystified by Effie's lively ways. He understood their only child, Ishbel, much better than did his wife, who dressed her

47

daughter in flowing Liberty smocks and showed no concern for her education beyond taking her to visit art galleries and talking to her in an individual brand of French that owed its accent and syntax more to the banks of the Clyde than those of the Seine. On the insistence of Douglas, who had achieved high office in Glasgow Cathedral and was on intimate terms with the Primus, as the head of the Episcopal Church in Scotland is known, Ishbel was sent to a hearty public school for girls where she wore conventional clothes and walked everywhere in a crocodile.

Douglas died during the war of food poisoning, acquired through eating chips fried in fat alleged to have been procured from the hunt kennels. He had been visiting the troops on leave at the seaside. He had never been suited to that sort of thing and rubbed his hands with too much eagerness and smiled too keenly when his pastoral duties meant he had to show the world what a good sort he was despite his dog collar. The chip shop was shut and the proprietors, some enterprising Italians, were interned as dangerous aliens. All Ardrossan was in a rage.

Effie's second widowhood was unrelieved. She had money enough, as her father had been big in shipping and her inheritance amply provided for her and Ishbel to continue living in a large, solid terrace house near Kelvingrove. Milroy looked after them. It had entertained Effie to tell people that Milroy had a past and had been a great beauty and had, indeed, sat for Sickert. Milroy was once in service in London quite near Fitzroy Square, which Effie felt was evidence enough.

Ishbel had done quite well at school and fled to Edinburgh promptly to marry James Innes, a rising young lawyer with an undistinguished war record, who was greatly disliked by her mother not only for his keen Presbyterianism but for his extreme dullness. Effie felt, quite rightly, that her daughter had never been disgraceful, and that no one should settle down until they had lived a bit. She herself was quite content to live in gloom in her later life, secure in the knowledge that her earlier years had been thrilling. Ishbel and James detested Glasgow and Grannie Lammont's dark house, which was all brown, green and maroon tiles, and felt that Andrea would be well punished by a week spent there.

48

The fog was so thick that Andrea could not see the other end of her room clearly. The mist swirled in through the windows, which were healthily open. In view of Andrea's sudden leap into adulthood, Milroy thought it appropriate to appear with a window pole and shut out the Glasgow night and close the heavy plush curtains. The stove was alight but was as warming as the canvas log effect on the electric fire at home. Perhaps there would be a fire downstairs and something hearty for tea. Milroy was famed for her solid pancakes and scones. Effie was overwhelmed with jam in epic quantities every few years when a mad Ayrshire friend, Lady Neilson, brought her baskets full of jars of the stuff. She did not believe in removing stones. One was warned lest one should break a tooth.

'I was thinking, my dear, that we should have an outing.' Effie was smoking a Capstan with her boney legs splayed out before the fire. 'We will go to the Kelvingrove Art Gallery tomorrow and see the Dali and then I wonder whether you would like to come with me to the pantomime one day?'

'Oh, no thank you, Grannie. The art gallery would be just fine.'

'Oh dear, I really did want to go to the pantomime. Perhaps Milroy will come with me after you have gone.'

Andrea felt awful. How impossible it was not to be rude. She seemed to have a talent to offend everyone most of the time. 'I'm sorry, I didn't realize you wanted to go. I thought you were just doing it for me.'

'No, dear, I love the pantomime. The *commedia dell'arte*, Punchinello, le Grand Guignol! *Je les adore!* You must learn to rejoice, be glad for absurdity. Revel in folly, weep and laugh with mankind. Do not let Edinburgh deprive your spirit of humanity.'

'No, Grannie.'

God, how embarrassing, thought Andrea.

Effie imagined that one of the reasons for Andrea's banishment had been Ishbel's pregnancy, an event of which she thoroughly disapproved. She had long since decided that breeding should be discouraged beyond replacing oneself and this James and Ishbel had speedily done. There was absolutely no need to clutter the globe with whims.

She had resolved to make Andrea's stay as pleasurable as possible. She hardly knew her grandchildren and was pleased to discover that she found Andrea to be quite interesting. The glasses were unfortunate and it was sad about the spots. She did not like to ask why her hair was so short but assumed it must have had nits. The thought of Ishbel having to deal with a child's infestation gave her a wry thrill. She enjoyed the idea of having someone young about and liked to be relieved of Milroy's company for a while.

The unchanging pattern of her existence was not unpleasant, merely tedious. At seven she dined or supped and would never admit to having high tea, though the meal hardly varied from week to week. Monday meant eggs, boiled very lightly and tasting of fishy water. On Tuesday, the day of Andrea's arrival, it was kippers. The best day was Wednesday, Milroy's day off, when Effie would indulge her passion for mutton pies bought from the butcher's shop with tiled scenes of thriving cattle around the walls, grazing in ecstasy, ignorant of their grizzly fate. Thursday brought another egg, poached this time to the consistency of rubber. Friday was a finnan haddock, and every weekend Milroy roasted a joint to a cinder and boiled a fowl till its elderly flesh fell from its bones. With a constant stream of milk puddings (the remains sustained the cat), and bowls of stewed fruit to ensure regularity, Effie and Milroy kept their sparse bodies nourished. Their souls were nurtured by Effie's attendance at Sunday Matins in the Cathedral and Milroy, who harboured a crucifix beneath her uniform, went to Mass. Thomasina, a dour old biddy, who was employed intermittently to mend, was a devout adherent of the Free Church and sneered at Milroy's popery, and was affronted by her participation in betting and games of chance.

Milroy had won a modest prize on the pools and spent it by buying a television, which she and Effie would watch in her pokey sitting room at the back of the house. It was an amicable arrangement and suited them both. With less of the house in daily use the fuel bills and Milroy's workload were both reduced, and they relished the companionship. Milroy would get irritated by Effie's habit of interrupting *Panorama* to switch to the independent channel in the hope of catching the advertisements, but years of service meant she knew her place and she solved the problem by offering it up to the Mother of God. She was chastened because she was loved.

In Andrea's honour the dining room carpet had been put to the Hoover and the kippers were eaten in splendour beneath the counterbalanced lamp, covered in threadbare velvet, tassels and intermittent beads, that hung over the massive mahogany table. Andrea hated kippers, more so than ever since they reminded her of the MacInlays.

'These kippers are unnecessarily boney, Milroy.'

'You say that every time, madam. They are created as God planned the herring, and the fact that they come from Loch Fyne rather than Mallaig makes no difference,' said Milroy firmly, as she left to eat hers in the kitchen with the *Evening Citizen*.

'I see you don't care for kippers.' The fish bones that protruded from Effie's thin lips matched the bristles on her chin.

'It's just that I am not all that hungry, Grannie,' Andrea lied. She was very hungry indeed.

'Don't lie, child, even in the cause of politeness. Would you like some scones? Milroy would be delighted to have her baking appreciated. In the meantime we will give your fish to the cat. That way face and feelings are saved. Life is for living, not for wasting on eating stuff one dislikes. I can never see the point of forcing children to eat distasteful messes. After all, if they were starving they would eat anything offered. Though, of course, one should endeavour to avoid rickets and try to preserve the teeth.'

Andrea was delighted and fell on the scones with a greater eagerness than would have been considered proper by Ishbel. Cat, who was exceptionally stout and had no other name, ate the blancmange too.

'Do tell me, what have you done to mortify your mother about your hair? I could not understand her grievance on the phone tonight.'

'I refused to have horrid old-fashioned curls. There was an awful rumpus at the hairdresser's. A friend cut it for me instead. Mum was very cross and Dad had to pay.'

'Well done! Never submit to the dictates of fashion or the restrictions of custom. Throw off the veil! Wear the trousers!

51

Spurn all whalebone and the tyranny of tight lacing, and combat foot binding at all times!'

'Can I have another scone, Grannie?'

'*Bien sûr*,' Effie answered in purest Sauchiehall Street French.

'I understand from Milroy that you have become a woman.' Effie and Andrea were standing in front of an allegory involving Nature and several Muses or Graces and more than the usual amount of breasts. They were visiting the Kelvingrove Art Gallery ostensibly to view Dali's *Christ of St John of the Cross*, but Effie would keep getting distracted.

'I wonder whether I should tell your mother. She sounded so peeved last time I spoke to her that I would hesitate to mention something so base. The refinement of Edinburgh has quite wrecked her for anything unsuitable for a tearoom. She is like a new convert to Christianity, twice as zealous as those born to it. I never told Ishbel anything when she was young because she went to the sort of school that dealt with everything in the form of a graph or in terms of some dumb beast. My mother mentioned something to me about fish swimming over each other in the water and it all being very beautiful. I assume you do not require enlightenment?'

Andrea muttered something about knowing all about it, and stared fixedly at the cavorting nymphs.

'Mind you,' Effie continued, 'any worthwhile woman can keep everyone happy, including herself, by just following her instincts. Don't you agree?'

Andrea was baffled and put about to find an answer that might stop this worrying conversation.

'That,' Effie pronounced, pointing with disdain at the classical frolics, 'is abominable! That enormity is what encourages the wrong people to take up art. It is rubbish like that which causes the ignorant to buy art and thus junk becomes popular. So wrong, so very wrong to expose foolish minds to bad art.'

Effie did not divulge what art was good. However, Andrea rightly assumed that her grandmother would not tolerate any argument on the matter. They paused at a picture of a butcher's shop. Effie sighed contentedly. She seemed to think the dripping side of meat qualified as good art, so Andrea, keen to please, gazed at it with feigned delight. She had rather liked the Arcadian revels and had been fascinated by the extra bosoms.

Effie had seen enough of the carcase. 'Incidentally, apart from your quaint hair, how have you managed to displease your parents so much?'

'They were told I had got drunk. Only I hadn't . . . well, not really. I enjoyed dancing and felt happy and someone got the wrong idea.'

'A male someone?'

'I'm not allowed to say. I had to swear to keep quiet.'

'How thrilling! Did you have a wonderful time? I remember the first time I found out that I could attract men. It was on a picnic at Largs in 1910. Reggie Cuthbertson squeezed my hand. I was utterly delighted, even though I couldn't stand Reggie.'

'I didn't like it at all,' said Andrea. They were now in front of a very murky landscape in which a couple of lost souls appeared to be destined to atone for former misdemeanours.

'Have you been molested?'

'Sort of.'

'Have you been violated?'

'I don't think so.'

'One generally knows if one has been violated, unless one has been renderd insensible or is shockingly inebriated. Were you very drunk?'

'No, not at all. Please don't ask me any more, I swore never to tell.'

'On the Bible?'

'No, the prayer book.'

Effie was silently assessing the virtues of a stout child in a large hat and appeared to be absorbed. After about a minute she suddenly turned to Andrea and asked if it had been a Church of Scotland prayer book.

Andrea said she thought it was.

'Doesn't count!' Effie announced in triumph. 'All those trite rhymes where the psalms should be – that so-called holy book is a travesty and no oath sworn thereon can be valid. Now tell all! Who was this boy?'

53

'It was a man,' Andrea whispered.

'How disgraceful. And what did he do, this filthy Lothario?'

'Please, Grannie, I'd rather not say, not here anyway.'

'All right, I won't stir up painful memories though I long to know the story. Just tell me, how did you see him off?'

'I bit him.'

'Bravo! Serves the bastard right.'

The uniformed attendant had to ask Effie to be quiet. Museums were temples of silence and not to be used for outbursts of anything, especially bad language.

'I'll have you know, my man, I am the artist's widow,' she pointed at a work labelled Sisley, 'and if it wasn't for people like me you wouldn't have a job.'

The attendant did not seem equal to the argument, and without questioning her veracity or her logic shuffled back to his seat by the door. Andrea was surprised about her grandmother being the widow of a Mr Sisley. She had always been told that her painter husband had been called Hamish Dunlop, famous only for depicting damp animals doing nothing until the tram had run him down. Effie always said it was ironical that the side of the very machine that put an end to such a brilliant native talent was embellished with a crest under which was written: 'Let Glasgow Flourish!'

'There now! What do you think of that?'

Christ was hanging from the cross, head bowed, and the painting was executed at such an angle that the viewer was presented with the top of His head. Perspective foreshortened the crucifixion and the light seemed to shine from the back and shoulders of the body suspended above a nocturnal landscape containing small figures.

'I don't like it,' said Andrea. 'I can't see it.' Her eyes could not adjust to the unusual angle. To her it looked like a grotesque bat.

'Never mind,' said Effie. 'It isn't worth bothering about. He is a dreadful man, you know. The only time I met him he was stuck in a diver's helmet and being most awfully uncouth.'

Andrea was taken aback.

'I thought it was meant to be Jesus.'

As they were making their way to the exit she wondered what

54

had happened about the painting by the Spaniard with the moustache that she had been told she was to see. She thought it best not to ask, as she had endured quite enough art.

'This afternoon we will take a cab to the Broomielaw and then as Milroy is out, we can have mutton pies.'

The prospect of pies and a trip to the docks seemed to have smothered Effie's curiosity. She had resolved to tell Ishbel about Andrea's experience. She hated injustice and could not bear the idea of her granddaughter being wrongly accused. However she could not, for the life of her, imagine what this elderly fellow had seen in this dumpy, spotty girl, but then some folks do have weird ideas . . . especially in Edinburgh.

'Remember, Andrea, I do not wish for burial.'

The sight of cattle being off-loaded from the Dublin boat seemed to put Effie in a reflective and morbid mood. The poor beasts had suffered a rough and cramped crossing after which the abattoir would hold few horrors. Effie and Andrea had taken a walk along the Broomielaw in order to work up an appetite for mutton pies. Having watched all that steak and kidney on the hoof, anything containing beef would have been tactless.

Death was a problem but not as disturbing as speculation about the afterlife.

'If heaven exists, or any of its less exalted colonies, I wonder who I will have to share my eternity with.'

Andrea assumed that her grandmother was fretting about whether it would be Dunlop or Lammont; both excellent men in their own ways, and most unlikely to be denied access to the eternal city.

'Perhaps you will get to be with both your husbands,' Andrea suggested.

'I sincerely hope not! Not unless I am thoroughly rejuvenated and have forgotten all that I have learnt. The older I get the happier I am, in fact I wouldn't mind sharing my hereafter with Milroy, only she will be off somewhere else with all those saints and sacred hearts.'

'At school they say we make our own heaven.'

'Typical of modern education! What a load of lazy nonsense.

No one has any imagination these days. Just because death, eternity, life and human nature are all great imponderables, does not mean one should not ponder on them. That way new ideas are born. Talking of which, I must show you my collection of pictures.'

Andrea groaned within. She was not mightily taken with difficult art, preferring pictures of things she could recognize. A good likeness was something she appreciated. She had heard James and Ishbel talking about Effie's collection when they had been speculating as to the size of the haul they would get once she was dead. Heaven forbid, they said, that she should die but it was as well to be prepared and, having done some crude sums, concluded that Ishbel's mother, whom they loudly hoped would live for many years, was worth a packet. School fees and other expenses would be worries no more.

A small girl dressed in baggy jodhpurs and her elderly, tweedy father were also watching the cattle being unloaded. He, for all his healthy ruddiness, had an air of immense unhappiness, but he was trying his best to enliven the pallid child beside him. She was pinched and skinny and held his hand tightly. Her only animation was in her eyes, which darted amongst the goaded cattle searching for something.

The beautiful dappled grey pony was unloaded last, its neat hooves skidding on the cattle droppings and its eyes rolling in fright. Fear can be transmitted between beasts and this animal was so terrified at the sight of the trailer that it plunged and reared, presumably thinking it to be the transport to doom. Nothing would persuade the pony to enter till a docker, well used to herding obstinate cattle towards eternity, applied an electric prod to its rump. It reared again, its unshod hooves flailing dangerously, broke loose, and galloped in panic towards the dock. No one could stop it as it jumped off the edge. There it lay on the lower deck, crumpled and dying with a broken back.

The child screamed. The longed for present, the consolation prize, was waiting for a merciful bullet.

Effie went straight to the little girl's distraught father and took charge.

She held the child firmly in her boney embrace and cooed like a

56

great mother dove. Andrea had never imagined that her sharp grandmother could be so compassionate.

'Hush now, this is soon going to be over. Your poor pony is going to a better place. You should be pleased that the kind man is going to see that it never suffers any more.' No attempt was made to remove the child. She had to learn the tough lessons as well as the joys of life. Had such a calamity happened to Andrea, she would have been whisked away and distracted with inadequate treats.

Two shots and the life was finished, the flailing stopped and the pony looked skywards with expressionless eyes, no longer terrified.

Tears fell copiously from Andrea's eyes. She had not been able to look until a tarpaulin was placed over the dead body. Somehow the small pony seemed bulkier prostrate.

The elderly father came to his child and held out his arms. Stooping down to her height, he said, 'Daddy will get you another pony, my darling.'

The child looked at him with the scorn that was going to colour her face in years to come. 'No thank you,' she said with composure. 'You don't get new people when they die.'

'Go with your daddy, sweetheart,' said Effie, 'and be nice to him, like a big girl. Look . . . he is very sad too. You must be kind to him.'

'Thank you.' His eyes were damp. Obviously, he doted on his daughter. 'Come along, we'll go home now.'

'Mummie won't be there, will she?'

'No, darling, she won't.'

'My, that was a tragedy.' Effie eased herself into an armchair. She talked as if they had just come out of a weepy film. 'One must learn to encounter such events with equanimity.' She looked at Andrea severely. 'I don't know whether it is entirely Christian but I always like to think that there is bound to be someone in a worse fix somewhere. After all, even that child was not in Belsen.'

'But Belsen was ages ago.'

'Not when you are my age. Now, what had I been saying? . . . Ah yes, I want you to remember that I wish to be cremated and my ashes scattered on the Broomielaw within sight of my father's yard. I do not want to be buried with either of my husbands. There is to be no interment for me, not even if the City Fathers gifted me a pitch in the Necropolis. If I am to be an unquiet spirit I wish to haunt the Clyde. I love the cranes and wee blue sparks of the welders working at night. I think it is the most romantic place on earth. I cannot be doing with the mawkish sentimentality of carved angels, broken pillars and draped urns. Will you remember?'

'I wish you would write it down, Grannie.'

'You have been made too cautious. It is the chill of the east coast. People in Edinburgh do not take risks. That is why Glasgow has more life to it. Fortunes are made in Glasgow to be slowly suffocated in Edinburgh.'

While they were looking at the pictures Andrea asked whether Effie really did think that animals went to heaven.

'Of course. Why ever not? You said yourself that you are conveniently taught that you make your own heaven. I would find it singularly non-heavenly without Cat, and that wee girl would undoubtedly want her pony with her.'

'But supposing you were an animal that hadn't meant much to a person, like a pig?'

'Pigs mean much to me. Without a pig one would be deprived of bacon, which would be a dreadful loss. I dare say that animals make their own arrangements about the hereafter. Us humans are far too keen to imagine ourselves to be superior. Have you ever thought that we might only be a colony of bacteria on the molar of a more advanced creation?'

Andrea had not.

'I was quite the centre of an artistic coterie.' (Effie pronounced it to rhyme with lottery.) She was pointing at a violently coloured portrait of herself in a large black hat. 'I never really took to the dance, I always found it so affected, despite dear Mary Morris and her Celtic ballet. I abhor bare feet on British legs, most unsuitable in a country so good at cobbling.'

Effie continued her soliloquy. Andrea was the audience and not required to converse. Each painting was a friend. Some of them were stacked against the wall. No one had bothered to hang them, and anyway their colour was often so loud and crude that it would have looked too startling on the brownish paper beside the heavy faded curtains.

'Now, I know I can't have treasures in heaven, unlike those misguided pharaohs, so I have decided to leave all my pictures to you.'

Andrea tried to give the impression of being deeply thrilled but was actually profoundly bored and hoped that her grandmother was going to live a good long time before these monstrosities got handed on.

Mutton pies happened at six.

5

Rogano's was only half full when Effie and Andrea lunched there before the pantomime. The brass and polished wood shone, but the company seemed flat. This was no slice of exciting society that sat, sober-suited, discussing business over fishy dishes. Pictures of lobsters, cooked and red, adorned the walls, and the restaurant itself resembled the darkened dining saloon of a pre-war cruise liner all tricked out in Art Deco. Effie had not been there for a long time but the waiters made a show of remembering her. It gave her great pleasure to introduce her granddaughter, though she would need more than two martinis to be proud of this spotted lump of a descendant.

Andrea thought she would never be embarrassed again after Effie had questioned her in Porteous, the bookshop, as to whether she had read *Lady Chatterley's Lover*.

'Do not bother to buy it,' said Effie. 'I have a copy at home. I bought it in France before the war. It is a most ill-informed piece of writing by a thoroughly nasty man. Personally I found it neither enlightening nor arousing. I expect you have tittered over it at school with your little friends.'

Andrea had read it – or rather she and Susie had read the dirty bits, which had left them both quite unmoved and fairly mystified. It had been easy to find the erotic passages in the book, which had been passed round the school disguised in the blameless dust jacket of *The Diary of Anne Frank*, as it fell open automatically at the steaming prose. The goings-on of her ladyship and Mellors seemed most improbable and therefore not enthralling. Susie and Andrea had gone back to mourning Buddy Holly and having fantasies about the curate who had prepared them for confirmation.

'I am sure you know where to find the dirty bits,' said Effie loudly. She mauled a pile of newly published books that she would not be buying. 'The rest is even more tedious.'

There were a few minutes to go before lunch and a bookshop was just the place to waste them at no expense. Andrea would have liked to have bought *Honey*, which was giving information on backcombing for maximum effect, but she had no money and did not wish to ask Effie for any, who evidently believed that one did not spend money in bookshops, which were, like Andrew Carnegie's excellent libraries, created to provide the public with free access to the written word.

The pair walked out. Andrea stumbled in her confusion, but Effie was impervious to the unprofitable disruption her visit had caused.

Seated in Rogano's, Effie had been minded to order oysters, but mercifully, despite the R in the month, they were not to be recommended. Andrea could not warm to the idea of swallowing live, jellified lumps of creature tasting of sea water. Also, she had never felt confidence in them after Kirsty's story about the man and the sneeze and the handkerchief full of oysters.

Effie decided on lobster. Andrea knew she liked that because she doted on lobster paste and tried not to feel that she was waiting outside the prison gates during a hanging while the hapless beast was being boiled.

The morning had not been wasted, as Effie had insisted on getting Andrea some new clothes. They had bought, or rather Andrea had chosen and Effie had paid for, a tomato-coloured needlecord pinafore and a truly wonderful black polo neck sweater. The effect was marred by the fawn knee socks and school shoes, so they had invested in some black stockings and black patent leather shoes, which Andrea knew would be much frowned on in Edinburgh. However, they were both well pleased with the effect, even if it did pall a bit under the dismal camelhair coat.

Because she was happy, Andrea looked better, though she could have done with a tip or two concerning backcombing. No matter what she did she could not create a solid dome of hair with slender fronds in front of her ears and a dense fringe falling to her eyebrows. Susan's haircut had been more or less accurate, but the effect displayed in every hairdresser's window eluded her. Maybe it was her head that was at fault.

Effie had miserable sparse hair but a delightfully shaped head and so hid the former and made the most of the latter by always wearing a hat. All her hats, and she had a great many, were black.

Martinis made Effie voluble but talkativeness was not conversational and Andrea was able to sit in a trance while she listened to her grandmother's former triumphs. The lobster got eaten to the accompaniment of stories that got more and more improbable, concerning the droves of admirers that had doted on her when young. It was strange that Effie had opted for the good cleric after the painter had been squashed by the tram. All Scotland – indeed, most of the world, it would seem – had been at her feet, clamouring to become her second husband.

After the war and her second widowhood, she had evidently resigned from being pursued and had nourished herself on increasingly apocryphal memories. The tales, while never exactly repeated, were like the Van Dyck multiple portrait of Charles the First, all remarkably similar. Most of her lovers had met unfortunate ends through spectacular accidents, insanity or by becoming alcoholics. One really choice fellow had done all three by drunkenly falling down a ravine in the alps whilst under the impression that he was Hannibal. No attempt was made by Effie to lower her voice as she mentioned their names, but none of the businessmen at lunch were of the same milieu and no one seemed interested in slander.

'Are you happy now that you are old and living alone with Milroy?' Andrea asked thoughtlessly in order to fill a vacancy in the diatribe.

'What is happiness?'

Sadly, this was not a rhetorical question. Effie waited for an answer.

'Well, I suppose it is getting everything you want.'

'Rubbish. People who have everything they want soon get fretful. Happiness is found through endeavour and desire to achieve. The pursuit of happiness is a constant struggle to gain satisfaction and self-respect, at least when you are young. That is why so few marriages are happy. Everyone expects to be given rapture; no one feels they should make an effort. Mind you, as I get older I seem more content than ever I was when I was searching for bliss. Constant hot water and reasonable health keep me merry. While you are young you must try to achieve your ambitions, aim for the top, struggle up the cliff face and enjoy the endeavour, for there is only fleeting satisfaction to be had in achievement and no delight in the descent. Excelsior!'

One or two heads turned in curiosity at this outburst but Effie did not notice as she was initiating Andrea in the art of using a toothpick.

'It is entirely permissible to pick one's teeth provided one does it with discretion, and the establishment has seen fit to furnish you with the equipment. Do you know why no one spits any more?'

Andrea did not have time to tell Effie about Neil, who was famous for his spitting, which he did frequently from great distances with astonishing accuracy.

'Spitting disappeared from our culture with the death of the spittoon. I predict that smoking will stop when ashtrays are no longer provided. In fact I have a theory that we have a desire to empty the bowels or the bladder in direct proportion to the amount of acceptable and congenial lavatories in the vicinity. Personally I never "go" abroad.'

'Do you travel abroad often, Grannie?' Andrea asked, hoping to change the subject as now the restaurant buzz had become silence as fifty pairs of ears were strained to hear more about Effie's interior. To have talked of bodily functions in public in Edinburgh would have been a social catastrophe.

'No, I haven't been abroad since the war. So much healthier to be regular at home.'

Effie had a talent for making the most of misfortune and it struck her as quite logical to forgo foreign travel in favour of predictable plumbing. She never spent her money with obvious relish, believing rather that she already lived in the best of all possible worlds, and preferred to travel by proxy in books, films, theatre and, lately, the television. She was terribly keen on programmes about savage beasts in distant parts and doted on the underwater doings of Hans and Lotte.

'What is your idea of happiness, Andrea?'

'I don't really know.'

'Come now, tell me. There must be something you want to achieve?'

'I would like people to believe me,' she said wistfully. 'I would also like to have contact lenses, but I know I have got to wait a bit for them, but what I really want to do is to see the mummies in the British Museum.'

'So you shall,' said Effie. 'You see, I believe you! I can't help about the lenses – I would prefer to be boiled in oil than to have to touch an eyeball, and even to talk of them makes me heave – but I can get you to the mummies. You and I will travel on a sleeper to London and do just that. Or maybe we should take one of those swift Vanguards, though this time of year is often too foggy for air travel. What fun! We will go just as soon as we can book the berths. Down one night and back up the next and you can gaze your fill on the mummies, though I fear you may find them somewhat shabby, and, I fancy, they smell a bit. Not of putrefaction, of course – your Egyptian embalmer knew his trade – but because of being so dreadfully old. You will tell me if ever I start to smell, dear, won't you? We will use the Sesame Club as our base, where I was once mistaken for Edith Sitwell.'

Andrea was overwhelmed, and didn't know what to say. She just hoped that her grandmother's scheme was more reliable than the tales of her past. She had longed to see the mummies far more than she had ever wanted a black polo neck sweater, and now she was going to have both. Bother the joy of striving, here was happiness on a plate.

The Alhambra in Glasgow was large, brassy and very full of people and red upholstery. Effie and Andrea had their seats in the stalls, for which Andrea was heartily glad because once before she had been singled out for special jibes when she had been part of a party in a box. She made sure that she sat in the seat nearer the centre of the row to be spared the likelihood of being invited onto the stage to assist in a trick or sing a song.

The story concerned an incredibly fair lassie, who spent much time being awfully good, badly done by and in desperate need of her true love, a well-known Scottish tenor who sang of Boony Doon and Islay in all spots including fairyland and the demon's den. The comedian had remarkable teeth and a face like a horse. He did the usual things with water, runaway rats and custard pies. Sometimes he appeared disguised as the lovely lassie's dotty grannie. Andrea loathed seeing grown men trying to make people laugh by making fools of themselves. The wearing of funny hats never made her feel any happier and she hated thrown food. Effie roared with laughter, sang raucously and clapped her hands in time to 'The Skye Tramping Song' while her granddaughter scanned the programme for a clue as to how much more was to be endured before the finale. Even the prospect of the mummies failed to obliterate the horror of the exploding wedding cake that revealed the lassie's grannie all togged up for the nuptials with a teapot on his head, singing of much gay stepping out arm in arm and row on row for Marie's wedding.

The evening was wet and it was dark when the pantomime ended, so it took quite a time to find a taxi to run them home. Effie pronounced herself to be quite shattered, although she hadn't enjoyed herself so much for years.

'Neither have I,' said Andrea.

They both knew she lied.

Milroy had been given some extra time off to visit her married sister in Dumbarton who, being greatly under the weather with her joints, found a good gossip to be most cheering in January when everything conspired to enhance her arthritis.

Andrea went to brew some tea while Effie sat slumped by the gas fire in her smaller sitting room. An electric wireless with exciting foreign capitals on its dial stood on the side table solidly encased in Bakelite. Effie switched it on to hear the news and it hummed as it warmed to its task.

As Andrea fought with the exploding gas rings on the mottled grey stove and put the heavy brown enamel kettle on to boil she was startled by a piercing ring. Above the door was a glass-fronted box and in it she could see that a red flash was quivering beside a section marked 'Smoking Room'. She assumed that Effie had called her and ran up to see what was the matter, tripping over Cat on the stairs.

'I can smell burning rubber.'

Effie was still sitting by the fire but appeared most agitated. A breezy BBC woman was giving staunch advice on some worthwhile subject over the air.

'Please investigate, dear.'

There was no sign of any burning and Andrea could smell nothing beyond the faint fumes following the ignition of the gas. Eventually Effie let her return to the kitchen to rescue the kettle that would be fairly hopping with boiling water. Still she insisted that there was an odd smell. She also complained of a headache. Andrea said she would find some aspirin and bring it with the tea.

The kitchen was large, dark and subterranean, and far from those co-ordinated masterpieces advertised in *Ideal Home*. The cupboards overflowed with items that Effie had seen on the commercials; she would even have bought Brand X if she could. Food was sparse and rather elderly, but Andrea dug some digestive biscuits out of a cream-coloured tin and discovered some fruit cake sitting on a crumby doily. She found aspirin behind the clock where they had been living with a large supply of Andrews liver salts, a holy picture and the paper boy's Christmas tip. She cut some bread and failed to make it either thin or symmetrical. Once the tray was complete, she carried it upstairs, carefully avoiding Cat who seemed unnaturally alert. Effie was still tuned into the Home Service but was, in fact, noisily asleep.

Andrea could not wake her and decided to leave her to rest. She would wake her for the news. Though they were slightly musty, Andrea found the biscuits to be rather nicer than the lobster and ate quite a few before she looked at Effie again, whose snoring had become very loud and irregular. With disgust she noticed saliva coursing out of the sagging mouth and then saw that water, or worse, was forming a puddle on the floor. She prayed that Milroy would come home soon.

Effie opened her eyes but did not seem able to move.

'Would you like some tea, Grannie?'

Her answer sounded like a roar, then Effie was sick. It just came out – there was no retching or heaving, which seemed to make it even more revolting. Effie had turned into a leaking sack. The stench was awful.

Andrea found a tablecloth and wrapped it round her

grandmother so that only her head stuck out and all the horrors were hidden beneath, she tried to wipe her mouth with a napkin but the stream was continuous. In desperation Andrea looked at the time and resolved to ring home for help ... once the cheap rate started. Only ten minutes to go. She knew she must not squander money on peak time calls.

She went to see whether Milroy had returned, but her room was empty and there was no sign of anyone coming down the terrace from the bus stop when she lifted the curtain to peer down the street from the bay window.

Effie was quieter, the breathing seemed to be shallower, but she shook all over as she gazed at Andrea without blinking.

The clock struck six.

'Stay where you are, Grannie. I will ring home.'

The operator took ages to organize the reverse-charge call.

James answered the telephone. 'I don't think we will bother your mother with this just now. She has had quite enough to put up with from you lately and she is enjoying herself in North Berwick with Auntie Mary. Why don't you just go back and wait for Grannie to wake up? Old people need a lot of sleep and I expect all your gallivantings have worn her out. Milroy will be home soon, I'm sure.'

The exchange lady might not care for such things as wet floors and the stink of vomit and faeces being talked about on her telephone, so the call ended with some inconsequential chatter and instructions to be good.

Andrea knew at once that Effie was dead. The jaw had dropped, the eyes were staring yet sightless, and the awful breathing was silent. Something told her she should feel for a pulse but she could not bear to touch the body. Remembering a scene from a film involving a mirror, Andrea held the silver sugar basin up to Effie's mouth to see whether it got clouded by her breath.

It was the same operator, and she was no quicker the second time when she was asked to arrange for the charges to be reversed. James refused to accept the call. He hated extravagance and felt that his children should learn to write letters.

Andrea sat in terrified despair. Who was there to ring? It was too late for the ambulance, there was no fire and one never involved the police. Suddenly she realized that with Effie dead and no longer able to pay her bills she could ring James without reversing the charges and involving the chatelaine of the exchange.

James answered. 'Andrea dear, you must be more self-reliant and not so easily agitated. You are a big girl now.'

'Grannie is dead.'

'I see,' said James. He may have been shaken by the news but it was not in his nature to betray surprise or alarm. 'Stay where you are, I will organize everything.'

'I can't stay here alone, Daddy. She is dead.'

'You can and you will stay there,' he said firmly. 'I will sort everything. In the meantime, do not make any more calls. Do you understand?'

As James hung up he heard Andrea sob and he felt, just for a moment, that it was not at all right for his mother-in-law to have done that in front of his daughter while her maid was out. Glaswegians are so inconsiderate. He would have to cancel his plans for the evening too.

'Don't hurry back. Andrea and I will be just fine.' Effie had told Milroy to make a day of her Dumbarton jaunt, and that is what Milroy had done. Seven o'clock came and still no sign of her.

The wireless played on. Evidently Hugh Gaitskell was not so chipper either. Andrea found the noise welcome. It prevented total isolation. The fog did not help. She feared that a howling might start. She needed to let fresh air in and Effie's soul out so she prodded with the window pole till she managed to open the sash. The fog came in and the light from the red-shaded standard lamp became diffused. She kept the curtains open as she hated the idea of being shut in with the corpse, now waxen white and strangely smooth. The jaw hung down and the eyelids drooped.

It was usual to have the dead laid flat and to put coins on the eyes – at least that is how it always was in stories – but Andrea was not going to touch any cadavers apart from covering poor Effie's vacant face with a velvet cloth that she had always used for the card table. The gas was extinguished. It would not be needed for

68

warmth any more, as Andrea could not bring herself to mount a vigil in the same room as that sinister mound.

She had loved Effie. Probably she had been more fond of her than she knew, but now she was dead. She had gone from that hideous body, which was now just a hulk, like a once-gleaming car after a crash. Andrea had an irrepressible notion that the heap might erupt, so she left the sitting room, locking the door behind her. The wireless continued to mutter to itself.

Andrea felt safer and less isolated sitting on the front door step. Huddled against the chilly night, she prayed for her own, not her grandmother's, deliverance.

'Whatever are you doing there?'

The voice was thick and strange. Andrea turned, and since she was sitting in a pool of light shed by the porch lamp, she could make nothing of the house interior behind her. The voice belonged to a barely discernible figure in the hall.

'Go away!' Andrea screamed as she tried to jump to her feet.

'Whatever is the matter?' said the voice.

'Who are you? Keep away!' Never had she felt such fear. Later she was to wonder how those in the Bible appeared to retain their composure when receiving visits from On High.

Milroy was neither fiend nor angel. She had let herself in the back door, as befitted her station, and was wearing her outdoor coat and not her black dress or familiar starched cap.

Andrea ran down the steps into the street and straight into the arms of the doctor whom James had rung and asked to attend.

'Whatever is all this carry on?' Milroy was now illuminated by the porch light. Her face looked flushed.

'Oh, Milroy, I'm so sorry,' Andrea sobbed. 'I'm so sorry.'

The doctor was baffled but assumed this to be the right address. In any case, he could scarcely leave this scene with things as they were.

'What is wrong, Miss Andrea?'

'Grannie is dead. It was horrible. She died during the news. I am so sorry.'

Milroy looked at her in disbelief and tried the sitting room door. After unlocking it she entered and turned on the light.

'Don't be silly, Miss Andrea. Look, she is here. She has been having a wee hiding game with you while she listens to the wireless. What a rumpus! Look here . . . Abracadabra!' Milroy swept the cloth off with a flourish.

But Effie was still there. She was still dead.

Milroy laughed. She worked from a chuckle through a crescendo of hysterical screeches till the tears streamed down her face and she rocked herself with mad mirth.

The doctor, now certain that he was at the correct address even if it was that of an institution for the deranged, decided to deal with the living first. He had not needed seven years of training to see that Effie was dead and nor had medical school taught him the best cure for hysterics but, despite any new teaching to the contrary, he gave Milroy a resounding slap on the face and ordered that she pull herself together. Milroy's jowls flapped and her streaming eyes looked with loathing at the young man. However, the trick worked and she was quiet.

'Now go and make a cup of tea!' he commanded with great authority.

'Yes, sir,' Milroy answered, her outburst concealed beneath her usual restraint.

Andrea fell in love instantly.

He was of sturdy build and had gingery hair and freckles, which was not the stuff of James Dean but a thousand million times more gorgeous. Having established that there was nothing he could do for his senior partner's late patient he rang for the undertaker.

'Come with me,' he said kindly to Andrea. 'You have had a horrible time. It is Andrea, isn't it? Let us go and see what has happened to that cup of tea.'

Very little, was the answer. Milroy was seated at the kitchen table surrounded by several empty miniatures of Haig weeping into a very wet dish clout. She had covered her head with a towel that bore the legend 'Udder Cloth', and she clutched a half-drained glass of neat whisky.

'You had better take a grip on yourself, woman. Away and wash your face in cold water and come back when you are more composed. I am going to talk to this young lady.'

No one had ever spoken to Milroy like that.

70

'Mrs Lammont was my life,' she said reproachfully.

'Quite. Well, she needs you to help her in death too,' he said more gently. 'Be off and get yourself sorted.'

'Is she drunk?' Andrea asked, fascinated.

'Very,' the doctor replied.

Andrea had not cried at all. The fact of loss and the finality of death had not struck. She was still in fear of that awesome heap. Nothing would ever make her look on her grandmother again. Death must be concealed and covered.

Ian was the doctor's name, and for all his youth, he was magnificent and treated Andrea with all the respect due to an adult. He did not interrupt her history of the evening's events. The death of a woman in her seventies following a massive stroke (only he, being a Scot, called it a shock) was not unusual, though there would have to be an inquest. He was satisfied that there would be no further difficulties. He had not known Effie personally but she had been a patient of his practice, in which he was the newest member, for a very long time. Effie had died because her time had come. It was a wonderful way for her to go following a great day out with a favourite granddaughter.

Andrea, anxious to be truthful, pointed out that she was Effie's only granddaughter. She was also worried in case her end had been brought on by over-exertion and that she would be blamed for causing such exhaustion. Furthermore, she wished the doctor to know that pantomimes were not to her taste. She felt sure that he would agree with her in the dislike of such foolishness. He was bound to share her aversion to silly clowns and over-egged antics.

'Your grandmother died at the end of what she thought was a wonderful day. I am sure the outing gave her the greatest pleasure even if you did not enjoy yourself.'

'I told her that I had a lovely time.'

'Well then, she died a happy woman. You should be proud of yourself.'

Andrea knew that Effie had detected her lie. Regrets were useless; she could never atone for her affectation. Though her death may have seemed grotesque and agonizing, the divine doctor tried to make Andrea understand that Effie probably had

71

felt or known nothing at all beyond sensing that she was in her own home surrounded by everything familiar and beloved.

Ian patted her hand. She gazed enraptured at the freckles on his wrist and then began to cry, but not with grief. He might have put a comfortingly avuncular arm around her had not James arrived at that moment. Due to the fog, he had driven from Edinburgh with extreme caution, but even so, his entrance was too soon. What a lump of heaven was thus denied.

James took charge, and things moved along at a pace.

Conveniently, a copy of his mother-in-law's will had been entrusted to him, because of his unfailing prudence and reliability. This document was consulted and instructions were given for when and how the body could be released for burial. In the meantime Effie was removed to the mortuary. The covered stretcher on which she was carried out looked empty because she had been so very lean. Milroy gave a good impression of sobriety and said she would be fine on her own. She must care for Cat and ensure that the blinds be kept down till after the funeral. James would take Andrea back to Edinburgh where Ishbel was being robustly comforted by Auntie Mary, who was having a wonderful time being a brick.

'Grannie wanted to be cremated.'

Milroy crossed herself.

'Rubbish,' said James. 'There is nothing in the will about that.'

'But she did. She told me to tell you that she wanted her ashes to be scattered on the dock side.'

'What nonsense, Andrea!' James was in no mood for silliness.

'She didn't want to be buried with either of her husbands. She said so.' And then, softly, she added, 'I was to have the pictures.'

'While there is no call for mawkish sentimentality, Andrea, your mercenary attitude is quite inappropriate.'

6

By happy chance there were slots still vacant in Effie's family lair. Thus the difficulty of selecting with which husband she should share her eternal rest was avoided. The lair had been designed for a whole dynasty of ship builders, but had only been occupied by Effie's parents, her aunt and a stillborn child whose provenance was obscure. Two of her brothers had been slaughtered in the Great War when they were scarcely old enough to possess razors, let alone bayonets, and though buried in Flanders were commemorated on the granite obelisk. No one ever mentioned Effie's remaining brother, Uncle Roland, who had disgraced his family and hopefully met a sticky end in foreign parts.

Andrea was excluded from the goings-on. There was nothing she could do. The Browns had her to stay as Ishbel was prostrate with grief, and burying was men's work. James took Neil to the funeral and they held cords as the coffin was lowered into its hole, which was tastefully lined with white ceramic tiles like a public lavatory. Effie, whose Episcopalianism was quite staunch, would have been incensed by the ritual with the cords, but her father had been a member of the Church of Scotland and to be buried without cords in the English fashion entailed the hiring of two further pallbearers, which James considered to be a flagrant waste of estate. Milroy was the only woman at the grave side. The cemetery was 'doon the watter' and overlooked the Firth of Clyde.

After it was all over everyone assembled at Effie's house and Milroy served up every old crumb and stale biscuit she could find.

Ishbel had not wasted the time during her mother's interment and had prudently collected any loose jewels and small valuables and stowed them away amongst the household cleaning materials that she thought she might need to remove to Edinburgh. The rest of the house defeated her. She could not contemplate the chaos of trying to empty such a barracks of belongings. She would tell James that her health was not equal to such an upheaval. Satisfied that she had removed the tastiest items from the grasp of probate, she collapsed in the dining room to await the return of the burial party.

She was deeply discouraged. The sight of all those lurid pictures had depressed her. The memories of childhood spent in this house were not pleasant even when viewed through the lapse of twenty years. Ishbel found Glasgow vulgar.

Few people had even attended the service. Many of Effie's friends were, of course, dead. Those that had outlived her were not aware of her death as it had been thought unnecessary to put an announcement in either the *Herald* or the *Scotsman*, let alone *The Times*, which would have been an absurd extravagance.

Netta Neilson, who lived in Ayrshire and was a bit strange, had rung up. Ishbel had always known Lady Neilson and had never cared for her, despite the title. She had quite a battle to convince her that Effie could not come to the phone for a chat.

'Mother is dead,' Ishbel shouted very loudly.

Netta, and probably most of the terrace, heard. 'Oh dear. I am so sorry. Oh dear, oh dear, so few of us left. I really loved your mother. She was such a good friend, such a kind person and so entirely out of the ordinary. I must come to the funeral.'

'She is being buried just now,' Ishbel bellowed.

'Oh . . . if only I had known. I would have liked to have done something. She was one of my oldest friends, you know. Oh well, it is too late now.'

'Yes,' said Ishbel. 'Goodbye.' She hung up and eyed the funeral tea with disgust, including Netta's dangerously stony damson jam.

Thomasina was in charge of the door and opened it with a face of suitable doom when James and the rest returned. Neil had found the funeral quite interesting, but wished that Andrea had been there too. He did not share her enthusiasm for mummification and embalming, but he found the procedure of disposal quite enthralling. As with the most esteemed Glasgow bodies, Effie had been buried by Wylie Lochhead in the best possible taste. There were no transatlantic indulgences, no cosmetics or open coffins. Effie was returned to her maker without her false teeth or wedding rings and took nothing out of this world except her second-best nightdress.

The old family lawyer, a revered and doddering man, had attended the proceedings with his young partner of only sixty-two. They made up a chorus of condolence and had a repertoire of comforting eulogies that provided a suitable background of subdued murmur. Together they spent more time assisting at the departure of their clients than serving their legal needs while they yet lived. 'A sad day, a sad day,' they muttered, adding that they would not see her like again.

The senior partner of Ian's practice was also there. He was not in the habit of attending his patients' funerals but he said that he had been privileged to have counted Effie amongst his friends as well as attending to her professionally. He apologized most profusely for having been away when Effie had died but also said he was relieved to have found such a splendid young man to join his firm. Ian had been an excellent choice, he said, and a doctor in whom one could have supreme confidence.

'Where is your daughter, Mrs Innes? I understand she behaved with remarkable good sense. It must have been quite an ordeal for one so young.'

'We thought it best for her not to come to the funeral,' said Ishbel. 'She is, as you say, very young and also somewhat immature.'

'I was told she was most composed and responsible. I see your son is here. He seems to be a fine lad too.'

'Oh yes, Neil is far steadier than Andrea. We felt it would be for the best to spare her any further unhappy memories. She will soon forget the loss of her grandmother. Whereas I am afraid that I, as a daughter, will never get over the death of my mother.'

Ishbel dabbed at her tears with a lace-edged handkerchief that she had found while emptying Effie's dressing-table. A half-chewed fruit gum was stuck over the embroidered initial and the humiliation of shoving a sweet in her eye caused her further mortification.

James suggested that she should go and have a lie down before their return to Edinburgh. He told the doctor that he was taking the greatest care of his wife and that promising morsel of the next generation that she carried in her womb.

'I trust you will give my regards to your daughter. She sounds like a grand girl and a credit to you all,' the doctor told Ishbel.

After the funeral, Neil returned to Edinburgh in the convenient company of his godfather who had an office in Glasgow and with whose family he would stay for a couple of nights. At home, Neil got on surprisingly well with his godfather's son, though at school, being his senior by a couple of years, he would have nothing to do with him.

Cautiously James drove towards home. Ishbel was exhausted and taciturn as she sat beside him, mournfully dressed all in black except for the fur hat that he had given her by way of a condolence present. Unlike Moira MacInlay, Ishbel when hatted looked much worse than the Moscow-bound Prime Minister. The beauty contest was a walkover to Supermac. She put James in mind of a crowned crane that he had seen at the zoo.

Evidently more than bereavement was putting her out, and by the time they were passing the mast at Kirk O' Shotts she had told him the cause of her concern.

'I cannot face the prospect of clearing that house. Even if I were in good health it would be too much for me. How mother could have left me with such a task beats me.'

'But she also left you with all her things.'

'Junk mostly! Have you seen those pictures?'

'That reminds me, Andrea said that she had been told she was to have them.'

There was a silence and James assumed that Ishbel had not heard him. 'She told me when she said that your mother had wanted to be cremated. Of course we could do nothing about that as it was not in the will.'

Ishbel was on the point of explosion. Never had she heard of such nonsense. How could that scheming child make up such lies! How dare the little creep try to grab stuff for herself! Had she no respect? Did she not realize what a catastrophic tragedy had occurred?

James endeavoured to calm his wife by saying that Andrea had not seemed at all keen about having the pictures either and was merely relaying something that Effie had dementedly told her a day or so before her death.

76

'Andrea will get what I choose for her. Neither of the children are mentioned in the will so I will divide their inheritance as I think fit.'

'Right you are, dear.' James overtook a duotone Morris Traveller. 'Look, number 666!'

'We are not with the children now,' Ishbel said scornfully, 'so please don't try to divert me by saying it will be 999 when it is upside down in a ditch.'

'No, dear.'

By the time they were nearing the outskirts of Edinburgh at Ingliston, James had hit upon a fine scheme. He proposed that Ishbel should retain Milroy and put her in charge of Effie's house, which she could let as furnished flats. That way nothing would need to be disturbed or disrupted. The contents could remain in situ and everyone would be happy including Milroy, who would undoubtedly prefer to stay in her old employment to being a pensioner living in dreary Dumbarton with her sickly sister. That at least was James's view of her future, and he did not expect his mother-in-law's maid to express any other.

Ishbel agreed with him. She even stopped scowling. It was a good and sensible plan and would spare her much aggravation.

She dabbed at her drippy nose and inspected the hanky. Muttering about the elderly and their disgusting habits, Ishbel extricated her mother's discarded fruit gum from the linen and flung it out of the car window into the horrid January night.

'Did you not think it odd that Mother had no photographs of her grandchildren on display?'

James had not noticed. He had been doing sums in his head concerning the likely value of the silver frames and had not noticed their contents.

'Did you ever give her any pictures of Andrea or Neil?'

'No, why should I? She never asked.'

They were nearing home and it would be pleasant to arrive in benevolent mood. James said how nice the old doctor had been and how gratifying it was to hear such good reports of Andrea's behaviour.

'Don't be absurd,' Ishbel hissed. 'That man is a socialist!'

Andrea was still staying with the Browns when term began. She had to be driven many miles from Lasswade in the south to her school on the north of the city each day, but no one complained. Major Brown's wine business was not really so very far out of the way, all things considered, and he courteously maintained that it would be a pleasure to make the detour. Mrs Brown lied staunchly about Andrea's school being so handy and convenient for her as she had to visit that area frequently in the line of duty. Bunty Brown did good by wheeling a comfort-laden trolley briskly round the Royal Victoria Hospital and dispensing encouragement and cheerfulness to the incurables along with grubby library books, Spangles, Refreshers, stamps and sickly scented soap. Andrea preferred the days she was compelled to go by taxi; the heartiness of the Brown clan could be overwhelming.

It was nearing the end of January when she returned to Magdala Crescent.

'Hello, who are you?'

A woman with a bitter look and a cigarette glued to her lipstick came out of Andrea's room. She was pulling a vacuum cleaner by the wire like an unbiddable dog.

'Who might you be?' the woman countered. 'And mind where you are going with your great feet. I won't have any stoor made by no stuck-up young lasssies. So mind your manners. I am Mrs Orr to you, and don't you forget it.'

Andrea thought she had never seen such a thoroughly unpleasant person before. 'I am Andrea,' she said as nicely as possible, which was not nicely enough.

'So this is your room that I have been sorting. Well, now it is done you make sure it is kept tidy. I am not chasing round after the likes of you.'

It was the first time that Andrea had seen her room since it had been painted. She had achieved a blue wall but it was saxe, not navy, and the toadstool lamp had been replaced by something nasty but adult, made out of wood and probably by the blind. The Mickey Mouse and Pluto mats had gone from the floor and a fleece-shaped, greyish sheepskin lay where the cartoon chums had been. The new carpet, which had been laid on the old lino, stopped the dead sheep from sliding at speed. The corpse crept towards the door instead. On the whole she was pleased, despite the anaemic walls and lack of fluff in the fitted carpet. If she remembered to say her prayers her knees would bear the imprint of the hair cord. Gentle Jesus was still suffering little children above her short utility bed, which was pleasingly familiar. The rest of the room looked stark and uncluttered, almost institutional.

Mrs Orr was cleaning the bath with Andrea's face flannel, which she had peppered fiercely with Vim.

'I use that to wash my face.'

'Well, you will just have to wait till I am through with it,' Mrs Orr replied.

Would the spots improve if scoured? Andrea had her doubts.

'Where is Mrs MacBryde?'

'Gone to a better place.'

'What?' Andrea was horrified. 'And little Christine?'

'There is no one here called Christine that I know of. Now clear out my way. I have work to do. But I want you to understand that I know my rights and I am not going to be exploited and I do no ironing, or heavy lifting.'

Downstairs, Ishbel explained that Mrs Orr was now the new daily and they were all lucky to have her. Andrea must bear with her and behave herself.

'But she is so rude. And she used my flannel to clean the bathroom.'

'I won't have a word against her, Andrea, do you understand? She is invaluable, a treasure, though it is a shame that she will not iron.'

Ishbel convinced her family that she was quite incapable of performing any housework apart from simple cookery and flower arrangement. Her dread of being without a cleaner made her a prey to the likes of Mrs Orr.

'When did Mrs MacBryde die?' Andrea asked. 'That woman said she and Christine had gone to a better place.'

'That is a matter of opinion,' Ishbel answered. 'As far as I am concerned they might as well be dead.'

Andrea was relieved to know they were still alive; she'd had her

79

fill of death. Bereavement was far more awful than she had imagined when she had been mesmerized by rites of passage.

Apparently Mrs MacBryde had been poached by Moira MacInlay and she and little Christine now shared the accommodation that had once been home to Juanita, who had been sent back to Spain in disgrace following the incident in the MacInlay bed at Hogmanay.

Juanita's dismissal had been a highly colourful affair with many accusations and denials, and the best Blair was quite offended at being absolved from the sin of deflowering a hapless virgin even though Juanita maintained she had been seduced by the rampant youth and would now be regarded as fallen and no longer marriageable. The truth was quite the opposite. She wore a locket containing a photograph of her younger daughter round her neck. Besides, Hector (and at least one other lusty male) knew that she was no innocent. The Blair suffered from a loss of reputation but not of allowance.

No one knew how Mrs MacBryde had heard of the job. Ishbel put it down to Moira's Jewish guile. Her fear and loathing of Jews was equal to that which she felt for socialists. Her heaven was very small, containing remarkably few mansions all filled with right-wing, white Anglo-Saxon Protestants.

'I am sure Moira MacInlay is a gentile,' James had said in an attempt to appease his wife.

'Oh yes, she is awfully genteel, but that doesn't stop her being a Jew. You only have to look at her flashy mother.' Ishbel made a gesture outlining a hooked nose. 'She has a dress shop in Troon.' This evidently was a foolproof test for non-Aryan blood, and far more reliable than anything devised by Hitler's henchmen.

'Your prejudice does you no credit.' James could still recall the appealing face beneath the hat at kirk. 'Besides, she is a fervent worshipper at St Cuthbert's. You should try not to be so anti-Semitic.'

'Don't be so disgusting! Remember my condition and have you forgotten my terrible grief?'

No, James could hardly forget. Nor could he understand much of what went on at Magdala Crescent these days. He contrived to spend long hours in the office.

*

School was most welcome, even though it was the worst term of the year. Sometimes Andrea would get a lift from her father, but more often than not she would have to take the bus, which was inclined to dawdle, so to be sure and get to school on time she would have to leave the house while it was yet dark. No excuses except fatalities and epidemics were sufficient to absolve a pupil from lateness at assembly.

Kirsty MacInlay always devised ways to make herself look striking in her dark red uniform. Her sweater was large and long, her skirt short and narrow, and her hips and legs were shapely and slender. Andrea's uniform was rather shrunken and her body somewhat swollen, but the two girls were not in the same class so the unfortunate comparison was not too obvious.

At their school, Fiona and Marion Brown wore unflattering green, which did not worry them at all as they knew they were destined to leave at the earliest chance and be sent to the Dough School in Atholl Crescent. Kirsty was booked to finish her education in Switzerland. Andrea had no thoughts about her future excepting those that involved a further encounter with Dr Ian Robb.

She thought of nothing else as she travelled past Comely Bank and Ravelstone Dykes. She became withdrawn and dreamy and her work suffered. She devised all manner of chance meetings. Sometimes she would rescue him from hideous accidents, sometimes he would loom out of the wintry mist and spring would suddenly blossom all round. She thought she might become a doctor too, and thus they could meet professionally, but her grasp of logarithms was most rudimentary and would never get her the requisite Highers to qualify for a career in medicine.

Maybe she would be a nurse. Her biology was quite good, especially if it involved putting the granules into drawings of the amoeba and its pseudopodia. Ian would be welcome to do everything in Chapter Fourteen of the biology textbook, and much more besides, including all the activities of Lady Chatterley's lover. Tingles crept up her spine and through her stomach and between her legs down to her toes, which she would screw up with anticipated rapture. Oh God, how she loved him.

81

This must be the more interesting stuff of growing up. The other was plain tedious except that now she could be Off Games every four weeks, which was a real bonus.

Even without her old best friend, Susie, time spent at school was bearable. Life at home was grim.

After a week or so at home, Andrea thought she ought to attempt to be amiable.

'I could do some ironing,' she volunteered.

'There is a good girl,' said Ishbel. It would be excellent for her daughter to learn the ways of pressing a shirt – such a skill might get her a good man one day.

'Would you pay me? I really could do with some money?'

'What for?'

'Well, clothes and things.'

'I suppose the next thing will be make-up?' Ishbel managed to make it sound like narcotics.

'Well, yes,' Andrea admitted.

Ishbel withdrew her good opinion. 'You have a nasty materialistic streak,' she scolded.

Andrea felt as low as the level of her funds.

Back in her room, Andrea started to go through her things. She thought she might as well try to see if some miracle discovery of a forgotten treasure could be made to cheer her. However, when she opened her cupboards the interiors were as pristine as the outside. No old books or toys, no ancient loves. All her friendly teddies had disappeared. Brumas the bear, Ellie, Molly the Golly and Big Theo – they were nowhere in her room.

'Where have you put my toys?'

'In the brock where they belong,' said Mrs Orr. 'Now mind your manners and don't let me hear you running to your mother tale-bearing.'

'You can't have thrown my teddies into the dustbin!'

'I was told to tidy your room so I did. I do my job properly. I was asked to clear out the junk and junk there was by the binful.'

Andrea ran downstairs and out the back to the shed that housed the dustbins. It was swept and clean. The men had collected the rubbish that morning. All her friends had been flung away. She had loved them since before she could talk. They would be hurled into a burning fiery furnace along with all the books and plays she had started to write, her Pelmanism cards, the backs of which she could read by the creases, and her ancient and familiar toys that she had been keeping for the new baby. Everything had gone, the whole of her childhood been thrown away. The only remnant, apart from the books on the shelf, was a hateful doll with which she had never played. It sat stiffly on the wardrobe dressed in spangled net.

'Andrea, what is it now? Can't you see that I am worn out? Have you got no homework to do?'

'Mum . . . Oh, Mum, please!' She knew that tears irritated Ishbel beyond reason, but this was real grief. 'All my teddies have been thrown out! I loved them so much.' She flung herself face down on the sofa and sobbed. Ishbel was touched by her misery and laid a frigid hand on her heaving shoulder. 'Hush now, lovey,' she said with unaccustomed sympathy. 'I know Mrs Orr did it for the best. You are such a big girl now, and they were all so tatty.'

'But I loved them. You don't throw people away when they get old and torn.'

'Now you are being ridiculous. Of course they are not like people. They were just silly stuffed bits of material for little children to play with. You wait till you lose someone you love like I have, then you will know real grief. Come on, pull yourself together. You really are a silly great girl. One minute you are asking for money to spend on cosmetics, the next you are weeping for a few childish stuffed toys. You must grow up. Now, let us talk about something else. You have never told me how you like your room since it has been done up.'

'I liked it more as it was.'

'Well, you should have thought of that before. You can't have everything. A girl who wants to wear make-up can't keep on playing with old toys. A time has come for you to put away childish things.'

Ishbel did not say with what Andrea was to replace the childish things, and volunteered no compensation, though the next day, for some extraordinary reason, her daughter's plight touched her and she bought her a rather cheap blue bear with a contrived cute face. Ishbel put such folly down to her pregnant fancy.

Andrea gave the smirking beast to Neil to use as a target for his air gun.

Later, when Easter came, she saw Big Theo. He appeared to be crucified, tied to the front of the dustcart for a mascot. She pleaded with the bin men to give him back to her but they said totting was against Union rules. Theo gazed benignly on the world with his single eye, but Ellie, Molly and Brumas had perished in the municipal incinerator.

In the absence of anything else to cuddle, Andrea allowed Petunia to share her bed and surreptitiously renamed him Ian.

7

If you are poor, people are sorry for you. They have flag days, collect from door to door and put money in boxes, coin-clutching hands of money-eating metal blackamoors, and netting Christmas stockings placed in shops in the hopeful expectation of contributions towards the childrens' home at Rhu, or limbless soldiers. If you are the child of a comfortable family and possess all your limbs, no one is sorry for you and no one gives you money except the occasional relative.

Neil was complaining about his lack of funds. Both he and Andrea were given some pocket money but it was a paltry amount because prudence had to be instilled into them at all costs. Even so, these meagre hand-outs were often withheld as all misdemeanours were punishable by fines. Neil envied his friends who got beaten with the slipper for their sins and thus still had money to spend on lurid sweets, bubble gum and comics. This was another grievance: any money that did come their way had to be spent sensibly, which precluded gobstoppers and *Beano*. Bubble gum was taboo and considered the ultimate in common behaviour and a sure mark of the worst elements of the working class, like wearing curlers in public and going greyhound racing.

Neil had once attempted to get taken on as a paper boy but, rejected as being too young, resorted to trying to make a living by returning empty Macpop bottles to the shops. When his parents heard of these exploits they were full of indignation and stopped his pocket money for a fortnight. So Neil was broke.

The Innes family was not poverty-stricken, just obsessed with seemliness and sense. Extravagance and ostentation must be shunned, there must be no splashings out on the flashy trappings of wealth. Holidays were taken in the pursuit of health or knowledge, never for the self-indulgence of rest, sunshine and

85

gratification of the appetites. All the sheets had their sides put to middle despite the linen press being stacked with immaculate virgins still wrapped as when they had come from Belfast. There was no joy to be had from the possession of wealth but, on the other hand, there was no need to give it all away; the camel would find another way through the needle's eye. The impoverished and unfortunate were succoured by the collection of milk bottle tops, old newspapers and used stamps. Rattled collecting boxes always received at least half a crown and often a note went into the collection on Sunday. The lower orders – and that meant everyone except the aristocracy, who were ancient, noble and excusably mad – were to be pitied and marvelled at for their profligacy. Imagine the absurdity of Jessie MacBryde taking a bus trip to the Low Countries and James's secretary announcing that she intended to visit the Costa Brava! What ostentation, what foolishness! Ishbel and James agreed that no good would come of such splurges. What was wrong with Rothesay, they would like to know? Neil and Andrea certainly had passports, but these unsullied documents had been procured merely as insurance against unexpected voyagings.

Since Effie's death little had been distributed from her estate beyond payment for the funeral and associated expenses of demise. There was no hurry; rewiring and chimney pointing could wait another season. No other expenditure was planned, though maybe it would be necessary to buy some more varied and practical education for Andrea so that she could take her place in the adult world armed with useful accomplishments. They would never stint on Neil's schooling. He was to board at a splendid public school near Perth after the summer, where he would mingle with the best and learn to be a man. The new baby would make great demands on their resources and the impending inheritance was a real bonus. The child, if a daughter – God forbid – would be called Euphemia out of gratitude to her grandmother for her prompt popping off. The fervently hoped for son would be called Jamie.

Dreary February was passing slowly. Andrea and Neil were filling in the time before Saturday lunch by reading. He was immersed in Andrea's Christmas present to him, the comic annual, even though he had read it all several times, and Andrea, who thought about nothing else, was trying to gratify her romantic longings for the good Dr Ian Robb by following the adventures of Susan of St Bride's in *Girl*. As romance it fell short of the mark. Her poetry books were no better, being designed for children and concerning Meg the Gypsy and the land of Counterpane. Neil promised to go down to the newsagent's after lunch and see if he could get something more amusing. As both their purses were empty, Andrea considered that a forlorn hope. She would continue writing her whodunnit, which was proving absorbing but difficult. All her characters would keep getting murdered or meeting awful accidental deaths – all, that is, except for the devastating amateur detective, a Doctor Roy, and the narrator, a brilliant Scottish girl and most attractive sidekick sleuth called Anthea Ingleby.

'Where did you get that fiver from before Christmas?' Neil asked suddenly.

'I was given it,' Andrea replied.

'I know that, but who by?'

'I can't say.'

'Why not? Is it a secret?'

'Yes. Now shut up and go away.'

'No, I won't until you tell me where you got it from.'

'I can't.'

'Right then, I will tell Mum and Dad that you stole it.' Neil stood at the door of Andrea's room poised as if to go downstairs.

'You wouldn't dare!' Andrea shouted at him. But she knew he would. He was a determined child, and ruthless. One day he might do well; right now he wanted some spending money. 'I can't tell you because I swore I wouldn't.'

'What, did you promise to cut your throat and all that rubbish?'

'No, I had to swear on the Bible, only it wasn't the Bible it was the Scottish prayer book. I was told I would be hanged if I ever said anything about it.'

'No one gets hanged for that, silly! God might strike you dead but that would be all. Now tell me, or I will go and see Mum right now.'

Andrea remembered that Effie had said that the Presbyterian

prayer book was not particularly valid when it came to oaths. She supposed it wouldn't matter too much if she only told Neil the source of the fiver. He was very unlikely to want to know the reason for the gift. Neil could be boringly persistent and if Ishbel or James thought she had been thieving there would be hell to pay.

'Oh, all right then. I will tell you if you promise not to tell anyone else. You have got to swear it properly on the real Bible. That way you will burn in Hell if the secret gets out to anyone while you live.' Andrea had been given three Bibles for her confirmation and she chose the impressive leather-bound one that had been sent by an agnostic godfather she had never met. Neil swore a most elaborate oath of Andrea's invention, and then she told him that Hector MacInlay had given her the money as a present.

'Really? How very interesting.' Neil used his theatrical Nazi commandant voice.

Ishbel bellowed up the stairs that lunch was ready. Without enquiring they knew it would be fish pie. It often was on Saturday and today the wafts had been particularly penetrating. The prospect was cheerless, especially as they knew that a vile semolina had been organized for pudding.

Afternoons on winter weekends were long and boring. Neither Innes child was sporting enough to be in a school team, and the ice-rink was horribly crowded on Saturdays. Not that either of them was particularly keen on skating, it was just that they were expected to do something active. Lolling about was an evil habit. Recently James was unable to make it home for Saturday lunch (he had urgent work to complete), so the stilted and compulsory walk was avoided. Ishbel put her swollen feet up and slept.

'Look what I have got!'

Neil had returned in triumph. Andrea was ecstatic as he had brought her a *Marty* and a *True Romances*, forbidden delights both. Neil had a *Dandy*, a *Beano* and a *Beezer*, so this Saturday transformed itself into a spell of paradise. In addition he had procured a bar of Caramac for Andrea, who tried to convince herself that it was not acne-inducing chocolate, plus a sherbet fountain and two vast gobstoppers for himself.

Andrea devoured both the bar and the magazines with equal gusto. The tales were trite but entirely satisfactory and stuck to a formula that provided exactly the right amount of pages of strip cartoon. Blondes and brunettes fell for our hero, who was sometimes hideously misunderstood and taken for a rotter. The heroine did much weeping and confided in fickle scheming friends all set to foil any romance. By the final page, opposition had been routed and the heroine would be pictured in a heart-shaped frame enjoying a real whopper of a kiss from the craggy hero. Sometimes she wore a wedding veil. All was to be ever after awfully happy.

Sated with slush and sugar they thought they might go and see about tea. Before they went down they took care to hide their treasures. Very little was safe from prying Mrs Orr unless it was out of reach. Her doctor forbade her to set foot on a step ladder so all banned delights lived on the top of Neil's wardrobe. There was masses of junk up there.

'Where did you get the money to buy this stuff?' Andrea had been longing to ask Neil this as she had believed her brother to be skint, but it seemed a rather rude question when she had enjoyed such good presents.

'Ver do you sink?'

'Oh God! You didn't . . . did you?'

'Didn't what?' Neil replied his eyes wide and his face a portrait of innocence.

'You didn't ask Mr MacInlay for it?' She knew she had made a mistake in even suggesting such a course. How could he have got any money from Hector in such a short time? She wished she had kept quiet, but it was too late now. The seed was planted.

'No I did not,' Neil replied. 'But that is a super idea.'

'No it is not!'

'Don't you want to know how I got them?' Neil asked, and then without waiting for an answer he said, 'I lifted them!'

'Neil Innes, how could you? . . . That is disgraceful. You will ruin us all. Think of Dad and his reputation.'

'What reputation?'

'He is a Writer to the Signet . . . and an elder. It would break his heart if he found out that his son was a thief.'

'Well, he should have thought of that before.'

'Before what?'

'Oh, never mind . . . nothing. Anyway you are in it just as much as me, and you are older. I expect they will have you for receiving stolen goods.'

Andrea went quite white. 'Oh no, this is awful!' She had had a feeling that Neil was light-fingered when some money had gone from her piggy bank last summer, but was horrified to find that he went shoplifting. 'You must promise never to do it again. It is the most terrible thing you could do – short of murdering and spying.'

'I wouldn't need to do it at all if I had some money,' said Neil. 'Anyway, Dalziel minor got caught stealing and all that happened was that his father was told to stop beating him with the slipper and talk to him instead. Dalziel minor says it is awfully boring and he preferred the slipper. Apparently it is something to do with him coming from a broken home. Mrs Dalziel has gone off with a gentleman from Cuba.'

'But you don't come from a broken home, Neil.'

'No, not yet.'

'What on earth do you mean? Mummie doesn't know any Cubans and she is busy having Daddy's baby.'

'Well, I could say that we were awfully upset by Grannie's death.'

Andrea thought that was a most unlikely excuse, though she had been greatly bothered by Effie recently. Awful dreams disturbed her nights. Once a furniture van arrived full of pictures for her and in the middle was an open coffin. Her grandmother spoke to her from where she lay all blueish white. 'You promised me I would be scattered by the docks,' she said accusingly. No one understood. Andrea tried to extract the body and fit her into a wheelbarrow, but Effie melted into nothing and all that was left was a dead horse on the ramp of the van. Another time she was in a cemetery with Milroy. She knew she was looking for Effie's grave but Milroy insisted on listening to the Dales on her portable wireless. No one would help. Time was short and all the gravestones were engraved with shopping lists, not epitaphs. Occasionally the dream became a nightmare which she could not remember when she awoke, sweating and shaking with an inexplicable fear.

Andrea slept on the top floor alone and no one could hear her if she cried. At these times she would weep into Petunia's fur but a live cat was easily irritated, unlike a familiar teddy bear.

Susie wrote a letter to say that she had received a lavish Valentine card with a Windsor postmark. Indeed, the whole letter was much taken up with showing off and point scoring. Evidently the school lake (a modest pond) had frozen in the extraordinarily icy spell and Susie, who had often been skating with Andrea at the Haymarket Rink when they were younger, had been the envy of all; her three turns and figures of eight had been a minor sensation. After the freeze most of the school seemed to have got the flu and all the dormitories had been transformed into wards in which the local Red Cross, idle since the war, having restarched their caps, swanned about with enjoyable efficiency. It had been the greatest fun, once the fever had departed. Last of all, the most gripping news was about a strong rumour that next year Princess Anne was to be one of the new girls.

When Ishbel got to hear of this she was filled with remorse.

'Why did you prevent me from sending Andrea south to school?' she remonstrated with James, who disliked having either his porridge or his *Scotsman* interrupted.

'As I recall, my dear, you felt that the financial outlay was out of all proportion to the likely return, and that we decided Andrea was receiving adequate education in Edinburgh without going to the inconvenience and expense of travel to England.'

Ishbel then blamed her mother for having lived too long – the windfall might have sent Andrea off to mix with royalty. Imagine the social coup of attending a speech day under royal patronage. So much more convincing than buying Smedley's vests from Jenners of Princes Street. She could see herself on James's arm in a print silk frock smiling chummily and passing the fancy cakes to those of the Blood Royal. In fact, this grievance preyed on Ishbel's anguished soul till she had to resort to stronger sleeping pills. Euphemia leapt within her reassuringly. Maybe there would be other princesses with whom the next Innes could mingle on the games pitch in thirteen years' time.

Andrea wished she hadn't mentioned it. She had only

volunteered the information to fill a gap in the conversation and to detract from a line of questioning about Neil's finances, a subject that bothered her a lot. In order to stop him thieving or blackmailing she had undertaken to pay him out of her own funds, which meant she had to walk to school and give him the bus fare. This was cold, nasty and very tiring, but anything was better than forcing him into delinquency.

Easter approached. The Browns were off to a point-to-point. Would Andrea like to come? Mrs Brown thought such events were the height of riotous entertainment and no one dared gainsay her. She had a large Land Rover, which normally towed her horse trailer. There was plenty of room for all, even if Cousin Malcolm decided to tag along, as Angus took up so little room and the girls were quite dispassionate about getting squashed.

Ishbel accepted the invitation without consulting her daughter. She felt that equestrianism should be pursued in the course of social elevation. After all, the Queen, given a spare moment, would invariably choose to be with a horse. Those who would be rich are advised to go where money is; likewise those who would be socially elevated should get themselves seen at equestrian dos. No need to ride, just be there and show enthusiasm. It would pay dividends in the end.

Ishbel insisted that no lady would attend such an event in trousers, so Andrea buckled on her ancient kilt yet again, and with the straining Shetland woolly under her school gabardine mac, set forth with lead in her heart and Ishbel's sheepskin-lined boots on her feet. She felt ridiculous especially when she arrived at the Browns' house to find everyone in jeans, giant sweaters and wellies.

Wee Angus, almost extinguished beneath a vast tweed cap, sat between his parents in the front, like the dormouse in *Alice*. Marion, Fiona, Malcolm and Andrea sat in the back with the picnic, most of which appeared to be liquid and alcoholic. Mrs Brown drove with aggressive panache and was evidently in a right old state of excitement at the thought of a bracing day of wind, mud and rural heartiness. Mr, or rather Major Brown read the paper and Wee Angus said nothing because he was trying very hard to fix his mind on things higher than vomit. Malcolm was forbidden to smoke, which made him peevish, so Andrea affected an interest in the passing scenery while the twins played a cheerfully childish game with folded paper fortune-tellers, which they had made themselves and which thus provided no surprises.

Spring had waved at Scotland for a few days in March, but by the time April had come she had gone off to burgeon elsewhere. Cross and disappointed lambs huddled up to their disillusioned mothers on the spartan pastures of the Lang Wang, which was the route taken after leaving the bings (slag heaps) of the Calder mines behind. It was a long way to go, but it seemed quite normal to the Browns to cross most of the Central Lowlands in order to enjoy themselves in hideous conditions. As they were to be near Glasgow, Andrea wondered if by any miraculous chance Dr Ian Robb would be there. Maybe he would be attending officially. Lucky the jockeys who fell from their horses were sustained by such a one. It was almost worth becoming a leathery lady rider just for the rapture of being rescued.

At the race course an incredibly elderly hunt factotum touched his cap to Mrs Brown and wished 'Miss Bunty' a very good day.

She replied with many enquiries as to the hounds, the puppy walkers, the scent, the wire fund and finally the welfare of Mrs George, the factotum's wife.

'She was gathered just before yon last back end.'

'Oh dear, I am sorry, George. Did it happen during cubbing?'

'Och no, we had her all awa' before the season started.'

'Jolly good!' Bunty Brown replied. 'Keep your pecker up, George! Now then, I suppose you are looking for our entrance money. Go round and ask the Major for it. It is always so convenient to be married and get someone else to do the paying.'

'Och, you were ever the canny yin, Miss Bunty.'

You couldn't help admiring Mrs Brown. The more the wind bit and the rain soaked, the greater degree of cheery bonhomie she demonstrated. The point-to-point took place on what she referred to as her home stamping ground and she was well known to every horsey type in those parts. She bellowed her greetings like a stag at the rut and her kissing of old friends put one in mind of a clash of antlers. Major Brown smiled benignly and poured large drinks for all. It was generally agreed that Bunty had done well for herself, though it was a pity that the son was so slight. Apparently Bunty had been a bit vague as to the symptoms of pregnancy and had insisted on riding throughout '45 when food was scarce and vitamins sparse. She only knew for a month that the bulge she carried was a baby and not a pot belly that could be vanquished by 'banting' and vigorous exercise. Despite his small size (Major Brown was horrified to hear that his son was no bigger than a five-pound salmon), Angus possessed a flourishing brain, though his physical development was hesitant, due perhaps to the sporting life he had pursued whilst inside Bunty. The Major had returned from Singapore and took his wife and son back with him when his leave was up. Throughout her next pregnancy, Bunty Brown reclined on the verandah of her black and white house surrounded by domestic help of all types consuming large amounts of Virol (sent from Scotland by her mother) and subsequently gave birth to the vastly sturdy twins.

A series of fellows, mostly kin of George, directed the Browns' Land Rover to a choice spot. It cost twice as much to park in this muddy field as it did in the one next door. The difference in price was to do with the class of the parker and bore no relevance as to the quality of the location. Both were slippery with tyre-marked mud and subject to gale-force gusts. It would have been possible to observe the racing from inside the car, but that was not to be as all available sitting space was now covered with the refreshments. A military groundsheet and a moth-eaten travelling rug were no match for the mud; the Browns sniggered at those, like the MacInlays, who arrived with folding tables and chairs. Hector was eager to show off his gleaming new Land Rover with its somewhat superfluous tropical roof. He never could grasp why the British aspiring rural classes considered battered to be best. Kirsty had disappeared to join the Blairs, who were no longer invited to share Hector's booze. Besides, she found the syco-phantic fawning of those in pursuit of his wealth and support hard to take. Moira sat in the front of the wonder vehicle, windows shut fast, reading *Vogue*, a large gin handily lodged in the optional bracket designed for trouble-free picnicking. She looked ravish-ing in tweed.

*

'Now, scamper off, all of you, and have a lovely time.' Mrs Brown even smiled like a horse. A skilled groom might tell her age from her teeth.

'Look! There is Auntie Pam!' Marion waved wildly at a woman with four little girls, who rushed up making baying sounds of delight as she approached her sister, Bunty.

Andrea realized at once that she had met Auntie Pam and her brood before, in the Kelvin Club, and Pam, with the aplomb of the well-trained military or diplomatic wife greeted her with warmth and said how much she had grown up since last she had seen her, though it was apparent to both of them that she hadn't the least idea who this ample child might be. The girls remembered Andrea well and started to giggle.

'How is Mother?' Bunty asked. 'I must come through to see her soon. Did Jasper get over the tapeworm?'

'Yes, thank God. The vets are wonderful these days. It is Uncle Jock who is getting her down. He really is quite gaga. He chooses to be deaf as a post most of the time so poor Mum has to shout, which unsettles the dogs. The worst bit is that he has started to worry about everything, from when the paper boy delivers to buying enough extra batteries for all his torches. Furthermore he has got awfully bothered about the Junior Bachelors' Ball of 1923. Some dotty old crow insisted that he had partnered her and he is sure he was in Ceylon looking at tea in that year.'

'Does it matter? Who was this ancient belle? He didn't father anything shameful, surely?'

'Of course not, Bunty! Not Uncle Jock, he doesn't know how! It is just that he will keep on about it. He has even started looking for old photographs to prove that he was in Colombo and not in Glasgow, but Mother threw all the albums on the bonfire when the rot got to them. She daren't tell Uncle Jock, so every day they spend hours in the attic searching for them even though she knows they aren't there. I'm telling you, it is hell. Perhaps Marion and Fiona could go and stay with her. She likes them. My girls are a bit wilful for her.'

'Who is that extra child with you?' Bunty asked.

Pam lowered her voice and made an effort to speak

confidentially. 'That is little Katriona Mackie – you remember, Glen's child. She is not at all easy, but I felt sorry for him so I thought we could bring her along. My girls can't stand her. It is almost like a litter rejecting the weak member. She has had a tough time, though. Did you know that Glen bought her a pony and it killed itself falling off the Broomielaw?'

'How dreadful! Didn't something happen to her mother too?'

'Hanged herself from the scullery pulley while on a weekend out from the Chrichton. She had taken to the bottle and they were trying to dry her out. She left a note saying she was bored. Now Katriona blames Glen for it all.'

'Well, he can be jolly boring,' Bunty admitted. 'What is he going to do now?'

'Advertise in one of the Highland papers for a wife. I reckon he will get swamped with capable sorts in the habit of being bored.'

'I doubt if anyone could take to Auchencaird, specially after the suicide. Highlanders are awfully fey, you know.'

'Well, at least he got rid of the pulley,' Pam conceded.

'Do you get the curse yet? Your bosoms have got even bigger.' Impervious to the lapse of months between interrogations the youngest of the Browns' cousins resumed her line of questioning. They were a persistent family.

Andrea quite lost her head and said she didn't know. Then, just in time, she spotted Susie. She waved and Susie, looking wonderfully worldly wise in heavenly jeans, ran over and kissed her. Andrea was astonished. Malcolm, who had been sulking, cheered up. 'Hi,' they said to each other when Andrea introduced them. It made her feel slightly more significant, especially when Malcolm suggested that they all go off together. Marion and Fiona were teaching their cousins how to work the fortune-tellers while their mothers gossiped, and Katriona thoughtfully swallowed the dregs from all the drinks glasses.

The third race was in progress when they met up with the Blairs and Kirsty MacInlay. No one had won any money, one horse had been shot and a rider had been removed in an ambulance. Ian Robb was not the official doctor, and the man who was had been most generously entertained out of several car boots before the accidents even started. Late in the afternoon he got no credit for instructing some jockey who had fractured his pelvis to pull himself together. The cup for the first race had been presented to the same cadaverous man who had won it the year before. His substantial frame lacked comfortable flesh and he resembled a walking corpse in order to ride at the required weight. His foul breath brought on by starvation caused the furred noblewoman who was presenting the cup to reel back as if drunk.

The Blairs led the way to a friend's trailer that was empty because its occupant was limbering up to run quite slowly in the ladies' race.

The ramp was up so they squeezed in through the small side door and sat in the straw while everyone except Andrea lit up. Kirsty and Susie shared a vivid pink cigarette that Mungo had pinched from his girlfriend.

Everyone seemed at ease. They chatted and giggled, told jokes that Andrea could only pretend to understand. Her face ached with trying to keep smiling. The races could be seen over the back gate so they poked their heads up to look each time a rush of hooves was heard and cheered a lot. Malcolm dropped his second cigarette into the straw where it began to smoulder.

'Quick, get some water!' the eldest Blair commanded.

'Don't be silly. Smother it with the horse blanket,' his brother shouted.

Andrea did not wait. She had seen a bucket of water outside and she rushed to get it, but took the door straight on and got stuck. Kirsty gave her a great push, which dislodged her so she fell headfirst in the mud and horse droppings outside. Meanwhile the fire had been put out by the resourceful lads and their pee.

'God, I hope I am never in a shipwreck with a fatty,' said Susie. 'Us women and children wouldn't have a chance with someone like you about,' she added to Andrea. 'You had better go and clean yourself up.'

'Come on, Susie!' The others called for her to go with them to see the slow horse attempt the ladies' race with an unwed Blair aunt on top. Andrea was not included.

'Don't worry,' said Angus, who had been quietly avoiding everyone. 'All manner of thing shall be well.'

'When?' Andrea snapped. 'That is what I would like to know.'

She was in no mood for poetry, and stumped off towards the car via the perfectly dreadful lavatory facilities.

'God knows,' Wee Angus answered philosophically.

Because he belonged to the generation that was devoted to nick names, Archibald Brown had always been called Buster. He had a benevolent sort of assurance about him that implied he had seen all this, and much, much more before. He treated everyone with a charming courtesy that made even the most insignificant person feel important and loved, and it was lucky that he was in the car when Andrea reached it. Her thoughts were low and gloomy and she felt inclined to cast about for a scullery pulley or to throw herself beneath a galloping horse with lethal hooves. Katriona, another reject, was absorbed in the Famous Five amongst the picnic in the back. Buster respected her desire to be solitary and made no effort to bring her out of herself. Andrea, on the other hand, was evidently in need of quite some attention when she fetched up, all covered with mud and manure with a voice on the edge of tearfulness.

'Andrea, how nice to see you. Have you come to cheer me up? I must say I do think the weather might have been a bit kinder. What about some chocolate cake?'

'No thank you, Major Brown.' The thought of the cake made her more miserable than ever. Normally she would have comforted herself with several slices but not now that she had been publicly labelled a fatty. 'I am never going to eat cake again.'

'Oh dear, you must not be so harsh on yourself. One day you might be somewhere which has no cake and then you would regret not having enjoyed it when you could.'

'I am going to get thin,' Andrea announced. 'Then no one will laugh at me and I will be happy.'

'Well don't overdo it,' Buster advised. He wondered whether his tales of his own enforced starvation as a prisoner of war would be of any relevance. He hardly ever spoke of his ordeals and experiences, they were private concerns and not to be flaunted.

The same applied to all his friends who had perished, and he did not search for sympathy by indulging in demonstrative grief for those he had loved. There had been one whole company killed or tortured to death. Buster was lucky, he had lived; he would never betray the horrifying grief that was with him always.

This little girl needn't know of his sorrow. He must cheer her up. She looked most awfully glum and such a thing should not be among the young. Even peacetime and plentiful supplies can not cancel the strains of adolescence.

'I wonder if you could help me with this crossword puzzle. Seven letters, fourth letter M, "Preserve close relation".'

'Mummify,' Andrea answered at once.

'Great heavens! You are a genius!'

'Ssh! I am trying to read,' Katriona announced in a peevish whine.

'Well, in that case Andrea and I will go to the beer tent, and take our puzzle with us. Will you be all right, Katriona?'

'Of course,' the child answered.

'Why is she so rude?' Andrea asked.

'She has had a hard time. Life has not been good to her yet. I hope she doesn't let her rotten luck poison the rest of her life. All will be well in the end.'

That was the second time in an hour that a Brown had expressed such optimism.

'I was there when her pony was killed. She was very upset but she was also horrid to her father.'

'Well, she is not like us, Andrea – damn lucky to be alive and to have such wonderful families.' Truly Buster and Bunty did think their family to be marvellous. Only outsiders lamented their misfortune of having a weedy son and a couple of battleship daughters. 'Come on, Andrea, I am going to buy you a drink to thank you for your mummification.'

Despite her muddied spectacles Andrea could see Hector MacInlay sounding down the car park towards them red-faced with well-fuelled wrath.

'Hello, Hector!' Buster greeted the obviously infuriated man. 'This is the life, eh? Grand day!'

Andrea hid most of herself behind Buster, but Hector was so enraged that he failed to notice her at all and only grunted at Buster while he stormed off towards the paddock. 'That man is becoming a fine golfer,' Buster remarked. He could find a virtue in a cesspit.

Buster had been decorated for his bravery and had been recommended for the Military Cross. Neither he nor anyone else ever referred to his brilliant record. Bunty's trophies, won for horsemanship, were kept well polished, and stood in significant array on the Browns' mahogany sideboard. Buster only had a scar on his shin, a tendency for his face to twitch when tired and a slight deafness as mementoes, apart from one golfing trophy for a discontinued competition that he kept in his office as a home for paper clips.

'Cheer up, chicken. We are all going home now.' Marion pinched Katriona's cheeks. 'What a pretty smile.' She made a face and Katriona stopped scowling. She actually laughed when Fiona started to sing 'Why am I so Starry-Eyed?' in the manner of Mr Khrushchev (or so she said).

It was ages before they managed to get out of the car park but nothing, not even being showered with mud when the ground-sheet was placed under the spinning wheels, could deter the Brown family good humour.

Angus felt most cheerful about the end of the outing. He was very tired of being asked by everyone whether he would be riding next year, and having pointed out to him that he was just the right shape for a jockey. 'A horse, however, is not just the right shape for me,' was his reply. Thus he had acquired a reputation for snootiness.

Andrea was thankful that now, or in an hour or two, she would be going home and could be miserable alone. She never did learn why Hector was so angry.

The reason for Hector's wrath was that Malcolm had presented himself at the MacInlay car and calmly asked him for some money. If he felt disinclined to hand over the cash, Malcolm said he would feel forced to ask Mrs MacInlay instead and it was a shame to disturb her, wasn't it? You see, Andrea Innes's brother told Kenneth Dalziel that his sister had been given a fiver by Mr MacInlay before Christmas and Kenneth told Katriona Mackie who told one of the Browns' cousins who told Wee Angus who had told Malcolm, and asked him what he thought it was all about. Malcolm said he was sure Hector had his reasons for his generosity and wondered whether he would like to repeat this largesse in view of Easter approaching.

It had worked well and Malcolm was satisfied even though he had to give some of the money to Kirsty, as she was the one who put him up to it. She had no illusions about either of her parents and thought it best to get what she could out of them. Her income was growing daily since she found that her silence was a saleable commodity. After all, who would want to know about the little MacBryde ninny sitting on Hector's knee, and Moira's long lunches at Dirleton.

8

'Men never make passes at girls who wear glasses.' Mrs Orr was waiting impatiently to get at the mirror in which Andrea was inspecting her spots. The woman had a way of always wanting access to anywhere that was being occupied. She sighed with frustration and drummed her fingers on the frosted-glass door panel.

'I am going to get contact lenses when I have stopped growing,' Andrea replied.

'Stopped growing! You are gigantic. Have you not done enough growing already or are you hoping that you will get tall enough to match your width?' Mrs Orr only appeared to get enjoyment out of being insulting. 'If you get much bigger you will have to go and live in the Usher Hall. Now hurry up and stop picking your face. You had better start looking for some blind fellow to have as a boyfriend.'

'I think it may be my glands that make me fat.'

'Rubbish, hen! There were nae fatties in Belsen.'

Andrea had weighed herself and found the answer most discouraging. She was nearly eleven stone, and she had no idea how it had come about except that she had grown a bit and possibly eaten a lot. She had found comfort in food and recently she seemed to need a lot.

For three days she gave up puddings, cakes and all sweets. She had a stomach upset as a result of over doing the fresh fruit, then weighed herself again. It was miraculous: two pounds had gone.

After that she began to diet in earnest. First she gave up sugar and then milk in her tea, then she stopped all biscuits and never had a second helping of anything. Another couple of pounds disappeared but then there seemed to be a halt in the weight loss. Then she tried even harder, only to find herself brooding on food more and more. The headache that she had most of the time was a reminder of her mortification and she felt that if it was absent the diet was not working, rather like a hair shirt being an *aide-mémoire* to those who would be pious.

She read recipes and dreamt of forbidden dishes lavish in calories. One day, a doughnut bursting with jam was too much for her. She ate it quickly and regretted it at once. Miserably she imagined that, as a result of this one indulgence, the pounds would all come racing back. Upstairs in the lavatory, with her transistor blaring and the tap running, she put two fingers down her throat. It was quite easy really. Ten or twenty heaves and all the sin was there in the bowl ready to be flushed away. She was purged.

After this upheaval, it was best to wait about ten minutes and then to have a fizzy drink. That way she could make herself sicker and get rid of even more. Her throat was sore and once she vomited a bit of blood, but on the whole it worked.

Easter passed and though she appeared to eat her eggs with relish they all ended up in the city sewage system sooner than expected . . . She learnt to replace the burden that her stomach heaved back with lots of water. She sloshed as she walked and her moods swung from manic elation to lethargy. She was below ten stone on Easter Monday and returned to school obviously much thinner.

'Clootie, there is nothing of you!' Kirsty exclaimed. It wasn't true but it gave Andrea a big thrill. 'You wouldn't get jammed in a horse box door now!' Kirsty then proceeded to tell all her friends about the incident at the point-to-point and made much of how the boys had to use their own fire extinguishers because Andrea was stuck fast. It made a good story and Andrea didn't mind. She was going to get even thinner. She was going to be like a stick insect before the summer was over.

'Darling, your breath is not very fresh.' Ishbel put up her cheek for the compulsory morning kiss when Andrea came for breakfast. 'Have you cleaned your teeth?'

Andrea had scrubbed hard in order to obtain the vital 'ring of confidence' that she knew she lacked. She was careful to spit every vestige of toothpaste out in case it was fattening. She bought Amplex pills, which were very small and very green and surely would not contribute to her weight, and yet still she worried. Her tongue was furred and she knew she had bad breath. She took to talking behind her hand and never getting close to anyone. Nothing mattered except her quest for skinniness.

At school she appeared to be working hard but somehow nothing was retained in her brain and when it came to exams her performance was dismal and her teachers and parents accepted that their fears were confirmed: Andrea was stupid.

At home she kept to her room. Sometimes she read trash, the story writing being abandoned, but mostly she lay on her bed listening to The Beatles and imagining encounters with Ian, or fantastic feasts. She had little energy left after walking to and from school, though she had tried to exercise herself into less bulk by lying on the floor with her feet held six inches from the ground. Her stomach muscles ached but it was wonderful to see how what was once convex was now concave. Her abdomen hung from her hip bones like washing on a line and bones appeared where her bottom had comfortably been and reminded her of her successful self-denial when she sat on hard seats.

Ishbel had other things more pressing than a fifteen-year-old daughter to worry about. Her pregnancy was going badly. Her age was against her and constant weariness crippled her, but even so, she found it impossible to sleep, and James had taken the zed bed in his dressing room of a night.

James was busier than ever, it seemed. He did mention that he was worried about their daughter to Ishbel, who dismissed his concerns by explaining that Andrea's change of shape and personality were attributable to her difficult age. Puppy fat was expected to dissolve and, after all, were not her parents both slender specimens? Neil knew Andrea was making herself sick, but she kept up the contributions of pocket money and he had other things to occupy himself, like cricket, in which he had begun to do well. James was proud of his son. Andrea would be all right too, especially as now they knew she was no academic and she had started to take such an interest in cooking.

It was strange how the thinner she got the more she liked to cook. She studied recipes for cakes and puddings and spent much time in the kitchen devising dishes that were utterly delicious if somewhat rich and over lavish. The family ate what they could, though even Neil was sometimes defeated by the gargantuan feasts Andrea produced. She never seemed to eat herself, though she maintained that she tasted everything as she went along and therefore had no appetite left by the time the dish came to the table. Mrs Orr fed her family on what she removed from the kitchen and hid in her shopping basket, which had wheels and was handy for ploughing through bus queues.

Auntie Mary lived in North Berwick but was maintained, like a car, in Edinburgh. She always concluded her visit with tea at Magdala Crescent where she offered advice to Ishbel on all matters connected with marriage, men, children, and their upkeep with particular reference to fresh air and regular bowels. Auntie Mary was a spinster and would return to her maker intact. Her practical ignorance was no deterrent to the proffering of theoretical expertise. On her last visit, in February following a dental appointment, she had been sorry to see that Ishbel had been letting herself go. True she was newly bereaved and Auntie Mary always held that a woman never recovered from the loss of her mother, but to serve cake bought from MacVitie Guest still in its corrugated paper case was tantamount to marital catastrophe. It would not be long before James went racketing off with loose women unless Ishbel made an effort to keep him brimful of home baking. Her own mother had died giving birth to her, so presumably Auntie Mary's whole life had been blighted by the loss. Her father had taken his time to remarry and even longer to have another go at reproduction, and when he and her step-mother successfully produced James, Mary was already the blameless captain of hockey at a hearty public school. Because of her excellent beginnings, Miss Innes always felt it necessary to set a good example to her half-brother and his wife.

May came and with it, Auntie Mary in pursuit of new corsets. The Spirella consultant had devised a system of preventing her bosom from resting on her lap when she sat, which meant that she carried a substantial shelf beneath her huge twinsets. Eating was hazardous due to the distance from plate to mouth, and keeping the eye on the ball in golf was almost impossible. However, nothing would deter her from taking her exercise on the links and captaining the ladies' team so she did the eighteen holes without benefit of support, which meant not only her drivers and niblicks were seen to swing. Her rigid shape was restored for savage bridge playing. She captained that team too.

On her visit to Edinburgh in late May, Auntie Mary was delighted to learn that Andrea was responsible for all the tea, including a plate of commendable scones.

'It is gratifying to note that the cake is home-made, even if it is a trifle loud in the icing. Domesticity is to be encouraged in one's daughters,' she declared.

It was disturbing, she said, to find Andrea looking less than robust. Peaky was the word she used to describe her niece.

'A change of air, a tonic and possibly some syrup of figs might put things to rights.'

What a shame it was that James and Ishbel had not insisted on their young learning golf. No good would come of loafing indoors. Had it not been for her daily woman being off sick with her piles, she would have suggested that Andrea be sent to stay with her at Muirfield View to get a good blow of bracing breezes off the North Sea.

Mary was unabashed about making personal remarks concerning her nieces and nephews. She was, however, quite determined not to sully the conversation with any reference to her sister-in-law's extremely obvious condition.

Ishbel was huge. The baby had stopped kicking, maybe from lack of space, and had taken to hanging very low and causing her considerable discomfort in the groin. Mary did not believe it was nice to refer to forthcoming happy events and one contrived to be blind to the expanding shapes of child-bearing women. Never was anything as indelicate as birth mentioned in mixed company. When Ishbel's time came, James would be expected to go with dignity to his club until all was over. Before she left, Auntie Mary did manage to refer to the confinement once. She hoped, with discretion, that all would go well with Ishbel and repeated, tactfully, that one never got over the death of a mother. She did not say when she would be returning to Edinburgh despite a visit to the oculist being scheduled for July.

'Fate is not to be tempted and life is ever a risky business.'

*

In spring Edinburgh is neatly gay with orderly bloom. As summer comes one gets to smell the brewery. It was an odour that Andrea would forever associate with her childhood. She did not find its heaviness unpleasant, though it seemed to penetrate everywhere, especially in warm weather, should there be any, in June or July.

On one rare warm evening towards the end of the summer term, Andrea found the heat too oppressive for fast walking and decided to catch the bus in order to avoid being late home. Though Ishbel never seemed pleased to see her, the scenes she created if Andrea got in late were epic performances. Such dramas were to be avoided.

The bus stop was beside a low wall whose railings had been loyally extracted during the war to be melted into weaponry, and it was here that Andrea found she was sitting next to Susan (late of Miss Fay's hairdressing salon). Neither was aware of the other at first, nor did they recognize each other immediately. Susan was now very blonde and made-up without restraint. Small fronds of lower lash were painted beneath her outlined eyes and her lipstick was so pale that she looked like a young ghoul. Andrea was very thin even though she hid her shape beneath an over-sized sweater.

'It's never you!' Susan exclaimed. 'You're that skinny I couldna recognize you.'

Andrea saw that beneath the pancake was her rescuing hair-dresser, the genius of the scissors whose efforts to turn her into Helen Shapiro had not been entirely successful and whose legacy lingered yet on her head. Such a style was not quick to grow out.

They were pleased to see each other though both were mightily altered.

'Have you been ill? You look kind of peely-wally. Here, have some gum.'

Andrea accepted the chewing gum and almost forgot to make a note of the calories it contained. After all, it was a lovely day and now that she had rested, she felt equal to the necessarily brisk walk home. One had to burn much energy to counteract the effect of the sugar.

'No, I've not been ill. I just decided to lose weight.'

'You have done that right enough,' Susan replied. 'You look like an advert for Oxfam.'

It was not meant as a compliment but Andrea was delighted. That was the look she was aiming for – without the swollen worm-burdened belly, of course.

'Did you go to London to be a hairdresser?'

'Och no. I had a wee problem.'

'What went wrong?'

'It is all right now. I just had a wee mistake that needed to be sorted. You know what I mean?'

Andrea did not.

'Anyway, I'm through with hairdressing and I'm a model now. I'm getting a place of my own as I can't stay with my mum any more. She chucked me out.'

'But that is awful! How can you manage?'

'I'm doing fine. Here comes the bus.'

'I'll walk,' said Andrea. 'I need the exercise.'

'You need a feed. You'll no get anywhere wi' nae boobs.'

'But models don't have boobs,' Andrea replied, looking at Susan's bust which had become quite voluptuous. Certainly this short peroxided girl did not look quite like the cover of *Vogue*. Maybe she did Maidenform bras or posed in hand-knitted cardigans for Paton and Baldwin.

'Cheerio then. Be good! And find yourself a man to feed you.'

Susan waved from the departing bus. Her fingernails were long and painted black.

Ishbel did not refer to girls who stalked catwalks and department store restaurants promoting clothes as models. They were mannequins and, sometimes, they were ladies too. Often they married well and prudently into wealthy foreign aristocracy, especially if they were employed by famous houses like Dior and Hartnell, where there was even a chance of revolving before the Queen. Less exalted girls paraded round Darlings clutching a placard proclaiming the provenance of their garments. This was not much of a springboard to social success, but it was not a shameful job. Models, on the other hand, especially in the scandalous climate of that summer, were to be regarded askance by the respectable classes. Andrea knew nothing of this. She was ignorant, so far, of the doings of Christine and Mandy.

Ishbel's baby was to arrive at a moment convenient for all. No spontaneous labour was to be countenanced. Birth was not permitted to start naturally, it was booked for the convenience of the staff. Furthermore, no baby was permitted to arrive during Royal Ascot or after the onset of grouse shooting, both great passions of Ishbel's gynaecologist on whom most of his patients, including Ishbel, had great crushes. He was so sympathetic, so understanding and so very, very expensive. It was the authority with which he reassured the apprehensive and flattered the otherwise hideous on the beauty of secret interiors that made all his ladies purr.

Ishbel's condition was causing concern. The circumference of her ankles and blood pressure increased daily. She was inert, lumpen and resigned to do as she was told. The nurseries were ready, the nappies heaped in folded piles and the pram, ancient and venerable in coach-built black, was already blocking the kitchen passage. The only problem that remained was the disposal of Neil and Andrea. Naturally they could not be at home; they must be removed and occupied elsewhere.

Neil went to stay with Dalziel. It seemed that Mr Dalziel was of the opinion that young Innes was a good influence on his son whose kleptomania was either waning (or his skill was waxing). The boys got on well and were to be dispatched to a cricketing course run by a curate who had been defrocked for having a flighty wife. Mr Dalziel and the curate had met because of their common misfortune. Mrs Dalziel was contemplating marriage with her Cuban and becoming Lucy Lopez, whereas the curate's wife spurned convention and welcomed all to her bed, and was currently conducting a mysterious relationship with an artist of debatable gender called Kit. The curate's match had been childless, but he was known for being good with the young, especially boys.

Andrea refused flatly to go to Auntie Mary, who had never been keen to have her anyway, and the Brown sisters were spending the beginning of the holidays on an exchange. Marion and Fiona were being sent under protest to stay with *la petite* Hedvige, and her sneering *frères au bord de la mer* on the very Cape Finistère that featured so frequently on the gale warnings. When there, Marion and Fiona found that Les Courtines all played *le golf* or bickered incessantly amongst themselves, so the twins learnt no more French than they had absorbed in the fifth form. They did acquire a taste for wine and an abiding dislike of Hedvige (who was nobly descended from a Napoleonic Swede), her *copains* and particularly, her sly *frères*, who enjoyed nothing more than a good mock of the two large girls and treated them and their lack of sophistication with a rudeness that only French teenage boys can muster. The parents Courtine, especially Papa who normally pawed any female within reach, did nothing to entertain Marion or Fiona, despite the fact that they were meant to be there to absorb culture as well as the language. *La petite* Hedvige was destined to be dragged all round every sight when her turn came to be exchanged.

Meanwhile, Bunty Brown was occupied with being the stunningly efficient and mightily keen district commissioner of the Pony Club during its week of camp. Keeping the young members on their mounts and off the bottle was tough enough without having to contend with juvenile lust. She was grateful when the week ended that her own children, though all equestrian dunces, were also sluggish in promiscuity. The modern horse lover, it would seem, was equally keen about indoor sports as they were about clearing fences and turning on the forehand. Such things had been so different in her youth between the wars.

Wee Angus, at home alone most of the time, was free to mourn Sylvia Plath and to wonder about existentialism. He had already resolved to embrace socialism, or Rome, or both. So Andrea could not stay at Lasswade during Ishbel's confinement, and even before it was discovered that Susie was in Cannes with Penelope Cohen (whose barrister father commanded three times James's fees), she had firmly refused to go and stay with her former best friend.

'But you used to be inseparable,' Ishbel argued. 'This time last year you were hardly ever apart. What has gone wrong?'

'Nothing has gone wrong,' Andrea replied. 'It just isn't the same any more.'

'I hope you aren't jealous,' said Ishbel. 'After all, you wouldn't have done very well at boarding school. It would have been a waste of money because you are not clever enough to justify such a financial sacrifice. Poor Susie must be most upset about Princess Anne being sent to Benenden instead of East Downland Hall.'

This royal decision had caused Ishbel nothing but delight. She had sent a compassionate postcard depicting Ailsa Craig in a squal to Susie's mother the day the Queen's choice of school was published.

'Well, I couldn't care less where Princess Anne goes to school, as long as she doesn't do it here.'

'Andrea! Stop being so disloyal.' Ishbel's tone implied that the Tower and the block were Andrea's destiny.

'Why can't I go and stay with Milroy?'

'In Glasgow?'

'Yes. Why not?'

Ishbel could think of no reason to refuse this bizarre request except that it would confirm her daughter's insanity. But it did solve the immediate problem.

While Ishbel packed herself several front-opening night-dresses, Andrea dreamt of chance encounters with Ian Robb while roaming in the Glasgow gloaming.

Just before her departure for Glasgow Andrea bumped into Kirsty MacInlay. The authorities were readying Edinburgh for the festival, and the scaffolding for Tattoo could be seen rising on the Esplanade below the Castle from Princes Street. The girls decided to get some refreshment in the Chocolate House.

'I'm bored.'

Kirsty was finding life impossibly tedious. No schoolfriends were left in Edinburgh once term had ended except the dreary ones without imagination. All the decent boys, like the Blairs, were busy elsewhere and seemed to have lost interest in her. Malcolm had been returned to his parents at their foreign posting and brother Mungo, the crammer having given up on him, had been banished to the Macpop factory to learn the business from the bottom. This was a desperate move on Hector's part to try to turn his son into the heir of his dreams. Though Mungo was starting at the bottom, he contrived to sink further. He showed no aptitude for commerce or enterprise. He wanted to drop out, but, as Hector correctly observed, his son had never done anything out from which to drop.

'What are you doing these holidays?' Kirsty had ordered a hot chocolate but Andrea had a black coffee.

'I'm going through to Glasgow while my mother has the baby.'

'What is she having the baby for?'

'I don't know. It just happened, I suppose.' Andrea was no longer worried about these things. She must have grown up a bit, or else she didn't care any more.

'I wish my mum and dad would have a baby. It might stop them quarrelling about how they are going to get rid of Mungo and me. It beats me why they had us in the first place.'

'I thought you were going to school in Switzerland.'

'Oh that.' Kirsty was dismissive. 'Do you know why I'm being sent there? I'll tell you. They think I will come back a lady. They think that I will get asked to stay in smart houses like the kind that belong to the Blairs or the Browns' relations. They think that I will get married to some smart fellow with a family that goes back to Bannockburn and doesn't have grannies you pretend not to recognize.'

'What do you mean? Your family is awfully smart, you have a lovely house and lots of grand friends. Don't you really say hello to your grannies?'

'Only when no one is about. Do you know what the worst bit is? It is that neither my father's nor my mother's mother seems to mind. They like to see their children pretending to be the highest in the land. They keep out of their light. They don't want to bring shame on their precious snobbish children. They are proud to be too common for their own kids. When my parents went to the garden party at Holyrood it had to be kept a secret in case one of the grannies wanted to see them in all their finery and showed them up in front of all the other hundreds of royal guests. Can you imagine how great it would have been if the grannies had turned up waving flags and shouting "Yoo-hoo" through the palace railings? Grandfather MacInlay is dead; he was run down by a train. I was told that he fell beneath its wheels at Waverley Station, which could happen to anyone. In actual fact he was working on the line and was drunk. He tapped wheels for a living. Grandfather Morris is never mentioned. Grannie Morris has a dress shop in Troon.'

'I know,' said Andrea. 'My mother told me.'

'You see what I mean? People in Edinburgh all notice that sort of thing. This place is fascist. It stinks. I want out.'

'You might like Switzerland,' Andrea suggested.

'What, all that guff about opening doors nicely and what to do with your gloves?'

'There must be more to it than that.'

'Well, let's see, there is how to lay a table, how to write to a duke and what not to talk about.'

'What not to talk about? I can never think of anything to talk about,' said Andrea. It was surprising how well they were getting on. Three months ago Kirsty would never have been seen dead in the Chocolate House with Andrea. It couldn't just be desperate times calling for such measures.

'Oh, you must never talk about religion, politics, money, disease or sex. Which just leaves the weather and the bloody scenery. God, how I dread this farce! All I want to do is be a bloody doctor and they won't bloody listen. "No wee girl of mine is going to end up as one of those clever women in flat shoes."'

'That is what my Dad said to me when I told him I wanted to stay on and do Highers. Even the Head spoke up for me but Dad would have nothing of it. Though it didn't stop him giving a stinking scholarship for some "impoverished wee girl to study for a good career". I'm the one who wants to study, I want to have a profession, I want to get a good job, but do you know what he said to me?'

Andrea said she didn't.

'Tell that to the Marines!' She ordered another hot chocolate. Andrea refused a further black coffee, which she didn't like anyway but had no more than ten calories to it. She calculated that she would have to sprint all the way up the Royal Mile twice if she wanted to shed two cups of chocolate.

'What about Mungo?' Andrea asked. 'What has he got to be?'

'That is the worst of it. Mungo wants to do nothing. He would be great on laying tables and folding napkins, but oh no, he has got to follow in Dad's flaming footsteps if he can't make it to Lord Advocate, Moderator or Vice Chancellor of the University.'

'I didn't know you wanted to be a doctor. I knew you were clever, though.'

It was true, Kirsty had always done well at school, it was just that no one had ever associated her with the earnest girls who were set on an academic path. Kirsty was a trendsetter, a troublemaker, and no one had ever thought that her difficulty with authority stemmed from a frustrated urge to be allowed to study seriously.

'I want to be a nurse,' said Andrea, 'but I haven't told anyone. I don't think they would mind, so long as it wasn't too expensive.'

'Lucky you,' said Kirsty. 'I'd give anything to be able to follow my vocation.'

Andrea wondered whether 'anything' included Kirsty's beautiful complexion, her self-confidence, her sex appeal or merely her leather skirt and new tape recorder. She had never thought that she would be Kirsty's object of envy, and felt a bit of a fraud. After all, she really only wanted to be a nurse in order to encounter Ian Robb in some life or death situation. Their eyes would meet, love would bloom. The patient would probably die.

'Do you want to come shopping?' Kirsty asked. 'There is this new place down Rose Street.'

'I haven't got any money,' Andrea explained, 'but I'll walk to the shop with you.'

'Why don't you ask Dad to give you some more then? Everyone else does ever since he paid you that hush money.'

Andrea couldn't believe this. How did Kirsty know?

Kirsty went on, 'Don't worry, Clootie, the man is just an old goat. I'm not blaming you at all. Just don't tell your brother anything you want kept a real secret. Mind you, I'm only guessing that he tried to buy your silence because he had been groping you. Am I not right?'

Andrea admitted she was. 'I am really sorry. I didn't want anyone to know. It was just that Neil kept on pestering me about the money and I did only swear not to tell on the Presby prayer book.'

'Don't apologize to me!' said Kirsty. 'I couldn't care less what the old fool does so long as he keeps on paying out. I get money from Mum too, especially if she has not told me where she is going when she is all tarted up and where she has been when she returns all in a heap. God, how I loathe them.'

'But you can't hate your parents,' Andrea protested.

'Why ever not? People who decide to get married often end up hating each other, so why should you have to love people you aren't able to choose? Tell me, does your father do divorces?'

'I suppose so,' said Andrea. 'He seems to do most things.'

'I thought so,' said Kirsty. 'That explains a lot.' She expanded no further.

After a pause, Kirsty asked, 'Do you really want to go and stay in Glasgow?'

'Yes,' said Andrea, luckily resisting the temptation to tell Kirsty about her crush on the doctor. 'But I worry about Petunia.'

'Petunia?'

'Petunia is my cat. He is getting very old. No one else likes him much.'

Kirsty began to sing, 'So you've got a little cat, and you're very fond of that, but you'd rather have a bow-wow-wow.'

'No I wouldn't,' Andrea replied.

'I was just singing a rude song, silly,' said Kirsty.

'Like "Eskimo Nell"?' Andrea asked.

'What does a nice wee girl like you know about "Eskimo Nell"?' Kirsty was astounded and somewhat put out at Andrea's apparent knowledge.

'My brother, Neil, can sing all twelve verses.'

'There are forty-two verses,' Kirsty replied, recovering her aplomb.

The Rose Street shop was newly opened and all done up in bright pine. The girls fingered the merchandise, tried on two peasant-type dresses, probed a pile of sailors' smocks, enquired the price of tin mugs and left, buying nothing.

'I'm bored,' said Kirsty.

9

Little had changed on the outside of Effie's house. It would have been hard to alter the appearance of such a solid and respectable edifice. However, Milroy had always insisted on the blinds hovering at exactly two-thirds up the window panes. Now they all differed. Such things must be tolerated if a house is to be let to several tenants. The rent came in prompt and complete and Milroy expressed herself pleased with the new régime so James and Ishbel were certainly not going to fret about the management of blinds. The same dismal plant grew in the pot at the top of the steps. It never had been much of a thriver.

Inside – well, that was certainly different. Andrea was amazed at the transformation. The cows still waded hock-deep in Highland swamps above the substantial fireplaces, but everywhere else was adorned with cheerful draperies and an enormous consignment of plastic roses, the kind that generally came free with Daz. Milroy must have bought them at Woolworth's or off the Barras street market, unless she had undertaken to launder for the whole of Kelvingrove in great vats of detergent to acquire so many bunches via the usual channels.

The two rooms at the front, the dining room and the one in which Effie had died, were transformed into common rooms for the tenants who, Milroy said, were all good hard-working girls and in need of pleasant surroundings in which to relax and entertain their friends. There was evidence of a well-stocked bar, and whereas the cantilevered lamp had once illuminated Effie's tedious meals, it now shone on a makeshift gaming table. Milroy had always been a one for games of chance and skill, which she maintained kept the senses sharp and lively.

Andrea was disturbed to find her visit less than welcome. Naturally, Milroy had not been able to refuse to have her landlord's daughter to stay, but she had tried in vain to say that all the rooms were let and there was no accommodation available.

116

However, James had insisted that a room be kept in readiness for any Innes unfortunate or stupid enough to have to spend a night in Glasgow, thus Milroy had no option but to accept the visitor and feign delight.

Her forced smile turned to an expression of shock when she saw the change in Andrea.

'Miss Andrea, I would not have believed it possible. What has happened to the bonny wee girl who was so taken with my baking? You have never been starving yourself?'

'Of course not, Milroy,' Andrea replied cheerfully. 'I have just lost the puppy fat.'

Milroy had changed too. No longer was she dressed in a modest afternoon frock with apron and cap. She was all aglow in shrimp-coloured crochet, a glimpse of her slip could be seen between the open work of the stitches, and round her neck, nestling on her bare flesh, was a gold pendant that declared the wearer to be called Teresa.

'You must not call me Milroy now. All my girls and their friends call me Miss T and you must do the same. I will call you Andrea. Now let me take you up to your room and then we will organize your evening for you. I am sure you like going to the pictures. There are lots of films for you to see and my friend Ina will take you. It will not be dull here, you will see.'

Andrea did not particularly want to go to the cinema. She had a headache and would have been happy to stay in with a book, but staying in was not to be. No more was there to be any mingling with the tenants. They were worn out with their work; they required to be allowed to unwind in their own ways. Andrea would keep to her room. Meals would be served there, and there was a chamber pot to be used at night. Milroy, or rather Miss T, was most insistent that Andrea was not to go tumbling down the stairs to her death whilst groping her way to the bathroom. Another thing was important: Andrea must decide, if possible several days in advance, about when she wanted to take a bath. Her stay was orchestrated like a royal visit.

She felt depressed but comforted herself with the knowledge that at least she was in the same city as Ian Robb. Tomorrow she intended to find out the location of the surgery. She would plan an encounter.

Elderly and unknown to Andrea, Ina had the air of a retired prison wardress and was undoubtedly in charge. She guided Andrea by the elbow as if escorting a malefactor to the cells. When she tried to be cheerful the result was neither convincing nor comforting, and her merriment was most alarming. The film, appropriately enough, was *A Tale of Two Cities*, which she had seen before, but Dirk Bogarde as Sydney Carton was still utterly divine. Andrea couldn't help thinking that Ina would have made a perfect Tricoteuse. Tomorrow they were to go to *Gigi* – she had seen that too – and the following night they must take a bus to Pollockshaws where Doris Day, Andrea's *bête noire*, was being shown in something decidedly transatlantic and hardly humorous.

Ina ate frequent choc-ices, which she bit through without a wince. Her teeth must have been of steel. Andrea had nothing, her headache became worse, and by the time Tweetie Pie, *Look at Life* and a silly western had supported the main feature, she too would have gladly laid her head beneath the blooded blade of Madame Guillotine. Ina dawdled on the way home and insisted on a pie and chips. Andrea ate some chips and felt better. Then she ate a whole poke full. It would take at least twenty heaves and a gallon of water to get rid of such a feast, but they were good. Her head cleared.

Back at the house she was escorted rapidly up the stairs with scarcely a moment to absorb the jolly atmosphere coming from below. The working girls were unwinding most effectively. In her room was a tray of scones and a cup of thick-skinned Horlicks which she planned to gorge and then disgorge in their entirety.

She bolted them, hardly savouring the taste, but enjoying the pleasure of eating despite the retribution to follow. Wait a few minutes – not long enough to cause the start of fat manufacture, but sufficient time to get the stomach in best chucking form. Andrea had the system finely tuned. She scarcely needed to put the fingers down her throat any more. She drank three tooth mugs of water and started out to find the lavatory.

Her room door was locked! She shouted but no one came. She

rang the bell and despite the red flash swinging most agitatedly in the frame on the kitchen wall, no one responded. The minutes passed, her waist was thickening and her thighs were swelling into two squidgy hams. She needed help. Maybe she could be sick out of the window as if she were in a car. The parapet made that option awkward. The only solution was to use the potty and then try to hurl the contents beyond the house. Luckily the window of her room gave on to the back yard and not the front and its railed area. There were plenty of visitors that night; she could hear the door bell ringing with great frequency. The working girls would not like their friends to be spattered with sick from a height.

It wasn't easy, and it was never pleasant, but she contrived to regurgitate all her self-indulgence and swilled the contents of the pot before throwing it over the parapet into the darkness. Seagulls are obliging and Kelvingrove is not so very far from the Clyde.

The next morning she had a sore throat. It became raw when she rasped it during vomiting. Her head ached but Milroy would have no lingering in bed. She dismissed the locked door as an oversight on her behalf and did not apologize at all. She was full of plans and had bought a ticket for a bus trip for Andrea to enjoy that very day. It was Tuesday and Andrea went to the Land of Burns.

On Wednesday she was sent to the Highlights of Kyle and Carrick, and on Thursday she was instructed to enjoy the Beauties of the Ayrshire Coast. Each jaunt had included a visit to Burns Cottage at Alloway. Bored with Russians, the custodian had hopes of her as a Robert Burns fanatic. On Friday, great excitement . . . Milroy had bought Andrea a place on the Mystery Tour. It wasn't very mysterious, and Andrea grieved the custodian by refusing to enter the cottage again. She compounded the crime by giving her admission ticket to a foreigner who muttered something to the effect that Ayr was hame to honest lads and bonny lasses, but the dire Scots, hard to comprehend from the mouth of a native, was incomprehensible when spoken by one from Minsk.

She hadn't had a moment to look for Ian. She had never been left alone. At night, after the cinema, she was always escorted to bed by Milroy who hovered outside the bathroom and saw that

119

she was in bed before locking her in. One must not risk being less than vigilant in these treacherous times. Glasgow was swarming with murderers and burglars, she said. (No mention was made of how Andrea was to cope if marauders entered via the window.) The gannets continued to feet on regurgitated food, and were reminded of their youth.

James had sent a message to say that Ishbel was having a total bed rest in hospital. The baby had not been induced to arrive as yet; births are not popular at weekends.

Saturday was spent aboard *The Duchess of Montrose*, who plied an excursion to Arran via Saltcoats and Ardrossan. She was not a swift vessel but Andrea was becoming accustomed to sitting quietly and being transported past sights. Mercifully a visit to Burns Cottage was not possible for seafarers, but the boat did chug by Effie's grave whilst sailing down the Clyde to the accompaniment of badly blown bagpipes.

On Sunday, too exhausted to protest, Andrea was hurtled round new territory, the trip was A Taste of the Trossachs, a welcome change that entailed nothing more energetic than sitting tight, singing about one's heart (in the Highlands), one's bonny (over the ocean), one's love (like a red, red rose) and stopping at a revolting café for repulsive refreshments.

Andrea had perfected the art of avoiding chattiness. She affected deafness and gazed intently out of the window, having fixed her mind on other, higher things.

She started from her reverie as they passed the Buchanan Arms at Drymen. Surely that was her father, hand in hand with Moira MacInlay in the hotel car park? She was certain it was them but the bus driver refused to stop, which was probably just as well. After all, James was Moira's professional adviser and he detested family interruptions.

Above the kitchen mantelpiece Milroy had hung three pictures: the Virgin, face forward with downcast eyes, her Son ascending to heaven and baring His sacred heart with an expression generally reserved for those with griping indigestion, and a profile of Pope John the Twenty-Third, which was newly draped in black. Like it or not, she could not warm to his successor, the sharp-featured

Paul. Above the sinks, near where she and Ina sat sipping strong tea, was a pulley laden with the tenants' undergarments. Bri-Nylon was evidently most popular, and the scantiness and transparency of the washing might have caused consternation amongst the neighbours if it had dangled out of doors. The washing line was reserved for sheets and other banalities.

'Yon wee girl Andrea worries me,' said Ina. 'You ought to get rid of her, Teresa. She's no' well.'

'Believe me, Ina, I didna' want her here at all. I'd love to be shot of her, but with her parents being my landlords there is nothing I can do. What do you think is wrong with her?'

'I think she has fallen.'

'Fallen down? She never said.'

'No, Teresa, I mean she is expecting. There is a wean on the way.'

'Och, Ina, whatever makes you say that?'

'I just know. She is for ever being sick and she is awful distracted. I bet you will find she has no' had a "visitor" for a couple of months.'

'Well, you should know, Ina. What shall I do? She must stay till after her mother gets back home.'

'I was wondering if she wanted it out.'

'I doubt she ever knew it wanted in. I think we had better leave well alone. It must have happened in Edinburgh so it is no our problem and anyway she couldna' pay.'

At that point a young, artificially blonde girl came in from the wash hoose and hung a pair of navy knickers on the pulley. Milroy and Ina had to remove their cups from the draining board as the collection of frillies was lowered and became entangled with the sink tidy. A condemned Brillo pad got hung from an ascending black suspender belt.

'Miss T, are you ever going by Pullars? I canna' get this ice-cream stain shifted?' She showed a mark on a serge gymslip to Milroy.

'Sure, hen. Just leave it there. In the meantime, how can you manage?'

'I will manage fine. I have an alternative get-up.' She left to find it.

121

'Who is that?' Ina asked Milroy.

'She calls herself Samantha but when she was doing hairdressing she was called Susan. Do you not mind her? She came through frae Edinburgh to you this spring past.'

'I'm that bad on faces,' Ina replied.

By careful artifice and convincing play-acting, Andrea was able to persuade Milroy of her poorliness. She had been very sick, she said, and furthermore she felt awfully dizzy and was fearful of removing herself from the vicinity of a good loo. In other words, she was not going to attempt a trip to Loch Lomond with lunch at Luss. She was sorry, but there it was, and with that she rushed to the bathroom again and heaved with many feigned raucous retchings till Milroy tapped on the door to ask if all was well. No, she said, it was not. She must stay in bed. Milroy agreed grudgingly that a coach trip over Rest and Be Thankful might not be wise under the circumstances.

She asked whether Andrea needed anything, also whether she was about to get her period.

'Maybe,' said Andrea. 'I haven't had one for ages, not since April.' She prayed that Milroy would summon Dr Robb. He would call round and fall in love with her at once. She must wash her hair in anticipation of his visit. Thank God the spots were dormant, though not extinct.

For the rest of the day Andrea was left in peace, and the house ticked on. The door bell rang all afternoon, and there were continuous comings and goings. Some of the tenants must work from home as the place never appeared to be empty of occupants. Cat had become so portly that he seldom climbed the stairs these days but sat in the bay window and observed the world passing by.

Ishbel had asked James to get rid of Petunia. The cat was old, inclined to fat and prone to lie on beds. The next place he would choose would be the crib, she predicted. Also his vermin-catching days were over. The children could be told that he had been run down by a car, not put down by the vet. Of all the tasks that James had intended to complete while the house was empty, this was the one he dreaded most. However, he felt obliged to see it through and had made an appointment with doom for the cat, who managed to become friendlier and more pleasant with each day that James spent as his sole companion.

'How is Petunia?'

'He is fine,' James answered. Indeed he was, he was sitting purring fit to burst on James's desk while he took the call from Andrea on Monday night. He had two days to live.

'Is he getting fed?'

'Of course.' It was intended that he should consume all the cat meat in the larder before he met his fate. Petunia's life, like Scheherazade, depended on his resources.

'I worry about him a lot. Please take great care of him.'

'I will,' James lied. 'Only you must realize he is very old and will have to die one day soon.' (Like Wednesday, he thought.)

'Oh please, Dad, please take care of him. I couldn't bear it if anything happened to him.'

Petunia jumped on his lap and settled comfortingly there.

'We'll see. Now you seem to be more worried about the cat than you are about Mum.'

'How is she? Is the baby coming soon?'

'Very soon, I expect. She is being cared for very well. You must not worry.'

'I don't,' Andrea replied honestly and then, because it was expected, said, 'Just be sure and give her my love.'

'How are you getting on? Are you having a good time?' James could not imagine how anyone could be faintly entertained by a trip to Glasgow but he certainly did not want his daughter returned to him just yet.

'I am not very well. I keep on being sick and I want to see the doctor. Do you think you could ask Milroy to send for Dr Robb? I know him, he looked after Grannie. I really feel dreadful and I do not want to go to the pictures again with Milroy's friend, who is mad and asks me awful questions. And I don't want to go on any more bus trips.'

'Bus trips?'

'Yes, she sends me on excursions every day. Yesterday I am sure I saw you and Mrs MacInlay in Drymen.'

'Of course you should see the doctor. You must be delirious.

Me and Mrs MacInlay in Drymen – whoever heard of such a thing?'

James laughed and Petunia squealed on account of being violently squeezed.

Apart from the problem of the cat, James found himself overwhelmed with domestic trivia while waiting for his next child to get on with being born. Reassuring old Nurse Glasgow, who had attended each previous infant Innes, suddenly declared herself to be unable to come to help. She said she was no longer up to the stairs. The truth was that she had been offered a slightly higher wage by decidedly higher society and was off to a ducal household where there were twice as many stairs but the pram was embellished by a coronet. A young girl, heavy with qualifications but light on experience, had been engaged instead. She was known as the shoddy substitute and liked to be called by her christian name, Marlene. She also wore jeans, smoked Cadets and said 'Ta'.

'Could things be worse?' Ishbel asked during a fresh attack of tearfulness.

'Yes they could,' said James crossly. 'We might have employed a homicidal maniac.'

'How do you know we haven't?' Ishbel replied. She had become very difficult during the last month and exceptionally unattractive. She wore no make-up on her beaky face and dirty pink ankle socks on her puffy feet.

The chimneys stacks were being repointed and the workmen, when they appeared, played their transistors so loud that the neighbours had formed themselves into a committee to complain. They told James that the tone of the terrace was being lowered, and despite the sherry of appeasement they said that they hoped James and Ishbel were not planning to rend the neighbourhood placidity with a squawking baby. James replied that he had specifically ordered the stork to deliver a meek and mild child. Irony was not appreciated by the Residents' Association.

Now there was this problem with Andrea.

'Miss Milroy, please will you get the doctor to visit Andrea? She is plainly not well. I believe the name of the doctor is Robb, who attended Mrs Lammont, you will remember.'

'I don't think Miss Andrea is that poorly. Just a wee bilious attack. There is a lot of it about,' Milroy replied. The telephone was in the hall, and since Effie's death had taken to lodging beneath the pink and mauve knitted skirts of a crinolined lady.

'If, as you say, it is just a bug going round, why did you tell me that you were all in such excellent health?'

'What I meant to say was, we are all just fine now. Last week we were prostrated, every one of us.'

'Well, I am sorry to hear that,' said James, 'but nevertheless I would like a doctor to see her. Especially as she seems to have been hallucinating.'

'Och, that is just her imagination. Too many visits to the pictures can do that to a body.'

'I think not, Miss Milroy.'

'Very well. I will take her to the surgery tomorrow.'

James balked at this. He and Ishbel disapproved of communal sickness and always believed that one caught more than was cured by visiting a surgery and sitting beside heaven-knows-who suffering from God-knows-what in an atmosphere hotching with germs. 'I wish the doctor to visit her. You cannot be too careful about contracting diseases especially in – er . . .' he was going to say Glasgow but thought that tactless and changed it to 'this time of year.'

Milroy agreed reluctantly. The doctor would be called if Mr Innes insisted. Which he did.

'And how is Miss Ishbel? Is the bairn no' coming yet?'

'Mrs Innes is doing well, thank you.'

'Och well, tell her I was asking for her and that I have lit a candle for her and the child.'

James was not entirely delighted with this news but he thanked Milroy for the gracious gesture most pompously. He would not be passing that message on any more than Milroy was going to say how the candle was very small and bought second-hand. The first time round it had been extinguished by a wicked draught. She had lit the charred wick while sending a prayer aloft to St Jude, who received most of her petitions on account of his patronage of lost causes.

125

All day Andrea lay in bed. It was hot and sultry outside, and her room on the third floor at the back faced south. A gull perched on the parapet and enquired after her health. He was not anxious for her wellbeing, just curious about the lack of semi-digested victuals on which he and his kin had come to depend. Milroy considered that colds should be fed and fevers starved so Andrea got nothing except Lucozade. When she was small she had made dolls' sombreros from the foil cap and transformed her subdued room into a golden grotto by looking at it through the yellow Cellophane. Now there were no dolls to dress and it would take more than amber wrappings to turn Glasgow into Jersualem the Golden.

There were forty-eight roses going up the wall and each roll of paper consisted of eight alternating rows interspersed with ribbons tied in bows every third row. The pattern did not work; especially as the section partially hidden by the mahogany wardrobe had been hung upside down. Like Mussolini, she thought. She had often wondered if he had been killed first. It was a question that she did not dare ask in case she was accused of being macabre, which was why she had resolved to keep her curiosity about mummies to herself.

All day she waited for Ian. He would come, she knew he would, as Milroy had told her that she had rung and asked most particularly for Dr Robb. She had also made it quite clear with snorts and hisses that medical science was not well served by the likes of him. She recalled his forthright manner concerning herself and her consoling drams on the night Effie died.

Andrea must wait; there were plenty who were far more urgently ill and afflicted with life-threatening and baffling ailments that must be attended first. She was being a nuisance and making a fuss. That was quite plain.

The house was unusually quiet. Maybe the nice weather had persuaded the tenants to bask in Kelvingrove Park.

At last, at about four o'clock, there was a knock on the door. Andrea had been dozing but was ready with her clean hair combed and her latest pimple obliterated. Milroy drew back the curtains letting in the blinding sun.

'Here we are, Andrea. I'll just leave you two the now. Ring if you need anything.'

She blinked through the dusty haze and the confusion of awakening and saw Ishbel.

'Mum! Mummie, how lovely! I have wanted you to come so much. Oh Mummie!' She surprised herself with the thrill she felt, and the love that had not sprung from her since she had grown out of childhood. 'But what about the baby? Shouldn't you be in hospital?'

The shape was right but the age and face were wrong. With bitter misery she realized it wasn't Ishbel after all. Nor, obviously, was this caller Ian Robb. Maybe one of the tenants had mistaken her room.

'I am sorry, dear. You must have been dozing.' The voice was calm and the accent subdued and lyrical, unlike the broad rasp of the Lowlands. 'I am Dr Robb.'

How could anyone play such a vicious trick? 'No you are not!' Andrea shouted. She felt an overwhelming desire to rage and cry and throw something at the impostor.

'I can assure you I am Dr Robb. You were probably expecting Ian, my husband. You see, we are both doctors and work in the same practice. We met at college and have been married for three years. I am just working for one more month though, because our baby is being born in October. I am sorry if you are disappointed, but I am just as qualified as Ian. More so in some ways. I have a lot of experience of working with teenage girls. Well, I was one, for a start!'

Andrea was sobbing so loudly that she heard very little of what was said. All she knew was that Ian loved someone else more than her. He had married. There was to be a baby and he hadn't even thought that he would have liked to come and see Andrea again. He had sent his wife. Andrea meant nothing to him at all. This woman lived with him, slept with him and they loved each other. She even smelt of him.

'Hush now, dearie.' Elizabeth Robb sat on the edge of the bed, encircled Andrea's bony body with her arms and tried to soothe her fearsome sobs, which eventually began to subside.

'Why don't you tell me what the trouble is, or have I got to guess?'

'I keep on being sick,' Andrea said at last.

'Well, I can see from here that you are severely undernourished. That is funny because Ian said that the girl who coped so well when Mrs Lammont died was a fine bonny sort of lass. When did you start losing weight?'

Andrea thought for a while. At least Ian had remembered her, even if it had only been for her substantial build.

'I was too fat to fit through a wee door in a horsebox and everyone laughed at me so I decided to go on a diet. That was a couple of months or so after Grannie died.'

'And things got out of hand? Let's have a look down your throat. Open wide . . . say ah. Show me your hands. I wonder what these fingers smell of?'

Andrea snatched her hand away and Elizabeth made no move to get it back.

'Now, if you lie down I will examine your stomach. My, my, that is quite empty. When did you last eat?'

'I had some cereal last night.'

'And did you need to put your fingers down your throat to get rid of it?'

Without thinking, Andrea replied proudly, 'I can make myself sick without using my fingers now.'

'I worry about our children sometimes,' Bunty sighed as she observed Fiona and Marion chasing each other round the scraggy lawn like a couple of boisterous hippos. Shrieks and yells caused rooks bound for bed to take off from the pines in vertical panic.

'But they are fine healthy creatures,' observed Buster. 'What could be better?'

'Well, at least they aren't like that dreadful French child Head Wig, who has done nothing but sulk since she arrived and complained about Wee Angus.'

'Why?'

'I gather Fiona told her that he was the dead spit of someone called Johnny Hallyday.'

'I take it she was lying?' Buster asked.

'On an epic scale, apparently.'

'Well, you can be thankful, Bunty, that none of them is like those horrors you had to cope with at the Pony Club.'

'Quite,' Bunty replied. 'Only they do worry me sometimes.'

Fiona was shoving grass mowings down Marion's Aertex-covered bosom as Hedvige strutted by, puffing on a disdainful Gitane.

'The twins aren't what you might term sophisticated. Sometimes I wonder whether they even know about the facts of life.'

'Naturally they do, Bunty. No one could be ignorant of those, living here with all your bitches forever whelping and the trouble we had with those lambs and that afterbirth.'

'Yes, but they don't seem to be very interested in you-know-what and they aren't really frightfully toothsome.'

'Don't you mean they are not very sexy?'

'Same thing,' said Bunty. 'You should have seen that Morag's neck by the end of camp. It was covered in dental impressions, all different.'

'Well, surely you don't want the girls to go about getting devoured.'

'Certainly I don't. When they get married they will be virgins.'

'Like you, my love.'

'Of course,' said Bunty. 'Can I have another gin, please?'

They sipped and stared at the misty evening. It would have been nice not to have lived so close to the city but money was not that abundant and this house, which they had inherited from Buster's aunt, was very large and had space for horses. On the whole, they were content to ignore the sounds of mechanical civilization that would have been absent in their ideal home.

'You weren't, though.'

'I wasn't what?'

'A virgin, Buster dear, when we got married. You knew exactly what to do and where to put it and all that.'

'Men are different.'

'Of course. That is another thing that worries me. I think you ought to do something about Wee Angus. I found him reading Oscar Wilde last week.'

'Jolly good stuff, some of it, and funny too, unlike that Sartre and his gang.'

'Don't be trying, Buster. You know what I mean. The boy ought to get in some practice with some clean and experienced female before he gets the wrong idea. He is very pretty, you know. One does not want him to be misconstrued. What did you do about losing your virginity?'

'I got drunk in Cambridge. Can't remember much. She was an obliging girl. She had protruding eyes. Then there was Spain, which was different, and then . . . well, then there was the war.'

'You met me during the war, Buster.'

He gazed into the distance and thought about Dolores of the massive thighs. Despite the hostilities, she had been a most friendly señorita.

Bunty interrupted his reverie. 'You must take Angus off and get him initiated. I insist. I have no wish to know how or where you propose to do it. I understand one used to go to Paris.'

'You have seen that Chevalier chap thanking heaven for little girls in *Gigi* once too often, dear. All of Paris is full of mean-faced young women in short-sleeved bottle-green sweaters.'

'How do you know?'

'Look at Head Wig . . . You wouldn't want that for your son.'

'Be serious, Buster, I mean it. There must be somewhere you can go. After all, look at what they get up to at Cliveden.'

'Angus is not a cabinet minister or a spy.'

'Buster! Please, you must take your duties as a father seriously. I will see that the girls know about not going alone with men in taxis and you will get Angus organized into being a normal capable male. Do you understand?'

'How, Bunty dear, do you propose I go about this?'

'Use your initiative. Ask someone at the club.'

'The New Club? You must be mad. That place prides itself on being the last bastion of the sotto voce and quite averse to carnality. The golf club is not much better, just full of people discussing their handicaps and prostate glands. I suppose I could ask one of those young fellows in the office. They drink with quite a raffish crowd at the Aperitif.'

'For God's sake, Buster, be discreet. I don't want people to think you are after some tart from Rose Street. Whoever you get for the job must be thoroughly vetted first. We don't want the embarrassment of having Angus required to attend the Special Clinic like Mungo MacInlay. His girlfriend had slept with half Midlothian.'

'Dear me, it must have been standing room only at that clinic. Talking of which, I hear you can have intercourse upright in a bus shelter for half a crown in Leith.'

'Buster, you are being exasperating. And another thing: please make sure that she doesn't intend to get pregnant. The Blairs have sent their eldest to a fish-packing station in Alaska because that Juanita says he is the father of her bulge.'

'Is he?'

'Perhaps, but he wasn't the only one. He was just the one whose name she could remember. This will be her third.'

'An accommodating race, the Spanish.' He had often wondered whether Dolores had given birth to his baby. Good God, the child would be over thirty by now, and he, Buster Brown, could be a grandfather! 'Why Alaska?'

Bunty explained that the Arctic Circle was generally considered to be too far for avenging brothers brandishing stilettoes in pursuit of a sister's seducer.

'One gets less trouble in time of war. Oh hello, Angus old chap. Good book?'

'Not bad. It is Nietzsche.'

'Oh yes,' said Buster brightly, 'that is about superman, isn't it?'

Angus nodded, he would have liked to have discussed it further, but Bunty interrupted breezily to announce that she thought Angus might be a bit old for comic-book heroes but she expected it was a good stirring tale, and there was nothing like a bit of manly adventure now and again.

10

An elderly woman, whose complexion resembled wind-blown rose petals, was waiting on the steps for the bell to be answered. Her seated heather mixture skirt indicated her social class, which was elevated, if faded. Once she had been a most effective and faithful ornament, and had drifted through drawing rooms being quite, quite charming. Her disarming fragility and inclination to girlish twitterings were pure camouflage. She had instilled confidence in suspect envoys and doubtful nobles and then, once they were enthralled by her pale English pastel looks, she had struck like a cobra and got whole embassies organized into charity bazaars, good works and generous contributions to causes that needed support. Beneath the crêpe de Chine she kept a soul of steel. Once widowed and rather impoverished, she had channelled her energies into horticulture. Her garden was renowned for its bounty, her baronial mansion was not.

'Good afternoon, my dear.' The bell was answered by a rather precocious schoolgirl.

Netta Neilson was impervious to structural faults like deafening pipes, interior gales and rot, but was offended by unhealthy plants and shook her head in sorrow at the straggled specimen that failed to flourish in its pot on the doorstep.

'Is Milroy at home?'

'There is naebody called Milroy here,' the schoolgirl answered, 'unless you mean Miss T, and she is away up the stairs with a visitor at the minute.'

She made to shut the door but Netta was stern and resolute.

'I will wait in the hall. Tell your mother that Lady Neilson would like a word with her.'

'My mother? Och, Miss T is never my mother!' the girl laughed, but Netta stood her ground and waited by the many-knobbed hall stand but did not use the mirror to inspect her collapsed face. Those days were over long ago, as was the way of life once enjoyed by her late friend Effie Lammont. Though she was short-sighted she was far from fooled by the plastic roses and scrutinized the telephone lady with pained disdain. The school-girl continued the conversation that the door bell had interrupted. She was evidently arranging a meeting with one of her friends. Netta pondered on the boldness of modern youth. Once the call was concluded the phone was again concealed beneath the crinoline and the schoolgirl turned to find Netta had entered the dining room and was inspecting the gaming table.

'Can I not help you? Miss T might be ages.'

'I have come for my jam jars. When she was alive Mrs Lammont ate a great deal of my damson jam but never returned the pots. I am expecting a bumper crop this year and will need as many jars as I can get.' Lady Neilson, who had once had a husband high in the colonial service, swept past Samantha and descended to the kitchen where she eventually found a cache of jars beneath the sink above which the tenants' lingerie dripped itself dry.

Only Milroy's special friends ever visited her kitchen, but Netta was as forceful now as she had been in Cairo in 1923 when most of the world was coloured pink. The sun did not set on such as her.

'Miss T, there is a body in your kitchen looking for jars. She says she wants to make jelly. I think she is fou or mad. She calls herself Lady Neilson.'

Milroy had just ushered Dr Robb out of the door at speed and now endeavoured to contend with this latest intrusion on the peace of her lodging house. Samantha did not wait for the scene that was sure to follow. Ferreting in the kitchen was forbidden and Milroy had a tough temper.

'Lady Neilson! Whatever are you about?'

'Ah, Milroy, I am looking for my jars. Perhaps you would put them in a box for me and call me a taxi? I intend to catch the train while the cheap rate is in force and have no time to spare. I hope you are keeping well?'

'Yes, your ladyship, thank you. And how are you yourself?'

'I mustn't complain.'

Indeed she must not, thought Milroy, as she crammed the jars into a large carton. The crinolined lady was lifted off her telephone nest and a cab called. It would take at least ten minutes. In the meantime Lady Neilson did a thorough inspection of the ground floor, quite undeterred by Milroy's offer of distracting tea. Had the taxi not been prompt Netta might have got up to the first floor but the thought of paying a higher fare prevented further probing.

'That plant wants dried blood,' she announced, almost knocking a dilapidated old man off the steps as she swept out. 'Jock! Whatever are you doing here?' Netta and Uncle Jock were old acquaintances. 'Are you looking for jam jars too?'

'No, Netta. Not really.'

'Dear me, Jock, don't tell me you are still up to the same tricks?'

He looked at this ancient girlfriend and wondered what she knew.

'Are you still just looking?' Netta asked.

Jock did not answer. The cab driver was getting impatient.

'Netta, tell me one thing. Where was I in 1923?'

'In Cairo, of course, on your way to Ceylon, to look at tea.'

'Thank God for that,' replied Uncle Jock, visibly relieved.

Netta and her jam pots were too late at St Enoch's and it grieved her greatly to have to find the extra half-crown.

Despite the typical sturdiness of prosperous Glasgow terraces, Andrea's sobs could be heard on the landing below. Samantha hated misery almost as much as she found unsatisfied curiosity unbearable. For over a week she had not had a chance to discover who it was that occupied the top back bedroom and now, with Miss T and the mad woman looking for jam pots, she felt she had a chance to find out what it was that had to be kept so secretively apart. Whoever it was had been very sick. You did not have to be clever to spot that.

The door was locked but the key was there. She knocked and waited. The sobs continued so she tried again, then she opened the door and went in. She had no desire to be caught on the landing by Miss T who had instructed all the other working girls that they must not, under any circumstance, communicate with the new tenant. She had implied that the girl was suffering from something infectious, but that was a load of blether, especially as she seemed to be allowed to infect whole bus loads and cinemas without restraint.

Andrea recognized Samantha first.

'Susan! How lovely to see you.' She meant it. 'I am really surprised! I thought you were through with school, and were being a model.'

'Good God! It's never you again! What in heaven's name are you doing in a place like this? Does your family know where you are?'

'Of course, this house belongs to them since Grannie died.'

'Are you telling me that your grannie stayed in this house?'

'Yes, most of her life, why?'

'Well, I'm amazed.'

Susan sat on the bed and looked at Andrea, who seemed so thin that there was nothing of her beneath the sheets.

'Are you still peely-wally?'

'I am getting better now.'

'Whatever was wrong with you?'

'I was sick, but I won't be any more.'

'I see,' said Susan. 'Have you been looked after by Ina?'

'She took me to the cinema.'

'I've never heard it called that before, but I dare say you will get over it. I was aye greeting for a few weeks but now I'm fine.'

'I wasn't crying about a film.' The tears started again.

'Come now, hen. You mustn't let men get to you like this. They are never worth it. I ken fine, they are only good for one thing . . . and I don't mean sex.'

'I loved him, he was wonderful.'

'Of course he was, pet. Wonderful at getting you into a state. Well, now you have learnt your lesson. Don't be used by men, just get into the habit of using them instead. Never give an inch till you have got your reward sorted.'

Andrea wasn't listening. She hadn't even grasped the astonishing discovery of finding Susan as one of Milroy's tenants. All she could think about was the domestic heaven of the two doctors Robb. She would have liked to have hated his wife but she was everything that Andrea admired. Clever and beautiful, and loved

135

by the most wonderful man in the world and, what was more, carrying a child that must, undoubtedly, rival the Messiah. Only this would be no virgin birth. The child would have been conceived in rapture that no pen could describe.

Samantha/Susan left Andrea and returned downstairs. She had an appointment.

Elizabeth Robb had intended to stop work at the beginning of June, but circumstances had combined to make life at home in their large flat intolerable. The spare bedroom was occupied, albeit for a fee, by Ian's cousin Mungo MacInlay.

Originally Mungo had been sent to Glasgow to work to the top of the Macpop business from the bottom, but he had shown no aptitude or enthusiasm, and seldom bothered to turn up for his shift. This left his foreman in a quandary, unable to sack the unsackable and doubting the prudence of reporting the owner's son for idle inefficiency. Blind eyes were turned, and Mungo stayed in bed till noon and then strummed his guitar between gasps of tobacco. He would shortly be breaking into the pop music world having formed a sensational group called The Clegs. So far the group consisted of one. The reek of cigarettes and the constant twanging made Elizabeth feel terrible. Music in any form was not her forte. Ian was addicted to jazz and listened to *The Riddle* far too often, though sometimes the flat resounded with a selection of Sousa, which was only slightly better than the persistent throb of Scottish dance music that had pervaded her childhood home or the fearful mouth music beloved of her mother, a keen Celt.

She loved her work and her husband, and would love their child, but she could not warm to Ian's family. Inspecting leaking colostomies was more enjoyable than sharing her roof with Mungo. He had to go. She told Ian that he must evict his horrid cousin but Ian felt that one should be staunch with one's family, however dreadful. Elizabeth replied that she doubted Ian would be so tolerant if Mungo had come from her impoverished clan. Ian was affronted and appalled and declared himself deeply wounded. Elizabeth replied that the truth always hurt. Ian threatened to go to the rugger club; Elizabeth replied that she

136

wished he would. He stormed out; she threw a Royal Worcester casserole after him. It was their first row, and Mungo strummed and smoked impervious throughout. Ian returned somewhat drunk and regretful to find Elizabeth tearfully sweeping up the shards of casserole which had been a wedding present from his Auntie Moira and Uncle Hector, but it was much better off in the bin. Their baby bounced in her belly with relief. Still Mungo remained.

It is not for a doctor to chat about patients, but she did wonder whether Andrea was known to Mungo, though she could devise no way of discovering anything from him as he was evidently resting his voice and made conversation by grunting. Her curiosity was satisfied when, on returning from her second visit to Andrea, she discovered that Kirsty had come to visit her brother and stay a couple of nights on the floor of his room. She was bored with Edinburgh – there was no one there, she said, and the whole place was put about by the impending festival. She also wanted to visit a friend of hers, Andrea Innes.

Andrea had been better. She had not cried so much, and had promised Elizabeth that she had eaten some cereal. Elizabeth sat with her while she ate some biscuits and then, because she had no more calls, continued to chat for another hour after their consumption. It was too late to throw up. The digestive system would have already grabbed the calories. After her initial reticence and resentment, Andrea had enjoyed having someone to talk with. Elizabeth made her feel that her life was important. She even appeared concerned about Petunia, and did not dwell on the imminent arrival of her new brother or sister. Much against her will, Andrea liked Elizabeth more and more. She could not continue to resent her for having captivated the most wonderful man in the world. His red hair framed his face like a halo, his voice was like heavenly music, his eyes were glossy lakes of liquorice and ginger. She dreamt of him as the hero of her life. She would not have imagined him getting drunk at the rugby club.

'Ask Andrea to come to supper,' Elizabeth suggested to Kirsty. 'Ian would love to see her again and it would do her good to get out of that weird boarding house.'

Elizabeth liked the idea of a family evening. She also liked Kirsty who seemed to be able to manage her brother, who had even put his dirty coffee cup on the draining board.

'Whatever do you want to be friends with that freak for?' Mungo asked Kirsty. 'I tell you, if that fat clot comes near me I'm off. She has as much sex appeal as a lump of lard.'

Kirsty interpreted Mungo's grunts for Elizabeth. 'He says he would love to see her. I'm going to call on her tomorrow morning. Can I ask her then?'

'Of course,' Elizabeth replied. It would be an interesting evening. She would be able to exercise some more wedding presents, which somehow during their three years of marriage had never got out of their wrappings. She was a doctor, not a cook, and Ian liked his food plain and copious. Tomorrow she would cook something with a French name out of her virgin *Larousse Gastronomique*. Better still, they might use the fondue set, but the thought of the boiling fat or seething cheese made her and the baby heave.

Kirsty made Mungo go with her to the pictures. They sat through *Psycho* even though they had seen it before. They both agreed that it was very boring and walked back to the Robbs' flat through Kelvingrove, passing quite near where Andrea was sleeping soundly, her throat soothed and a comforting scone digesting in her placid stomach.

'Here, Mungo isn't that Mr Mackie?'

Mungo looked back at the man they had passed who turned away sharply and disappeared down an unlikely alley.

'You are right. It was that one they call Uncle Glen. Does he not have a wee girl?'

'Yes, she is a real weed. His wife, her mother, killed herself.'

'How?' Mungo asked, brightening.

'She hanged herself from the scullery pulley.'

Mungo thought for a while. 'My, that takes some doing.'

By the time Andrea rang Ian and Elizabeth's door bell, her looks had improved considerably. She was thin to the point of emaciation, and her rather limp summer frock hung waiflike off her, but her eyes without glasses for the evening, were still a

138

mystifying green and the spots, for once, were obligingly absent. It took a lot of courage to walk up those steps and press the button marked Robb. She was waiting for the orchestra full of strings to surge through a crescendo of rapture, for lights to burst from heaven and a thousand white doves to be released.

'Come ye in, come ye in!'

A freckled, hair-stubbled hand, vast like a clutch of white puddings, was stretched out towards her. With one hand Ian shook hers while he slapped the other down square between her shoulder blades. Presumably this vigour went down well with his old college hearties, but it quite winded Andrea. He was shorter and broader than she remembered, his hair was more crinkled, and though it was bright orange his washy eyes were framed in pale sockets. He was most awfully hirsute, some of it overflowed his open neck shirt. The disappointment was dreadful and was made more poignant by the realization that this erstwhile idol had more than just feet of clay. Most of him was pretty lumpen.

Elizabeth, though exhausted, had enjoyed the novelty of cooking a supper party. She had used most of her virgin kitchen equipment and thus she felt the saucepans, garlic crusher, set of knives and electric egg beater had been made her own. She even laid the table with some pristine table mats depicting some catastrophic coaching scenes (will generations to come find cars in ditches and collisions attractive?) and contrived to utilize two wooden pepper grinders and three salt mills. However, she could only find a use for two of her five spice racks. The kitchen was a tip.

'Has my wee wifie been having fun?' Ian asked.

Elizabeth smiled through the steam of it all, but did wonder how much of that sort of remark she would be able to tolerate in years to come.

Kirsty had seen the chaos and kindly helped. She half washed most of the utensils, left them to drain and put them all away, but not in the places from which they had come. Then she said she must just pop out. Mungo flicked ash in a pan, but no one was to know once its lid was replaced and it was stowed amongst the biscuits.

Elizabeth could not believe that tomato soup (from a tin), lamb chops, instant Smash, frozen peas and chocolate mousse that had to be poured from a jug could be such a lot of work.

To start with, Andrea thought she would cry. The old revulsion and awkwardness assailed her just as it had at the MacInlays' supper party before the charity Christmas dance. She had nothing to say and nothing to do with her body. She felt as if she was hung about with spare limbs, like an unemployed spider. Ian offered her sherry. It was sweet and had been bought by Elizabeth, who had marvelled at its cheapness. Her family had it known that they were abstainers, and therefore Elizabeth had entered university never having tasted or bought alcohol and had graduated knowing a great deal about beer and cheap wine. While pregnant she was revolted by drink. The baby appeared to be taking after its maternal grandparents.

Above the mantelpiece hung a picture of a couple of gloomy cows idling about in a sodden gully. They seemed familiar and on closer inspection Andrea recognized the signature.

'My grandfather painted that,' she said.

Elizabeth came in from the kitchen. She looked huge, and exhausted, but her face lit up with delight on seeing Andrea. Secretly she had thought that her patient would never turn up and would contrive all manner of excuses to avoid the evening and its inevitable food. She would watch the loo assiduously and make sure that Andrea had no chance to send her supper down the drain. She had tried to disguise the decrepit leatherette sofa beneath a cheerfully dreadful stretch cover. The air hissed from the cushions like a gentle fart as Elizabeth subsided into the arms of the Missenden Settee.

'Would that have been the husband of your grandmother that died?' Ian asked.

Andrea said it had been her grannie's first husband. Then, as nothing seemed to come of that, added that he was run over by a tram.

Ian assumed a face of sympathetic gloom suitable to such a calamity. 'What happened to her second husband?'

'He was poisoned in a chip shop. He was a minister in the English Church.'

'That just shows,' Ian observed. 'In actual fact that picture was a wedding gift from my senior partner. He was very fond of your grandmother. By the way, what happened to the maid?'

'Milroy? Oh she is running the house as a hostel for working girls.'

'Like the YWCA?'

Andrea looked puzzled and Elizabeth replied, 'No, darling, more like the House of the Rising Sun.'

Kirsty rushed in saying she was sorry she was late but that she had been out to buy a present for Ian and Elizabeth to thank them for having her to stop for a couple of nights.

Elizabeth declared herself utterly and totally delighted by the gift of a perfectly splendid spice rack.

Mungo loped in behind his sister. His glasses were so dark that he got his gangling legs involved with the Risborough Easy Chair and almost tripped into Andrea's arms as she stood on the hearth rug affecting an intense absorption in her grandfather's painting.

'Are you fond of animals, Andrea?' Ian asked.

'I love my cat,' she replied. 'I don't know anything about cows.' She did not want to admit that horses gave her the terrors.

'I don't know anything about cows either,' said Ian. 'But I like that picture. They look quite benign to me despite their great horns.'

'Cows is great,' said Mungo, who was attempting to perch his glasses on the top of his head. 'You can do a lot with a cow.'

'I didn't know you were keen on agriculture,' said Elizabeth. Perhaps, here at last, was a little flame of enthusiasm that could be fanned to a billow.

'I'm not,' Mungo replied. There seemed little sign of the conversation exploding into a riot of chat.

Kirsty gave her brother a beer. 'You must be keen about something, Mungo.'

'I don't see why,' he replied. 'But I'll tell you one thing, I would much rather be working with cows than with this flaming Macpop.'

'Why don't you go to agricultural college then? I am sure Uncle Hector would understand,' Elizabeth suggested.

'Oh no, he wouldn't,' said Kirsty. 'Dad is great at supporting

141

student charities but when it comes to us he has very fixed ideas. Mungo could go to a stuck-up college in the south and come away talking like royalty and able to chat to a factor. He wouldn't want him to milk the cows himself. Like me – I'm to go to Switzerland to get turned into one of they debby bitches.'

'Do you not want to go?' Elizabeth asked. 'I've never been abroad. I should think it would be lovely. You surely don't want to hang around in Scotland all your life? You said yourself you were bored.'

'I want to be a doctor,' Kirsty said.

'I know someone who has been watching too much *Emergency Ward 10*,' said Ian with a patronizing jocularity. 'Or is it the strength of my personality that has influenced you?'

'Neither, you conceited jessie. I have wanted to be a doctor for ages.'

'Don't be ridiculous!' Ian persisted. 'Whatever would a smasher like you want with studying medicine? You would be off dancing all night or else you would get married and have loads of bairns and be far too busy being a grand lady to ever practice. No, my dear, you leave that sort of thing to us men. Look at Elizabeth. Seven years' training and what happens? She turns into a mother and then it will be nappies and coffee mornings and how many teeth has your wean got till she has forgotten everything that was taught her.'

'I beg your pardon,' said Elizabeth. 'Of course I am going to work once the baby is weaned. I can surely earn enough to pay a baby-sitter.'

'You will never get that rich as a part-time locum, my dear.'

'You wait, I have it in mind to become a psychiatrist in private practice, then I will get pots of cash.'

'I am dedicated to the National Health Service,' said Ian. It was hard to tell whether his pomposity was serious or designed to entertain.

'What a load of rubbish!' Elizabeth turned to Kirsty. 'You know Ian had intended to become a gynaecologist? If it weren't for his great fists he would have made a champion man of the womb. His chat line is superb, all the female patients dote on him. He could have delivered all the little lords and ladies and we would have been as rich as Croesus.'

142

'You need nifty wee hands to deal with cows,' said Mungo, 'especially if you get to do that artificial insemination. Mind you, you need even niftier wee hands if you are dealing with sheep. But sheep are no' as great as cows.'

This was rather more than Mungo had said for a fortnight and brought the conversation to temporary halt.

'Anyway,' Ian continued, 'I think you should put all such crazy ambitions out of your pretty head, Kirsty. I am sure it is all just a flash in the pan.'

Andrea could bear this condescension no longer. 'Kirsty told me about being a doctor ages ago. She is very clever and I know she would be brilliant at it.'

'Well said, Andrea! We women will stick together,' said Elizabeth. 'I will help you all I can, Kirsty. I think it is a grand idea. What is stopping you?'

'I told you, Mum and Dad want to turn me into a young lady. God, what a bloody anachronism!'

'And what do you want to be, Andrea?'

She thought for a while. Certainly the ambition to be a nurse had vanished with the mists of love. 'I think,' she said, 'I would rather enjoy being an anachronism.'

'I can't see you lobbing bombs at statues of folk,' said Mungo, the second beer making him less taciturn. 'You are the right size, though. You have to be lean and mean if you are to get to be one of those yins.'

No one paid much attention to Mungo, no one ever did. Only Andrea bothered to be bewildered. She had never felt moved to explode anything. Right now she wondered why she had wasted so much time adoring Ian Robb. Great God! He even had the same smell as his uncle and the thought of his tongue in her mouth made her feel just as sickened as when Hector had pounced on her at Duddingston Loch. Maybe she was not meant for modern life. Perhaps she was more suited to withdraw from the world and become an anchoress.

The dinner was fun despite the dire food. Nothing had worked – even the Smash had lumps like gravel in it. But Kirsty and Elizabeth were enchanted with each other. They had a similar wit and managed to keep everyone entertained. Even Mungo contributed in his own way. He had remarked that much could be got from a cow. He was referring to the cream in the pudding, but the remark was misinterpreted. The chocolate mousse was extremely dark and sloppy.

A plan was devised to make sure that Kirsty could return to school and her place in Switzerland taken by Andrea. The theatrical ploy involving swapped twins was hardly feasible. Disguise would cause concern; questions would be asked as to why Kirsty and Andrea went about masked. Disfiguring accidents were most uncomfortable.

'Why don't you both come straight out with it?' Elizabeth suggested.

'I wouldn't dare,' said Andrea.

'And neither would I,' Kirsty agreed.

'I find,' said Ian, 'that you can achieve anything provided you really want it. It is just a question of application.'

'You had to apply yourself a lot to get me to marry you,' Elizabeth remarked.'

'Och no, that was a doddle compared with getting into the rugby team.'

'But you only played once. You were the reserve.'

'So? I got there, didn't I? All it takes is determination.'

'And a discreet insertion of botulism into your rival's dinner.'

'I shall have to use blackmail,' said Kirsty. 'It normally works. Everyone is so bothered about their reputations in Edinburgh. They are easily unsettled. How did you get your parents to let you do what you wanted, Elizabeth?'

'I was fortunate; we all wanted the same thing.'

'Elizabeth is the heroine of her family,' said Ian.

'Mind you, it can get kind of cloying at times, but I was lucky. Heaven knows what would have happened if I hadn't done what they wanted. I expect they would still have loved me, though.'

'Nothing I do pleases our parents,' said Mungo.

'Well then,' said Kirsty, 'just carry on doing nothing.'

'What do your parents want you to be, Andrea?' Elizabeth asked.

'A credit to them.' She thought for a while. 'And off their hands.'

The rain made the walk back impossible. Ian would drive Andrea the few streets home. Besides, he wanted to see the transformation of the house since Effie's death.

'I am not saying that there is a red lamp above the door,' said Elizabeth. 'I'm just saying there would be one if it wasn't Kelvingrove.'

Andrea could not believe how little the prospect of a trip alone with Ian delighted her. The thrill was gone. In fact, she even found time to speculate on whether her new brother or sister had been born yet, and was her mother all right. Did Petunia still continue in the pink?

A chink of light could be seen between the heavy curtains but apart from the gentle strains of 'In a Monastery Garden' (the tweeting birdsong version), there was nothing to denote orgiastic doings when Ian stopped his Morris Minor at the front steps. He made to get out of the car.

'You mustn't do that,' Andrea said. 'Milroy would not be pleased. She doesn't want anyone to disturb the working girls when they are relaxing in the evening. I will just have to shoot upstairs once she has let me in. She spends the evening guarding the door, making sure that she doesn't let in undesirables.'

'And am I an undesirable?'

'No, of course not,' Andrea replied, though she no longer desired him. He bent to kiss her on the cheek, preceded by his uncle's odour.

She had let herself out of the car and was halfway up the steps before she turned and thanked him for the lovely evening and the lift home.

The next day she wrote a letter to Elizabeth. She had enjoyed herself enormously, she said. In accordance with convention, she did not mention the food.

Both Robbs agreed that Andrea had great potential as an anachronism.

In *The Pilgrim's Progress*, Christian became glad and lightsome when his burden tumbled from his back leaving him unencumbered by the trappings of this world and free to travel cheerily to the Celestial City with only hobgoblins, foul fiends, giants and temptresses to contend with on the road to Bliss. The morning after the dinner party, Andrea felt as if a great burden had been lifted from her shoulders and the new lightness was disturbing. She was out of love. There was a void in her heart. It was scrubbed clean and sterilized, no microbe lurked to cause a flutter. Her passion for Ian Robb had evaporated as speedily as it had materialized. The man was as any other, he was imperfect, yet another poor forked creature. He was a flawed mortal like all the rest, and furthermore, he shared much with his uncle Hector. This was no Doctor Kildare, no angel made man. Ian Robb was just another Scottish GP with a fondness for rugger and a leaning towards the jocularity of the golf club, an atrocious taste in music, and as much romance in his psyche as a bowl of cold porridge.

11

James was worried. He had much to concern him and not all of it relating to his wife and her imminent confinement. The MacInlay child, Kirsty, with her mother's eyes and her father's guile, had called by a few days ago to see whether there was any message she could take to Andrea, who had rung and suggested that Kirsty, who was dreadfully bored, might like to visit her in Glasgow. A kind thought certainly, but not entirely straightforward, or so it seemed to James. He had been preparing to leave for half an hour at the hospital, and thereafter he had hoped that his evening might improve, but that was not to be. Kirsty had unsettled him. She had asked after the cat. No one would want anything to happen to Petunia, she said, especially with Andrea so devoted to him. She doubted whether any cat would be good enough to replace him, though she had heard there were fine ones to be found in Drymen. Did Mr Innes go to Drymen often? He had replied that he never went there. How strange, Kirsty had replied, while staring at the cat basket that awaited Petunia like a tumbril. Her mother never went to Drymen either, preferring to spend her weekends in Peebles, which Mr Innes would agree was nowhere near the Buchanan Arms at Drymen.

'Whatever are you on about?' he had asked, quite forgetting his usual pompous line of interrogation.

'I will not be on about anything. Nothing at all, unless something happens to this cat. Then I will be on about a great deal. It would break my heart as well as Andrea's, and then there would be no telling what I might say or to whom. It must be a grand thing to be so important in society and to be so good, clever and honest. Fancy being a WS and an elder. The Lord Advocate and the Moderator must think a lot of such a one.'

His evening was ruined. The cat must live, so James took the basket that was to convey Petunia to his doom out with the dustbins.

He drank several weak whiskies and felt no better. His sister, Mary, rang and announced she had urgent and disturbing matters to discuss. She was abandoning her morning of golf and her afternoon of bridge to have lunch with James tomorrow. Apparently, the news was too grave to be trusted to the telephone.

Thank heaven Neil still appeared to be having a good time at the curate's cricket course. Andrea was a worry, though. She was not doing well in Glasgow, which was hardly a surprise. She would have been better off with someone steady like those nice Browns. That was another thing: what had Buster Brown meant when he consulted James about where to go to find a reliable and clean woman with experience? Buster was looking for one for a friend and he thought James might be able to help. He understood lawyers often procured such women for their clients.

Buster had meant that James's clients might need to cite adultery with such types as grounds sufficient for divorce. James took it that Buster had him for a pimp.

The evening would get no better and he decided bed would be best. Petunia was already purring on the pillow where Ishbel's head usually lay facing away from James.

The hospital rang just after dawn. Mrs Innes had cheated induction and gone into spontaneous labour.

James rang the hospital to ask after Ishbel. His day was already ruined by having to give Mary lunch. His plans were awry, and the obtuse letter from Mr Dalziel concerning the curate scarcely made any impact. Mr Dalziel had nothing against the curate as such, but he couldn't help having his suspicions. He did not expand, but left James speculating as to what manner of suspicion was worrying Mr Dalziel most. Maybe the man was not ordained, maybe he was a charlatan, or perhaps he was no good at cricket. At least he was generally considered to be good with boys. James wrote a note to Mr Dalziel, thanking him for his confidence and hoping that Neil and his son were having a good time even if their spiritual and sporting improvement might be less splendid than expected.

The nurse who answered the labour ward phone was calm and pleasant. Mrs Innes was doing well. Would Mr Innes be coming in? It was quite in order these days for fathers to be with the mothers at the birth of their children.

James replied that that would not be at all necessary, and hung up. Great Scot, whatever would they expect next? He was worried about Ishbel. He had been fond enough of her to have attended the conception of this child, but that did not mean that he had to be inflicted with all that mess and shrieking. He had seen enough films to know that men at births were superfluous and had to pace up and down while bossy women bustled about with kettles and towels till a cross cry was heard . . . or not, depending on whether the story was happy or sad.

He would walk to the club. The day was fine and exercise might clear his head. He walked so quickly that he decided to waste a while strolling in Princes Street gardens. The wallflowers, whose scent had been so penetrating, were now replaced with vivid formal plantings. James was no gardener. He found the scarlet salvias and orange tagetes to be rather jolly, and almost forgot his appointment with Mary and had to rush to his club, only entering it as the one o'clock gun was fired.

'You are late,' Mary remarked, offering a cheek made ruddy by east coast winds. Her features were grim but she consented to a sherry, which was a sign that either she was in cheerful fettle or needed a reinforcing buffer in the face of calamity. James rightly deduced that it was the latter. Having established that Ishbel was progressing satisfactorily, he returned to this business with his sister. He tried hard to expunge the disgusting information that his wife was almost fully dilated from his mind as he sat down at the linen-covered table and prepared to listen to Mary's grievances.

'I had it on the best authority. Lady Neilson, Netta Graham that was, knows about these things.'

James knew nothing of this Netta, either before or after ennoblement. 'You have lost me, Mary. Who is this friend of yours?'

'She was more a friend of your late mother-in-law. I know her from playing bridge in Ayrshire. She is a rotten player, can't count and has a memory like a sieve, but she is sound on shrubs.'

'Well?'

149

'She is also a woman of wide experience. She spent many years on the Park Bench Committee in Cairo.'

'Are you trying to tell me that this old lady from the west coast was a houri?'

'No, I told you, she was a Graham, from Drumslab.'

This interview was as unsatisfactory as the breaded cutlets, which had arrived in front of James and his sister, the vibrant orange contrasting merrily with the tinned peas.

'I am telling you, James. Netta Neilson knows a brothel when she sees one.'

'Surely not.' James was aware that his sister's voice was just as loud here as on the fourteenth green in a gale. Despite their excellent upbringings he could detect several prominent citizens were eavesdropping. 'Do you not think she meant bothy or even hovel?'

'No, James. Your only daughter is living in a house of ill repute.'

There Mary was wrong. A club servant summoned James to the phone. Euphemia Innes had got herself born during the grapefruit cocktail. He must go at once to the hospital, his half-sister must take herself and her revelations back to North Berwick. Greater matters needed his attention now.

On the contrary, Mary would come in the taxi too. Ishbel would need a woman to be with her at such a time, Mary insisted.

James was not the man to contradict her.

Nothing aroused Mary more than a cracking good crisis. Her capacity to condole was boundless, her longing to be capable was quite frightening, for she had no equal in compassion and no rival in the management of the afflicted. She irritated everyone. Her persistence let no issue pass without analytical dissection. James was not to be allowed time to celebrate his child's arrival without being reminded of his other parental burdens. However, in view of this latest excitement, Mary declared her intention of carrying on the mission of rescue to Glasgow herself.

'I will go at once. At least I mind about the welfare of my niece. I will go after I have seen Ishbel, who may also need me. I will go,' and here she gave a most martyred moan, 'despite tomorrow's foursome.'

'Bridge?' enquired James, who was not listening.

'No, golf. I was to play in a medal . . . only now I can't.' She gave vent to a sigh of sacrifice, her vast breasts heaved like the ocean deep.

'That is nice,' said James. The taxi had arrived at the hospital. He rushed in, leaving his sister to pay.

Ishbel needed no one. She lay exhausted and punctured by drips and drains. The birth had not been easy and her age had not helped.

Mary was shocked and felt that her sister-in-law should buck up, especially as there were others, albeit in the public ward, who would expect greater pluck from one of her class. Mary, being firmly virginal, knew what was expected and what should be done. Her mother had died in childbirth, which was tough, but she had passed over with commendable lack of fuss. Those spared death should pull themselves together. She patted Ishbel's hand as a concession to her fragility and caused the drip to jar and leave a bruise like a sacred stigma. Ishbel saw and felt nothing much except deep weary afterpains and a load of despair.

'How lucky you are to have another daughter. So much more companionable for the older woman, I always say.'

Tears seeped from under Ishbel's lids and coursed down her beaky nose to make small blots on the white theatre gown she still wore.

Staff had been intimidated by Mary, who showed no signs of obeying the instruction to be quick and leave Mrs Innes to rest. James was talking to the doctor. He had seen his baby daughter, who was more content with her new life than her reception warranted.

Once back at his wife's bedside, he said he wished to speak with her alone. Mary showed no signs of leaving until some small, frightened student nurse, who was deputed to take her to see Euphemia, ushered her out of the room.

'I'm sorry,' Ishbel whispered.

'So am I, so am I,' James answered. 'It is not your fault,' he added, though he felt, in his heart, that his wife was to blame. He never would acknowledge the part he had played in this calamity. He recalled the conception nine months ago with no more

151

pleasure than any of the other dutiful sessions of sex he had undertaken to have with his legal mate in recent years. He forgot why they had ever decided to try for another child. Maybe it was just to prove that they were not too decrepit to appreciate the new decade's joyous carnality. At least there would be no more children now.

Mary regarded her niece with detachment. Had she been a new set of golf clubs or a young rhododendron she would not have entertained the prospect of ownership for a moment. This specimen was not worthy, but nevertheless one had one's duty. One was a Christian, after all.

Once back at Ishbel's bedside Mary addressed her brother.

'Now, James, you are not to worry. This is unfortunate but not impossible. I have many friends and much influence. I can safely say that the child will be well cared for. Let us hope she doesn't live long. Those children seldom reach adulthood. No one need know, Ishbel dear.' The hand was patted again and the needle jogged. She saw that Ishbel was still tearful, which really was too bad. Comfortable words might staunch the flow. 'The babe is quite a pretty colour, sort of peachy like a prize begonia.' Mary had not been told of the jaundice that added to Euphemia's disadvantages. 'And at least her face is not terribly oriental, though I must admit the forked tongue is somewhat odd. Still, you are not to worry. I will organize everything and you will soon be up and right as ninepence and forget all about this.'

'I want my baby,' Ishbel replied. 'It is not her fault that she is a girl even though I know we all wanted another son. It isn't my fault,' she repeated. 'It is the man that determines the sex.'

James had not told Ishbel what he had learnt from the doctors. Little Effie was born handicapped. She would never be normal, her face was flat, her eyes were slits and her tongue slightly forked at the tip. She was what was known as a mongol. She had Down's syndrome. There is no remedy, no cure. The chromosomes are to blame.

'Your age was against you,' Mary continued. 'I read it in a magazine.'

'No it wasn't,' said Ishbel. 'Lots of older women have sons.'

152

'Sons or daughters, it makes no difference when it comes to being handicapped.'

'I am sorry,' said Ishbel weakly. 'I hadn't thought about the baby playing golf.'

'Neither had I,' said Mary, 'and furthermore I don't consider this the moment for flippancy. James, what are you going to do about your family? Sometimes I feel I am the only one with a sense of responsibility.'

'Mary, shut up!'

'No one, no one, not even when I was at school, has ever said anything as rude as that to me. How dare you speak to me, your older sister like that!'

'My older half-sister,' James corrected. 'Now please, Mary, leave us alone. I have a lot to discuss with Ishbel, who has been through enough already.'

Mary snorted as she gathered up her immense Burberry and prepared to leave. 'Very well, I will go, but these things cannot be kept hidden. You must do what Kipling said about disasters and those other things . . . impostors. You must bite the bullet. I will deal with the unpleasantness in Glasgow if you investigate the credentials of that curate. I also advise you to make arrangements for the care of that baby. It would be most selfish to expect the other children to put up with a child like that.'

'Like what?' Ishbel asked.

'Like she is, a mental defective, an idiot.' Mary saw that this was news to Ishbel, but felt no remorse at having been the one to tell her. After all, someone had to bear evil tidings and it might as well be a close and cherished member of the family like herself. 'Mind you,' she added by way of comfort, 'I understand that some of them can be quite affectionate.' She almost added faithful and companionable.

'You are talking about a child, not a dog.'

'A dog, my dear James, could be put down. You will have to put up with your baby. That is why I suggest it is put in an institution where they understand such abnormalities before your whole life is ruined.'

Ishbel let out a howl of grief. She had only just grasped the meaning of the conversation between her husband and her sister-in-law. Her baby, the burden she had carried with such difficulty and brought forth in such misery, was a catastrophe, a blight, a freak and would be better dead.

Before she became quite hysterical the ward sister called the doctor, who prescribed a giant dose of tranquillizer, which took immediate effect and lasted till long after new little Effie needed her first feed. In fact, Ishbel lay in a state of semi-torpor for several days and when they finally brought her baby to her, the child spurned her swollen and engorged breasts. The little mouth with its slit tongue refused Ishbel's nipple and returned with vigour to the bottle. At least she too could reject.

When Ishbel saw the little face turn away from her she was rent with a possessive determination to be loved by this child. It was the least her baby could do.

There was to be no night of celebration for James. He had few friends who would take him drinking, and this baby was not the kind that demanded its head to be wetted. He felt repelled by any female companionship; that sort of thing led to this sort of calamity. Solitude without austerity was the solution and so he spent the evening in the company of a host of Johnnie Walkers.

No calls interrupted his steady consumption and increasing gloom. At ten he had made a mental list of all the catastrophes that had been inflicted on him. He compared himself to Job, attempted to reassure himself that he was chastened because the Lord loved him, which was no comfort whatsoever.

He must find Mary and stop her from mangling the Glasgow arrangements. The last thing he needed was the return of his children. She must be stopped. There was no reply from the North Berwick number, which meant she had already attacked and was even now engaged in cleansing Kelvingrove of vice.

James's voice was already impaired and thick with muddled words. Conversation was not easy, especially as there was quite a party taking place in his late mother-in-law's house. It certainly wasn't Milroy who answered, but he was sure the number was correct. A youngish woman with a broad Scots accent denied that there was anyone of that name in the house. Nor did she know of an Andrea. Would Samantha do?'

'Is my sister, Mary, there?'

'Hang on, I'll get her.'

There was a slight pause. 'Sister Mary here. Do you want to come to confession, you wicked man?'

James was dumbfounded.

Receiving no reply, the voice continued, weedling, 'Are you wanting to hear about my sins? Or do you want me to make sure that you get a really severe penance?'

Two whiskies later the phone rang. James fumbled for the receiver. He knew that he was very, very drunk and in his effort to appear sober he spoke with exaggerated precision. Nevertheless his tongue got in the way and his brain sent confused messages to his larynx.

'The Dalkeith Police here.'

'What? Not the Leith Polishe Dishmisheth Ush?'

'No, sir. This is the Dalkeith Police. Is that Mr Innes?'

'Yesh, Mishter Innesh shpeaking.'

'We have your sister in the station.'

'Shishter Shushie shewing shirts for sholdiersh?'

'No, sir. Your sister, Mary. Would you have a word with her?'

'Shertainly not,' James replied. 'Shishter Mary is nothing but a Glasgow tart.'

Petunia had lost his litter tray and had utilized the mat in the cloakroom instead. James had discovered this when he had crept to the lavatory at dawn. His face looked strange and bloated, his eyes were kind of putrid. At first he had thought the offering on the turquoise candlewick pedestal mat was an hallucination, but his nose, though numb with whisky fumes, told him the mess was real. Mat and all went into the bin. Some things must be abandoned when all the universe is disordered.

Mrs Orr clocked in promptly. She was agog for information and keen to cook a greasy breakfast for James. On perceiving that his bed had not been used, that the study stank and appeared to have been the site for a debauch, and furthermore that the downstairs toilet mat had been jettisoned she gave in her notice. She had no alternative, she said, unless James was prepared to offer an explanation and reward her for her extra work and her subsequent silence. She shouted this through the bathroom door where he was attempting to shave away his sins and soak out the remorse by means of an overhot bath. James's reply was neither courteous nor conciliatory so she gathered up her belongings, pocketed all the house cigarettes, stocked up her wheeled basket from the larder and left. A note on the kitchen table was all that remained of Mrs Orr by the time James came downstairs clothed but not entirely in his right mind.

You Owe Me three and fourpence, Mrs Orr's curly writing proclaimed.

James picked up the note, crumpled it and threw it out of the window in full view of Next Door who were distressed by the deterioration of the Crescent.

Send three and fourpence, we are going to a dance. James found the thought of Mrs Orr on pleasure bent to be quite entertaining.

Send reinforcements, we are going to advance.

First things first.

The Lord that James worshipped sat on His throne shaking His head in sorrow.

'Oh Lord,' pleaded James in the manner of his forefathers, 'I didna' ken, I didna' ken.'

And the Lord looked down in His goodness and mercy and said, 'Och well, ye ken noo.'

James swore that he would never drink or fornicate again. Ever. Celibacy and abstinence were to be his chosen ways here onwards.

These things having been established, life must get itself lived, and that in an orderly manner.

Ring the hospital. Alert the monthly nurse. What else? Oh yes, perhaps he ought to go to work.

The office was submerged in paper, which was quite usual, but his sharp temper was a novel phenomenon for his secretary who quickly hid her copy of *Honey* under several wills and even changed the brackish water in the carafe.

Something hammered inside his head. It was called remorse. A

fiend goaded him from behind his eyes. It demanded appeasement. Action was needed. He rang his half-sister, she was not at
home.

He rang Glasgow. Milroy answered. She was correct, polite
and most obliging. Surely last night had been a nightmare
brought on by excitement and bad breaded cutlets. Milroy's
establishment was the epitome of propriety.

Andrea was brought to the phone.

'You have a little sister.'

'How lovely!' She meant it. In fact she was astounded to find
how much the news thrilled and affected her. She felt inclined to
be weepy. 'How really lovely. What does she look like? What is her
name?'

'She is called Euphemia like your grandmother. But, Andrea
. . . there is something else.'

'Is Mummie all right?'

'Yes, fine. I am going to see her later. But, Andrea, there is
something I want to tell you.'

'Nothing has happened to Petunia, has it?'

'No, the cat is fine.'

'Oh wonderful! When can I come home? I don't like it here
much, only it is a bit better now Kirsty is here.'

'Kirsty MacInlay?'

'Yes. She has come to visit her cousins because she is bored at
home. Please can I come home?'

'Won't you be bored?' James suggested hopefully.

'Of course not. I am not like Kirsty, and you and Mum are not
like Mr and Mrs MacInlay, always carrying on and making
everyone miserable. How is Neil?'

'All right, as far as I know.'

'Please let us come home. We can help with the baby. Oh, it will
be wonderful and I really miss Petunia. I thought he was going to
die while I was away. Can I come home today?'

'No.' James tried not to sound too horrified. 'Stay there, I will
come and see you.'

'Today?'

'No, not today but really soon. Tomorrow maybe.'

*

157

'Darling, I must see you.'

'I want to see you too.' James was resolved to end it. 'I feel we ought to talk.'

'Of course, it has been nearly a week now.'

'I think we ought to stop this.'

'Stop what?'

James put his hand over the receiver while he bid his secretary goodnight. He had let her go early and she had returned his generosity with a hand-knitted yellow matinée jacket she had made for his baby. It would look marvellous with the jaundice. He resumed the conversation.

'Listen, I am sorry. I have been wrong, very wrong.'

'Well, what about me? Do you think I have been wrong too?'

'Frankly, yes.'

'What had brought this on?'

'The baby. She was born yesterday.'

'But you said that would make no difference. You always said the baby wouldn't change anything.'

'The baby isn't right.'

'So?'

'I feel it is a judgement.'

'Don't be ridiculous. What about me? What am I to do?'

'Be a good wife, and I will be a good husband. Let us put all this down to being middle-aged and unhinged.'

'Speak for yourself.'

'Hector will stand by you.'

'But I can't stand Hector. I've had him, I want to have you.'

'Darling, sorry, you have had me too.'

'But not enough. Please, let us meet this evening.'

'I'll ring you sometime. I must go, there is someone to see me. Goodbye.'

Bunty Brown was ushered in by the temporary typist, who always spoke the truth and would never dare deny anyone access to James's office even if they came obviously armed with several cleavers.

He was sitting with his head in his hands and presented such a miserable sight that Bunty came all over motherly and managing.

'Dear, dear. This will never do. I just called in to congratulate

158

you. You must both be thrilled to have another daughter. I wish we could breed still, but what with the mumps and having my inside out it is just not on. Mary told me the wee girl isn't quite normal but then, when you think of it, which one of us is?' She chuckled merrily at this palliative. 'And by the way, Mary is fine. I rescued her from the rozzers and she spent the night with us and is now safely back in North Berwick. Cheer up, chicken . . . we will soon be dead.'

While James was still trying to console Ishbel, and before he recruited the bottle to perform the same service for himself, Mary had been wasting no time in her crusade against vice. She had decided to start for Glasgow on her mission of morality just as soon as she had organized her North Berwick life and fed the parrot. Because of the gravity of her journey she had covered the parrot's cage with a shawl from the East and doubled its dose of seed and cuttlefish, thereby ensuring total contentment and silence in its twilight world beneath the oriental embroidery. The parrot was called Anna Pavlova because it generally stood on one leg, though this posture lacked the grace of an arabesque. It could also 'die' with a thump on the bottom of its cage, not that this was done one jot like a swan. Pavlova's vocabulary was obscene French acquired during a Tunisian chickhood.

What Mary was going to do when she got to Glasgow was not clear, but fortified by indignation and a glass of Dry Fly she aimed her Morris Traveller towards the West. As the sun set over Dalkeith she became dazzled and collided with a sly bollard.

The police were raw and impertinent, her dignity was injured as much as the car, and she took the gravest exception to their line of questioning, which was why she fetched up in the police station refusing vehemently to walk down the line. This she would do provided she was permitted to undress first. She said she would only confide in a woman police officer. No male was to be privy to her problem of obstructed downward vision created by her upwardly hoisted bust.

There was quite a to-do, Bunty related, when she had arrived to reclaim her best bitch who had strayed, lured by lust. Various suitors were still prowling the vicinity of the police station and all of them were bad lots.

Bunty had recognized Mary's voice, which was never soft and low, even in prayer, and now that it was raised in anger her outraged speech was unmistakable. With great relief the constabulary reversed its machinery and Mary was discharged into Bunty's care. The desk clerk's joke about how he had thought Mrs Brown had only come to collect one stray bitch was well received over the midnight tea.

Mary later informed James that she thought Bunty was the only real Christian she had met in many a long day's march. Once back in North Berwick she resolved to stay there and let her brother's family sort themselves out, at least until her pride and car had been repaired.

She wrote several enraged letters about police insolence to various august bodies. Their replies all stated that her comments were noted.

When Bunty left James's office she instructed him to give lots of love to Ishbel and to say she was longing to see the little one, and that she envied the Innes family their new baby, which was true, and that she thought Euphemia was a charming name, which was a lie.

'Oh by the way, I am just off to get tickets for the Tattoo, we always take the girls. Would your Andrea like to come with us?'

'I expect she would love it. I know Neil would be really keen to go. It doesn't look as if we will be taking either of them this year,' James replied.

'Of course Neil must come, though he will be the only boy. Angus doesn't care for that sort of thing. Incidentally, talking of Angus, do you happen to know of any discreet, clean and experienced w . . .' Her voice trailed off and James looked at her expectantly. 'Window cleaner?' she said at last.

'No,' said James, he didn't, Ishbel was in charge of that sort of thing. Why did she require a window cleaner for Angus?

Just in case, was her reply. Just in case he failed to get into Oxford, she continued wildly, he could get an apprenticeship. 'Times are tough,' she concluded cheerily.

12

Never, not even when he had been forced to take his godmother to a tea dance, had Buster felt so thoroughly ill at ease. This engineered outing with his son brought back all the misery he had experienced when toying with dainty cakes between foxtrots. Now, as then, he was over-bright and glibly convivial. Much good had it done him then, and today his false chattiness showed no improvement. He had failed at Skindles before the war and now, in the late July of 1963, the fiasco was repeating itself at the Malmaison, over the way from Glasgow's Central Station. The episode at the tea dance was an abject failure and had been devised by his mother who thought that the rich godmother (a maiden lady of wealth with no sex appeal) would be charmed by her godson and make him her heir. The wealth was left elsewhere and Buster was condemned as a frivolous lounge lizard.

This lavish lunch had the mark of failure stamped on each crumb.

A large, but not crippling amount of wine was drunk, and though Buster's words came out quickly they got confused and signified very little. Wee Angus, while neither sullen nor rude, did not help his father in his confusion but ate with a steady application and let his parent burble on. Girls, women, natural appetites, and the need to be able to perform one's duty with efficiency seemed to be concerning Buster that week. Normally his father would chat about golf, or wine, or how to prevent slugs from eating dahlias. Maybe it was the west coast air creeping up the Clyde that altered his interests.

Angus drank three glasses of extremely fine claret with as much enthusiasm and as little response as if the red drink had been Ribena. Luckily the wine had its usual benevolent effect on Buster, who almost managed to forget how much more cheaply a similar bottle could have been supplied by his own firm without the expensive addition of an obsequious *sommelier* complete with dangling cup like a golden version of those chained to municipal fountains.

'The thing is, Angus,' Buster began, 'your mother, indeed your mother and I – yes us both – in fact, we . . . Oh God!'

Angus looked up from his overwhelming plateful of *boeuf en croute*. 'Yes, Dad?'

'Well, put it this way: do you know any women?'

'Of course I do.'

'Oh, jolly good.'

'Well, there is Mum and the twins and – '

'I don't mean quite that sort of know, or indeed that sort of woman. They are your family.'

'Well then, there is Mrs Blair and Mrs MacInlay, and that woman who came to stay last night, Miss Innes.'

'I don't think you quite understand, Angus. I mean like in the Bible.'

'The Virgin Mary?'

'No . . . Oh dear, this is not easy. Here, have another glass of wine. I mean have you got to know any women since your voice broke and all that?'

'Matron was quite nice to me when I sprained my ankle.'

Buster tried a new approach. 'What happens at school if one of the fellows wants to know a woman? Or indeed gets to know one?'

'Once they are in the sixth form they can ask them to tea and chapel every second Sunday.'

'Angus, listen. I am going to ask you straight out. Have you ever poked?'

'Poked a fire? Certainly if I have known the people whose fire it is for seven years.'

'No, no! Not that kind of poke!' Luckily the string orchestra was playing a rousing barcarole.

'Do you mean the kind of poke you buy sweeties in?'

'*No!*' Buster's fist came down on the table with enough force to cause the spare glasses to chink nervously. 'I'll ask you once more. Have you poked a woman?'

'In the eye with a sharp stick? Certainly not!'

'No, Angus, not with a stick!'

'Well, I may have . . . I can't remember. What is all this about anyway?'

'It is about you turning into a man, and I don't mean like Oscar Wilde.'

'I thought you liked his plays, Dad.'

'I am not concerned with his words, it is the deeds that bother me. What do boys get expelled for from school?'

'Bryson got expelled for being deviant.'

'Did he, by George? And what exactly did this dreadful Bryson do?'

'He decided to become a conscientious objector and refused to play cricket. What are we going to do now?'

Buster looked with horror at the bill for lunch, which seemed to have given birth to a litter of extras beyond the basic cost of a meal for two.

'You, Angus, are going to visit someone who will provide you with some well-needed education and entertainment. I am going to go to the zoo.'

'What on earth for? There is a brilliant zoo in Edinburgh.'

'Sorry, old chap, I wasn't thinking. We are going to take your mother's watch to Edward and Son to be cleaned and then I am going to the art gallery.'

'Oh great!' Angus's eyes lit up. 'I would love to see that Rembrandt again – you know, the beautiful picture of the young man in armour.'

'Well, you can't. I am going to the art gallery alone; you are going to enjoy yourself like a man.'

While Buster was arranging for Bunty's watch to be overhauled, Glen Mackie came into the jeweller's shop accompanied by a large blonde in stiletto heels and a plastic mac, from whom he contrived to disassociate himself on catching sight of Buster and Wee Angus. Stilted greetings were exchanged while the blonde pretended to be interested in a showcase full of presentation timepieces. Buster could not imagine that this female was the sort who answered advertisements in the *Aberdeen Press and Journal*. Bunty's sister maintained that Glen was forever seeking a second wife in that paper's situations vacant column. Maybe this was some secretary who was requiring a reward for long-suffering service to one so dull.

'Poor old Mr Mackie,' said Buster to his son after they had hailed a cab. 'His wife hanged herself from the scullery pulley.'

'Yes,' said Angus. 'Of course, I know his daughter.'

'Really?'

'No, Dad, not really.'

'Here we are. Hop out, old man,' said Buster brimming with casual joviality and merry man-to-mannishness. 'Have a good time. I will meet you at Queen Street at six thirty.'

Reluctantly Angus left the cab and climbed the front steps. He rang the bell and was admitted immediately. Only when the door had been shut behind him did Buster instruct the driver to take him on to the art gallery. Three hours should be more than enough time for Angus to discover lust. It was far, far too long for his father to seek solace in art.

'Just go up the stairs, my dear. Your friend is waiting for you.'

Angus was greeted and directed by Miss T, who was all splendid and glinting in a turquoise two-piece. She would have accompanied him to his tryst with carnality but the phone rang yet again and needed to be answered. Angus started to climb the brown stained wood stairs carpeted in a pattern that would never show dirt, being constructed of stains and marks in every hue. The dado was brown and the walls above distempered in a grubby cream. On the walls were hung Effie's much despised pictures.

Now, Angus knew a thing or two. His taste was singular, he doted on colour and vivacity – in fact, he was somewhat ahead of his time when it came to being retrospective. He could recognize what would enjoy popularity twenty years later, but was ignorant of the commercial zeal so essential to one who would make a fortune from art, which was a shame. His heart was gladdened by what he saw.

Peploe, Ferguson, Cadell, they were all there. The brightest canvases had been carefully hung in the gloomiest corners. Pink roses and blocks of velvet black mingled with sparkling glass and vibrant yellows in the still lifes. The portraits, one of which may have been of Effie Lammont herself, had a serenity and elegance cleverly married to great inspirational splashes of pure, bright colour. Whoever heard of such a thing, and in respectable Glasgow of all places, where industry and art strove to be heavy?

Bella was quite used to these appointments. She was a specialist. Over the years her ploys had become refined until she guaranteed satisfaction every time except in cases of gross physical immaturity or blatant contrary inclination. She reclined upon a sofa, fragrant with Ma Griffe and dressed in a cascading negligée with which she needed assistance. The ribbons got knotted and were fiddly to untie so she required help from the dexterous to undress. As her clients reached the landing she would call for help through the half-open door and then when they had entered her boudoir the business of initiation would begin. Bella was in no hurry; she was also very expensive and had to be pre-paid while being pre-booked. Angus was so engrossed in what he saw on the walls that he did not hear her enticing call, and he walked past the invitingly ajar door and continued up the second flight of stairs where still more treasures hung.

On the top landing he met his old friend Andrea, who was still digesting the splendid news about her new sister and preparing to pack for home. She could not now wait to be shot of Glasgow, its day trips, its lodgings or her previous infatuation.

Angus was ashamed to think that he had assumed his father had ulterior motives in sending him to this strange house. What a vile mind he had! All he was expected to do was to visit an old friend, who had obviously been horribly ill with a wasting disease. But that was typical of his parents, they were forever trying to ensure that their children had fun with others of their own age and they went to a lot of trouble on their behalf. It was sad that most of these plans bore no fruit. However, Andrea was very amiable, even if she had dwindled to half the volume of one of his sisters, and she seemed delighted to see him, which was rather pleasing.

'This is a surprise. I wasn't expecting anyone to come and see me. You can help me pack, though that won't take long. I am going home tomorrow.'

'Why don't you come through with Dad and me tonight? I am meeting him at the station later on. He has gone to the art gallery – or at least that was what he said.'

'Why do you say that? Is he not fond of art?'

'No, not so you would notice.'

'I wish I could come home tonight but Dad says I must wait for him to collect me, and I must not go home before.'

'You know something? I think our fathers are being awfully shifty these days. Kind of devious, as if they are conspirators. Why couldn't he tell me you were here? Why has he gone to the art gallery alone? After all, we could all have gone together.'

'But I've been,' Andrea protested. 'I went with my grannie before she died.'

'You could go again.'

'Whatever for?'

'I go whenever I can. I have only been to Kelvingrove once, but I have been masses of times to the National Gallery in Edinburgh. There is a wonderful picture of John the Baptist's head being brought to Salome at the feast. I could look at it for hours.'

'I couldn't understand the picture of Jesus. It looked like a frog.'

'*Christ of St John of the Cross?*'

'Probably. I think it was painted by a Spanish man with a moustache.'

'Have you ever been in an aeroplane?'

'No. Why?'

'Look, I will show you how to look at that picture. You stay at the top of the stairs and look down on me while I hang off the banisters below.'

Angus was fired with enthusiasm and it was quite a relief to Andrea to find him so talkative. It was also reassuring to find that his voice had broken. He was not quite so wee either, though he would never match his sisters for sturdiness. She looked down the well of the stairs where Angus was standing and hanging by his arms from the railings of the half landing two floors directly beneath.

'Turn on the light,' he called.

By throwing an array of brass switches Andrea eventually managed to get the right light to work and then she saw exactly what Dali had been after.

'I see now! How really clever. Of course it is quite easy now you have shown me.'

166

'Who the hell are you?' Samantha asked, mildly surprised to find Angus blocking the way to her room. She was returning from the cleaners with her school uniform (which formed part of her working wardrobe and was charged to expenses).

'I am being Jesus Christ,' Angus replied.

'Right you are then.' Samantha pushed past the Son of God and went into her room. She had long since ceased to marvel at men and their ways of achieving satisfaction.

Bella, however, was not prepared to put up with that sort of nonsense. Still dressed in her coffee-coloured boudoir gown she called down the stair to Milroy.

'I told you, Miss T, I don't deal with weirdies. There is a wee fellow up here who is getting himself crucified. I doubt he would be happier seeing Minnie. Where has she gone?'

'She is away out being bought a present.'

'Another one? My, there is an awful lot to be got from hangings.'

'Minnie is back from shopping with her friend. Listen,' Samantha replied. She had decided to join in, there was nothing much else to do. Some straining squeaks were audible above Milroy's transistor, which was blaring out the introduction to 'Runaway'. 'Can you not get Minnie some Three in One, Miss T? Or turn up your trannie? Yon record is great.'

'This is Angus,' said Andrea. 'He is a friend of mine from Edinburgh. We were going to play Scrabble. Does anyone want to join in?'

'Is playing Scrabble your idea of a good time?' Bella asked Angus. He replied that it was. 'Well then, Scrabble it is. Now Miss T, don't look so scandalized. This young man has come here to be entertained and that is what is going to happen. Where's the board?'

Milroy and Bella joined in, and for an hour or so, they all managed to be quite distracted and impervious to the strange sounds coming from Minnie's room. Even the somewhat depleted quota of letters (for like her jigsaw puzzles, Effie's board games had never been bought new or complete) did not impair their fun, despite the frequent moans, cracks and thumps.

*

167

At 6.30, as arranged, father and son met again. Both were ready for home.

'I am sorry,' said Buster. 'I forgot to give you money for the taxi.'

'Oh, that is fine, Dad. I was quite all right. I got a lift from one of Andrea's friends.'

Angus, because he was not the lad to betray a trust, did not say that Mr Mackie had been leaving the house at the same time and had not only shared and paid for a cab but had secured Angus's perpetual silence with a couple of fivers.

'Andrea? I didn't think that was her name.'

'Of course it was, Dad. But Andrea has never been called anything else except Clootie.'

'Was everything, er, satisfactory, Angus? If you know what I mean?'

'Yes, Dad. I scored a lot.'

'Well done! That is my boy. Well, there is no need to mention this ever again. Your mother will be highly delighted, as indeed am I.'

As a rite of passage, the losing of the male virginity is lacking in ceremony. For the female the entry into matronhood is a matter of gripping speculation and interest to all, especially in countries where brides are bought and sold depending on the intact nature of their hymen. At least in Scotland no one seemed to feel it necessary to parade blood-stained sheets off a marriage bed through the streets. It was, however, a comfort to feel that one's son knew what to do. One never knew when such a skill might be required at short notice. Buster would not have wanted his offspring to have been found to fumble. Like a wise virgin, Angus should keep his wick well trimmed and ready for service.

The train rolled reliably back to Edinburgh with Buster's mission accomplished. Gratefully, he thanked God that he had but one son, or at least only one son that he knew about. He fell to brooding on Dolores of the friendly thighs while Angus reflected on higher things and pondered on the relative merits of amenorrhoea and amanuensis as triple word scorers.

James was suffering. He blamed himself entirely for all that had happened. His perception of his place in the Almighty's Plan was rather more pivotal than his professional, parental, and spiritual status actually warranted. Nevertheless, he felt compelled to apologize for the lot. He was even inclined to guilt about poor harvest prognostications despite being in charge of only the office's miserable potted ivy and the shoddy variegated laurels front and back at home.

He had been feckless and what was worse, he had been exceedingly foolish. Fun, games and good humour undertaken on purpose for fulfilment or the entertainment of others were fine, especially if done in the course of rearing the young or alleviating tedium in those with scant resources, but to indulge in idiotic erotic passions purely for the gratification of carnal delight was enough to cause death by embarrassing shame. James would reform. Little Euphemia (Wee Effie) was an augury of the bonfire to come. If he were really to be granted time for amendment of life then that time would be filled with constant striving for perfection and the suppression of base nature.

Neil was coming home. The cricketing curate had seemingly lost interest and Mr Dalziel, who was planning to tramp about Skye and mope in solitude amongst the midges, had pressed James to take his son in at Magdala Crescent as well as Neil.

'Two young lads are as easy as one,' James had remarked to the nurse during his most recent call to her.

It would seem that she did not entirely agree and was not filled with enthusiasm about having not only a depressed mother with a congenitally sick infant to cope with, but also two obstreperous young boys, an adolescent girl and an incontinent cat to add to the fun. Nor did she agree about life being easier without domestic help.

James had resolved to be positive, and in this mood of saintly optimism he was most trying. He was making the best of everything. He welcomed misfortunes as proof of his sin being purged. Others, like the monthly nurse, did not. She had no wish to be shriven.

Moira MacInlay asked to meet James and was informed that he would be delighted to see her in a professional capacity only, and she must arrange an appointment for when he returned to work.

169

Or perhaps, if it was an urgent matter, would not his partner do just as well? Moira told him he was mad. He replied that he feared she might be right but who was to say, in this world, who was sane or insane?

He bought too many roses for Ishbel and held her hand while she cried interminably. His dogged devotion and sympathy were no comfort to her. She did not wish for consolation, she wanted rage. How could her life be blighted with this monstrous child that wouldn't even accept her milk? She had given the pariah life and it wasn't even grateful.

James cooed at the flat face of his new daughter and said she was terribly, terribly special. The ward sister never expressed an opinion but she did find his enthusiasm quite out of the ordinary.

Much to Neil and Dalziel's disgust, James arranged for Mary to be taxied from North Berwick to keep an eye on things while he went to Glasgow to collect Andrea. 'Then,' he said, 'we will all be a happy family again and just need darling Mummie and her little treasure to complete the picture.'

Mary, bearing a sloppy casserole, arrived at two. She was injured but determined to rise to the occasion like a martyr going to the stake, and started by being capable and clean. She assaulted several grubby lampshades with a soapy toothbrush. Such dirt, such neglect – dear Ishbel had been badly betrayed by skimpers.

Meanwhile Neil fed Petunia with the casserole. He and Dalziel had spotted the dreadful stew lying low in the larder. Apart from being created vile, it had travelled badly. Packed with stringy meat and gristled fat, the greasy gravy was enhanced with lots of limp carrots, which Petunia rejected.

'You must never neglect dumb beasts. There wasn't a tin of cat food to be had in the house,' Neil explained the end of the stew to his aunt.

Mary, naturally enough, was livid, but forgave her nephew because he was kind to the brute race. She also said that one should boil lights for pets and ordered a great many to be delivered from the butcher along with some offal and skirt with which, on the morrow, she intended to nourish her nephew and niece in the proper manner. She made a solid rice pudding to sustain the young – and finished the milk. The stew, being inside the cat, meant there was nothing for supper. Neil suggested fish and chips from the Haymarket Carry Oot. It was gripping to watch Auntie Mary exploding.

James found the fear of exposure to be far greater than his anxiety about divine wrath to come. Everlasting torment would be quite ghastly, but not as terrible as having his private life detailed in the *Scotsman* and ridiculed in the *Daily Record*. In England, it seemed, people were more prepared for idiosyncratic inclinations. He had marvelled that anyone, notwithstanding someone of public importance, had ever decided to attend an orgy clad only in a leather apron and mask. How could a masochist live with himself? Surely no one, however devoted to self-chastisement, could submit to the possibility of such public humiliation. James realized that perhaps he understood very little of the urges that toppled ministries and monarchs. However, he did know what would destroy him. He was an elder and an example to those inclined to be backsliders. He was a lawyer and knew the law, especially of adultery, as it was this very sin that helped him earn enough to be significantly prosperous. In fact, the birth of Euphemia had made him calculate just how prosperous he must remain if his family were to continue to thrive.

Tormented by anxiety, he drove west. The day was hot and his tweed suit, normally reserved for weekends, made him sweat. He could not be seen without a jacket in the city, even if that city was Glasgow.

He was filled with a dreadful foreboding that, once more, his half-sister was entirely correct. He had met Buster Brown in the bank that very morning and the man was quite beside himself with satisfaction. He had found the perfect solution for you-know-what. He winked and rubbed his nose in the way that is used to denote confidentiality. A delightful and discreet solution, but damned expensive. Still, cheaper than a trip to Paris, what? After all, only a skinflint could object to the fare to Glasgow if it meant such satisfactory results. Buster continued to talk to James in a stage whisper loud enough to be heard at the back of the Lyceum. Buster suggested that, in a couple of years' time, if James felt that some initiation was in order, he too might like to make the trip to

171

Kelvingrove with his son. Such a refined area for that sort of thing, don't you know? Dear, oh dear, Buster was quite forgetting himself – congratulations were in order. Well done, the proud father, there was life in the old dog yet! He slapped James upon the back. Had Buster enrolled in extra mural drama classes? He was certainly behaving like a citizen of Old London Town, or a Merry Peasant.

The nearer he got to Glasgow, the more ridiculous James felt. If Milroy was really running a bordello, how would one tell? Would he find the railings around the residents' garden draped with young females in skirts split to the groin? Would you ask for Fifi or Nana, having knocked thrice? Maybe public figures would be pleasuring blondes in petal hats in the backs of open cars all over the Botanic Gardens. Perhaps naked girls would be sitting astride kitchen chairs with knowing sexuality exuding from their every pore. Such doings seemed to fill the papers these days. He did so hope that Ishbel and the children would concentrate on the sorry state of Civil Rights in Alabama but, for good holiday reading, he feared that Governor Wallace and Dr King were as nothing compared to Christine, Mandy and Dr Ward.

If there was a red light above the door, then he would know. With great relief he noted no such thing. The fly-filled globe that had always been there was suspended still, and the sad plant existed yet in its tub, hovering between life and death. Furthermore no siren sat provocatively in the bay window sensuously a-stroking of a cat. One knew (he had been told) that such behaviour denoted carnal goods for sale in the coarser quarters of Hamburg.

Milroy answered the door. She wore her black afternoon frock and smirked with subservient modesty.

'Good afternoon, Mr James. I trust you had a pleasant drive. Miss Andrea is ready for you right away.'

Her cases were packed in the hall and she was just round the corner saying farewell to Cat.

Father and daughter kissed. As always, James said how she had grown, but this time, because Andrea was so anxious to be gone and so delighted to see him, she did not attempt to deny it or show

172

resentment. Normally the predictability of this remark irritated her enormously. She could not even retaliate with an observation concerning the thinning or greying hair, or indeed the broadening paunch. Children did not make personal remarks. Adults, on the other hand, seemed to be permitted to say what they liked concerning all physical changes in children.

'I expect you will want to be off directly,' said Milroy, grasping Andrea's suitcase and heaving it towards the waiting car at speed. 'You will not need to get stuck in the traffic. Well, cheerio, Miss Andrea. It has been a pleasure having you,' Milroy lied. She didn't lie well, but Andrea was dying to go and obediently loaded the rest of her stuff.

James was not as eager to be off as that. He needed to inspect the rones; it was always wise to check the guttering before the winter. Were the guards on the chimneys still? Or had wicked birds nested there this summer? He was minded to investigate a damp patch in the back passage that he had noticed after Effie's funeral.

'No need, no need, Mr James. The house is just fine.'

'I can see a nest from here.' A starling, one of millions, was looking down at its landlord. It must have been a hermit as most of its kin were busy deafening and bombarding the shoppers in Sauchiehall Street.

The damp patch was still there. Alarmingly so, as there was a bathroom directly above. Maybe a pipe leaked. Perhaps it leaked in the vicinity of the wiring. Zeal was the thing, care must be taken or else one's property might be consumed in flames or crumble to its foundations. He went up to the bathroom above. James was no plumber but years of the law had taught him how to look competent. He tapped pipes, looked puzzled, tapped again and said that a man must be sent for at once.

'Certainly, Mr James. I will see about it tomorrow. Things are always difficult during the Glasgow Fair.'

'There is a strange smell of festering food out the back, Miss Milroy.'

'Och, that would be the wicked gulls dropping food they have scavenged from the parks. Folk leave their picnics all over the place and then the birds drop them.'

173

'How strange. We get no trouble like that in Edinburgh.'

'That would be the east coast for you,' Milroy observed.

'True,' James concurred. Were beaks stronger or sandwiches more manageable in Edinburgh? Either way he was glad not to have to cope with this stink of stale vomit in Magdala Crescent.

Milroy waved and waved as the Rover retreated down the terrace. Thank goodness they were gone. Such disruptions were hard to tolerate and very bad for the budget.

'You should not read in a moving car,' James said as they headed eastwards. 'It will make you sick.'

All her life Andrea had been warned of this. Never once had she felt even vaguely car sick, and furthermore none of her friends had got appendicitis from grape pips or contracted pneumonia by neglecting to change their footwear. It was a shame that newspaper in the shoes never caused fainting either. Grudgingly she put the book away. It was not the sort of literature that would go down well at home. She wanted to finish it quickly just in case. It was the latest James Bond and even though Ian Fleming was Celia Johnson's brother-in-law (so outstanding in *Brief Encounter* . . . such a lady), the adventures of 007 were not accepted reading in Magdala Crescent. The cover alone was enough to cause a seizure amongst the cultivated. It was flesh coloured with two actual perforations representing bullet holes.

'Tell me what you have been up to,' James suggested. He wasn't really listening but he needed distraction. The weight of the world was overwhelming. A portico to some temple of commerce was on their left – Atlas and his twin brother, wrought in reconstituted red stone, had been recruited as caryatids. Neither looked happy with their lot, nor was James.

'I went on masses of bus trips,' Andrea volunteered. 'I went to Burns Cottage three times.' Her voice did not convey enthusiasm for the bard or his birthplace. 'I also went round the Trossachs . . . Remember I told you on the phone that I saw you?'

'In the Trossachs? Don't be ridiculous.'

'It looked just like you, outside a hotel in Drymen.'

'Whatever next!' James was gripping the wheel uncomfortably tight. This conversation was proving most disturbing. 'I expect you must have been sickening for the flu or whatever it was that you got. Fever plays terrible tricks on you. I remember I thought your mother was an angel when I had pneumonia.'

Andrea decided not to mention his companion. There was not much point in being disbelieved twice over. Besides, he did not seem pleased that she had dined with Kirsty and Mungo MacInlay so any mention of their mother might only increase his disapproval.

Just beyond the Wills factory James remembered what had slipped his mind. Ishbel had asked him to bring her mother's portrait back with him. She missed Effie more each day, she said. A woman needs her mother at times like these and what is more, she never gets over her death. Here she quoted Mary; she knew what weight that could carry with her husband. Somehow James had always felt guilty about his half-sister's motherless life, though even he knew that it was not his fault that her mother had died in childbirth. His own mother, Mary's stepmother, had been kind and useful, nothing more. He had got over her death at speed, but then of course he would, being a man.

'I am sorry, Andrea. We will have to go back. I'll just turn the car round. It won't take long.'

'Oh, Dad! Can't Milroy send the picture parcel post? Don't let's go back now, it will be busy.'

'What will be busy?'

'Glasgow, the traffic . . . look, it is the rush hour. We will not get through to Edinburgh for ages if we stop now.'

James agreed with her, but he was driven to return for the picture. He had promised Ishbel he would fetch it, and that was a promise he could keep. Unlike those he had flouted. He was aware of the retribution that awaited him whenever he broke his word.

There was nothing for it. Back they went through the streams of homebound office and factory workers. The Morris Minors and Minis were interspersed with the occasional Bentley, Jaguar or Armstrong-Siddeley of the more prosperous, while the tycoons travelled, chauffeur driven, in Austin Princesses or Rolls Royces. Sometimes James wondered whether he would be such a brilliant lawyer that his fees would run to the employment of a man to drive a car with leathery-smelling interior. What folly, what vanity, consider the lilies who get by without such frettings!

When they had negotiated the hubbub of the city centre and emerged into the calmer uplands of the West End beyond the Charing Cross, James was irritated to find that there was no longer a parking place outside the house, which was now looking more lively. The blinds were all awry and a light shone wastefully in the front dining room even though the sun was not yet setting. The wages of the working girl must be extensive for such extravagance amongst paying tenants. Andrea was sullen and silent as her father slid the Rover between two parked cars at the end of the terrace, a loud Jag and an extremely discreet Wolseley. She resolved to stay in the car and snatch a few more paragraphs while James fetched the portrait.

During the time since Milroy had wished James and Andrea a thankful farewell and waved her best white handkerchief from the front steps, the house had transformed itself from the restrained gloom of middle-class worthiness to a worldly frenzy of indulgence. A lavish array of cheering and inebriating bottles had appeared on the sideboard and the gaming table was uncovered.

Somewhat bewildered, James sat on Effie's old sofa. He shared the seat with a pink teddy bear. Like Christine Keeler, this toy had the expression of innocence but the bearing of experience. James was not at all sure of much. At least the light which still burned was not red. For this he was thankful. However, the array of bottles was a spot lavish for a hostel for working girls. Cliff Richard was singing loudly about going on a summer holiday, which should cause no anxiety as he was such an upright sort. But however commendable it was to have policewomen amongst the tenants, the particular young officer who had opened the door did not appear to be much like those normally found on the beat. That old duffer called Jock, who swayed quietly in the hall and smiled stupidly into space while concealing a book on art under his jacket, did not seem quite healthy. (James was sure he had seen him before; that foolish leer was awfully familiar. Maybe he was another of Bunty's numerous dippy relatives.) James told the policewoman that he had come to take a picture, to which she had asked how much he was willing to pay. When he said that the picture in question had belonged to his late mother-in-law the girl had gone off to find Milroy, only she had called her Miss T, adding that she thought James was a fly one. Cliff was now crooning about Juliette, who was not to forget something or other. Probably the remedy for holiday tummy.

Milroy entered dressed in a black lace cocktail dress of blatant provocative intent, which was not pacified by the pious hours the nuns of Carrickmacross had spent in its stitching. The spectacles that hung round her neck on a silvery chain were enhanced with glittering wings.

James rose to his feet somewhat amazed. 'Miss Milroy, you are dressed to go out!'

'Yes, Mr James, a charity whist drive. Mr Jock here, who was known to your late mother-in-law, is accompanying me.'

Jock ambled in. 'I only look, you know.' The old man's nervous tic might well have been a conspiratorial wink. James could not tell, but it was a relief to know that there was still a relic of the old times in Effie's house.

He explained about the picture. It would be no bother, Milroy would fetch it, but James would not hear of it. The Merry Widow had never been required to be handy about the home. So Milroy, Jock and James trooped off up to the second flight.

There is something about a hat and James was subject to it. Hats had to be atop delicate features and worn with confidence. Knitted shapes as favoured by stout shoppers were not the thing at all. He had secretly admired Mandy Rice-Davies in the petals she had worn to visit the Old Bailey, the flower of innocence upon a knowing stem. Effie gazed at him from beneath the blackest brim and looked magnificent, even if the lettuce-green and candy-pink flowers beside her added unwelcome vulgarity to the composition. However, he reflected that Glasgow was Glasgow and boys would be boys.

'Whatever is that noise?' A winching sound and some authentic groans were coming from Effie's old bedroom.

'What noise would that be?'

The groans were interspersed with the sound of a cracking whip.

The picture, having been lifted from the rail, was to be taken downstairs to be wrapped for the journey.

'It sounds as if someone is in pain, Miss Milroy.'

'Not at all, Mr James. It is just wee Marie from the labour exchange practising her judo.'

'I'd like to watch that sometime,' said Jock.

Milroy, after years of sensible flatness and secure buckles, had taken to wearing patent leather stilettoes, which she bought off the Barras. They were not stairworthy and the lethal heels became unmeshed in the tatty fringe of the landing rug. To the sound of ripping, she tumbled shrieking down the ten steps to the floor below. Now there was a noise of real pain and also real anger. Not only was her ankle turned, but the saintly lace was torn under her armpit where years of housework had made Milroy stout and muscular.

Doors opened all round, but the only person who seemed able to assist was a well-developed schoolgirl. Samantha had been a Girl Guide before she took to other ways of lending a hand. A nurse, who closely resembled the policewoman, was no use at all and disappeared as swiftly as an older woman, who was all overflowing in a coffee-coloured negligée.

Milroy was more shaken than injured, and Uncle Jock was instructed to go and make some tea. This was quite beyond him and he couldn't resist a quick peek into the room from whence this advanced schoolgirl had come.

'Watch out, you old fool!' A man dressed only in academic gown and mortarboard had been watching the scene through the hinge of the door. Jock had all but squashed him against a knobbly ornate Burmese chest. With nothing but black serge between his back and the well-wrought handles, the pain was not to be endured. The man, red in face and hair, stood infuriated in the doorway. In his hand he held a cane such as was wielded by Mr Quelch or Jimmy Edwards in *Whacko!*.

'Good God, Hector! What on earth are you doing?'

'Do you two fellas know each other?' asked Samantha. 'I do doubles but at twice the price. How about it?'

James knew now that Lady Neilson's suspicions were well founded. Mary's information had been correct. He looked with disgusted horror at the ridiculous figure of Hector MacInlay. He also realized at the same moment that it was now in his gift to ruin him. Who would take a City Father seriously who had to indulge his fantasies with a Glasgow whore?

Hector stood his ground, though he wrapped the gown round him and removed the mortarboard.

'There is no need to tell anyone about this,' he said shakily.

James delighted in Hector's confusion. 'Oh?'

'I've got nothing to be ashamed of,' Hector bluffed.

'Oh?' This was beginning to be fun. Maybe James would get noticed as an advocate after all. Could he impress the Master of the Rolls? Might he become a star like Mervyn Griffith-Jones, QC? He resolved to get himself called to the bar immediately he got home.

'Mr James,' Milroy interrupted, 'would you like me to give the rent to you in cash as usual, or would you prefer a cheque?'

'Well, just fancy that!' said Hector, recovering his aplomb. 'I would have thought that a man in your position would shun the idea of living off immoral earnings. Still, it is canny to get paid in cash. No doubt about that. Here, let me put some clothes on and I will help you carry that picture to your car. It looks a wee bit awkward for you.'

James had heard enough. He charged from the house, clutching the portrait, which he scratched badly on the area railings. The sun was setting as he started the car, and looking back he saw the reflection in the bay window. It glowed invitingly red.

13

Greet home-coming man with cheerful smiles and scented wafts. Keep news of the apocalypse for later. Man the breadwinner must be nurtured by woman the homemaker until he is happily settled in his favourite chair plus pipe and slippers. Then, and not before, he can be told of the exploded kitchen, evaporated pet, neighbourhood anthrax and the corpse in the cellar. To welcome him home, hot and weary from the toilsome world, woman must not be without fresh lipstick, combed hair or cheery endearments. Lack of these is death to a marriage. Keep your man by keeping your complaints to yourself. Thus spake the advising columnists.

Aunt Mary never had, nor would keep, a man. She was ready at the front door with her grievances. The first item on her list of complaints was Neil's language. It was so bad that he had actually used some words of which she had never even heard before.

James apologized, something would be done. He did not ask how his sister could assess the filthiness if the words used were unknown to her. She was sensitive to obscenity like others can detect auras.

The butcher would not deliver. The laundry had arrived and needed payment on the spot. No funds had been left for this eventuality and Mary had had to settle from her own pocket. The cat had peed (only she said it had lifted its leg) in her galoshes, and had James any idea of the state of the oven?

No, he hadn't. With great restraint he refrained from suggesting that his sister should inspect it more closely herself, having turned on the gas.

Where was the sherry?

Where indeed? This final complaint could be remedied. He would go to the off-licence and buy some. The departing Mrs Orr had probably basketed the last bottle on her final lap of dishonour.

Mary and Andrea faced each other.

'Well? Aren't you going to give your aunt a kiss?'

There was no alternative. Andrea kissed the ruddy cheek, she felt a whisker on her lips. Aunt Mary clasped her to her uplifted shelf. The affection of this embrace was as heartening as a chilled foot meeting a hot-water bottle gone cold.

'My poor, poor child. What you have been through! You must try and blot out that terrible experience and not let it poison your view on life.'

'But I have had a wonderful time,' Andrea lied. 'I did masses of things and met tons of friends. I can't wait to tell Neil. Where is he?'

'Locked in his room with bread and milk.'

'Whatever for?'

'Blasphemy . . . and insubordination!'

'Where is his friend Dalziel?'

'Who, dear?'

'The other boy who is staying.'

'Oh, him. What a dull child,' Mary replied. She couldn't remember seeing the small boy for hours. She had quite forgotten his existence. He was probably skulking somewhere. After all, he was very dull – simple even.

Andrea started up the stairs. Petunia had draped himself round her ankles. He at least was pleased to see her and asked no questions. She was immensely relieved to see him still alive and just as enormous.

The offy being handy, James returned soon. Tentatively, he poured his sister a glass of sherry.

'Oh, I don't want any now. I have made do with gin.'

Indeed she had.

'Now, James, what are you going to do about it?'

'About what?'

'That house in Glasgow, of course.'

'Well there is a damp patch in the hall, the rones need attention and the chimneys could do with a sweep. Apart from that, everything is fine.'

'Everything? What about . . . you know . . . the women?'

'Charming, all delightful. A very fine bunch of dedicated professionals. Nurses, policewomen, civil servants, you know the sort of thing, academics even – I had a glimpse of a gown.'

Mary looked puzzled. 'What about Lady Neilson? She was convinced it was a house of ill repute.'

'That woman has a filthy mind and an evil tongue.'

Neil was lying on his bed when Andrea unlocked the door. He had a sort of tearful look to him. He also smelt of gobstopper and tobacco.

'You've been smoking!'

'No I haven't.'

'Well then, you have been crying.'

'No I haven't.'

'Yes you have. Your eyes are all pink and you look all puffy.'

'All right, I have been smoking. You bloody women are all the same.'

'No we aren't. Here, haven't you got a fag for me?' Andrea had never smoked before.

'No. Dalziel has got them all.'

'Where is he?'

'In the garden, at least he was. I think he has run away.'

'Where to?'

'He said he was going to find his mother.'

'But she is abroad somewhere.'

'That is all right. He is going to stow away on a boat at Leith.'

'How will he know that the boat is going to the right part of abroad? He might fetch up at Aberdeen instead.'

'Who cares! Good riddance to bad rubbish.'

The cricketing cleric had favourites. Neil had not been one of them. On the other hand, little Dalziel with his cherub's curls and piping treble had been just the thing.

'What did you call Aunt Mary? She is awfully angry.'

'Good, I am glad.'

'What did you call her?'

'I won't tell you.'

'Very well. I won't tell you about what I did in Glasgow.'

'Nothing happens in Glasgow.'

'Oh yes it does.'

'What?'

'Tell! What did you call Aunt Mary?'

'A sodding whore of Babylon, a pissing gas bag, a buggy nit and a frigging cod.'

'Why a cod?'

'It was the rudest thing I could think of.'

'I think codpieces may be rude,' said Andrea.

'Well then, the whole bloody thing must be much worse. She deserved it.'

'I am sure she did,' said Andrea. 'But you won't be her favourite any more. No more half-crowns and ten-bob notes.'

'Sod off!'

'Don't you want to hear about Glasgow?'

'Yeah, okay, spit it out.'

She told him and he was enthralled. He had overheard people discussing the case of Dr Ward and cavortings that were alleged with Christine and Mandy. This was real. His sister had seen it. What went on in London was as remote as a debauch in furthest Siberia, but to be told of vice in Glasgow meant that such doings were no longer fiction.

'Tell me more!' he commanded eagerly, but Andrea's stock was exhausted. Besides, someone should be looking for Dalziel, who was, after all, only twelve and probably not quite up to being an effective stowaway.

She left Neil's room and relocked the door. She felt that she might be able to get the ear of her aunt if she appeared to be on her side.

'You bitch!' Neil shouted through the keyhole. His hammering fists could be heard beating on the door as she went downstairs.

James and Mary were arguing vehemently. Would life be ever thus?

'Dad!'

'Later, Andrea dear,' said Mary. 'Can't you see we are talking. You mustn't interrupt grown-ups.'

'Please, Dad, it is important.'

'Now now, darling.' James never called her darling. He must be very distracted.

'Listen!' she shouted. Brother and sister turned towards her in shocked disbelief. 'Listen. That little boy, Dalziel or whatever his name is, has run away to sea. He wants to stow away on a ship at Leith and go to find his mother.'

'Great Scot! That is all I need.'

There was quite a scene. James, who prided himself on being calm in a crisis, insisted on questioning his son before ringing the police. Neil's story was rather imaginative but served its purpose. Auntie Mary was beside herself with remorse. She had visions of the youth being sold into slavery, of becoming a eunuch in a harem, a catamite in Port Said, drowning, dying of smallpox or even being lured away by the Jesuits to become an altar boy, which would be the worst of the lot. It was all her fault, she said. No one disabused her of this conclusion.

It was quite dark when James rang the police. They would try to help. They needed all manner of details, which was irritating especially as no one seemed to know much about Dalziel except he was small, pretty and rather dim. His clothing was not memorable. Both parents were unobtainable, one on the continent with a lover and another on Skye with himself. Nevertheless, the force was alerted, the docks would be scoured. Had a complete search of the premises been effected prior to alerting the authorities, the inspector wished to know.

'Of course,' James replied curtly.

What with Ishbel and Euphemia about to be discharged from hospital, the unpleasantness in Glasgow, his doubtful chances of salvation and now this unnecessary child getting itself lost, James felt that the fates were conspiring against him. Thank goodness the nurse would be coming tomorrow.

'Oh by the way,' Mary said, 'I forgot to tell you, the nurse rang to say she won't be coming after all.'

'Cocoa in a crisis' was all Mary could contribute. They sat in the kitchen round the old table that had been veneered in Formica during the fifties, an action now greatly regretted by Ishbel. Norwegian wood everywhere was now the thing.

'What is this key doing here?' James asked, pointing to it on the table.

Mary explained that she had conscientiously locked all the outhouses because one never knew these days. James thanked her for her zeal but pointed out through clenched teeth that tomorrow was the day on which the dustmen called, and would need to get in to the bins to take the brock to the coup.

'James . . . it is affected to contrive to talk Scots. The lower orders do quite enough of that.' Mary, like many Scots who consider themselves mighty grand, had an accent whose existence she roundly denied.

With a dim torch to guide him, James went to unlock the shed. Petunia was already there, mewing most plaintively, pleading for access to the fine morsels often found festering behind that door.

Dalziel was in there too. The cigarette carton and the bottle of sherry beside him were both empty. His snores were raucous. He had run no further than the Haymarket before realizing the sheer folly and likely failure of his stowaway scheme. He had planned to hide in the shed long enough to worry Neil, whom he had begun to hate. When Mary had locked him in he had nothing to do except to finish the supplies that they had filched for a feast when they were still on good terms.

No one actually said that James had been wasting police time. Not openly did they, but the implication was there. James indicated that a substantial contribution would follow shortly for their excellent benevolent fund. That was as may be, the inspector answered. Notebooks were officiously pocketed and patrols stood down. His crimes becoming more heinous by the hour, James could sense the gates clanging to behind him, if not the noose a-tightening around his throat. At least he hoped he would not be charged with fornication by earthly powers. However, there would be no escape from the inevitable outcome on Judgment Day. He was booked in for ceaseless torment.

Dalziel, once aroused, was sick, complained of a headache and was put to bed. Neil was quite unmoved and appeared to see nothing but perversity in a small boy wishing to run away and find his mother. He hadn't seen his for a whole fortnight and was not in the least perturbed.

'You don't come from a broken home,' Andrea told him.

'Nor do you,' Neil answered.

'But I can't wait to see Mummie, and the baby, of course.'

'What on earth for?' Neil replied, trying hard to keep up his defiant stand. 'I suppose you know that the baby is a foreigner. It can't belong to us, it comes from Mongolia. Auntie Mary says it will be like that boy who helps the laundry man. I heard her asking how old it would have to be before it could go on the rounds too.'

At Christmas, Andrea's school usually entertained the residents in a home for the handicapped. Sibyl, one of the inmates, was a large, jolly, incontinent woman with slit eyes and a fat, flat face, whose strength was that of ten and who was given to wearing hideous knitted hats. Andrea remembered her well. She had felled several during 'Auld Lang Syne'. The bruised and shaken schoolgirls had been told that Sibyl had been born with mongolism.

'Off to bed with you at once.' Auntie Mary clapped her hands in the absence of a rousing whistle. 'If people were more responsible none of this would have happened. Personally I blame the parents.'

What struck Andrea most was her mother's sudden agedness. Naturally she had known her to be in middle life and past her youth, but for the first time, in the white starkness of the hospital bed, the grey hairs, wrinkles and deep lines of discontent and furrows of worry were frighteningly vivid. Her hair, normally so sensibly tidy, was rat-tailed and the blue brushed-nylon nightgown looked sad and soiled. Ishbel's breath was none too fresh and her temper was clearly vile. Nevertheless, Andrea was thrilled to see her again. She had missed her mother more than she had imagined possible and longed for the warm smile that had been bestowed on her when she was very young, before Neil had become the favoured one.

Andrea did not resent Neil's superior position in their mother's affection. She assumed that it was because he was a boy. Maybe if she had a sister instead of a brother she would have been jealous. Now she had a sister, but anyone could see that Euphemia was unlikely to oust others from Ishbel's heart. Confident of being best beloved, Neil treated his mother's devotion with disdain. Nothing would persuade him to visit her in hospital and he stayed behind with Dalziel, a friend once more, and planned a raid on the Haymarket newsagent while Auntie Mary rang every agency in pursuit of a third nurse. Price, she unwisely said, was no object (Mary was generous with others' money), and the rent from the Glasgow house would surely cover all expenses now she was assured that it was not derived from immorality.

When Ishbel saw Andrea she was terrified by her own feelings. She looked with horror at her eldest daughter and realized that she resented her for her youth, her increasing good looks, and for her life only just about to start, and as yet unburdened with the trappings of adulthood. Ishbel was gobbled up with jealousy.

Mother and daughter kissed but Andrea felt the stiffness and chill of a cheek that once used to be warm and spontaneous with fondness. She longed to ask what was wrong. What had she done to cause such iciness?

'Be careful where you sit, I don't want my bed all crushed and dirty. You had better wash your hands before you see Euphemia.' Ishbel noticed that Andrea's nails were still chewed and stubby. It was a relief to be able to say, 'Now that you are turning yourself into a young lady I am surprised that you still bite your nails like a baby.'

There had been so much that Andrea wanted to say to Ishbel. Now she could remember none of it. She washed her hands in a sink, operating the levers on the taps with her elbows as she had seen on *Emergency Ward 10*.

'Don't be so stupid and affected, dear. Sometimes I think you are no older than Neil. Only little children would play around like that.'

Chastened, Andrea sat down again. Her hands were damp, she did not like to risk contaminating a towel.

'Where is the baby?' she asked. Other mothers had small cots beside them; Ishbel did not.

'The baby is in the nursery. One of the nurses will show it to you.'

'Neil said that she is not quite normal.'

'What do any of you know about what I have been through?' Ishbel asked harshly. 'No, the baby is not normal. It is far from normal, and what is more it is not my fault. Why should I be blamed for what has happened?'

'No one is blaming you, Mummie.'

'Oh yes you are.' Tears once more started on their well-worn track down Ishbel's pale face. So many had come out of those red eyes – most hot with anger, some fuelled by self-pity, but none containing compassion, only hatred and resentment for the hideous misfortune of having a baby that was not perfect.

'Just you make sure that you never let any man get you into this kind of mess.'

'Daddy is not to blame either,' said Andrea.

'Oh no? Run along, Daddy's girl. Go and gloat over the monster. Show her your round eyes and good figure, and be thankful that you are not a freak.'

Andrea hated to leave Ishbel like this but there seemed no point in staying longer. Mother love was absent. No comforting child was needed.

'Put your shoulders back when you walk. Your slouch is getting worse.' Ishbel resumed her desultory flicking through the pages of the *Scottish Field*. She seemed to derive pleasure from mocking the pictures of the superlatively unattractive people whose weddings were recorded in its pages and she wished them all ill.

Andrea held her sister with trepidation. The baby, clad in hospital clothes, had been crying fretfully when she entered the nursery. Other small and poorly babies were in incubators in the room beyond where Euphemia lay in a solitary cot. All the rest had been parked beside their mothers. The nurse in charge was glad of a visitor. She doted on all babies, loved them to pieces till they went home, and then transferred her affections to the next newborn. Andrea hadn't held a baby before. It felt awkward and hazardous.

'Go on,' the nurse urged, 'talk to her, she likes that. Isn't she lovely?' She bent over Andrea as she sat with Euphemia lying in her arms and twitched the cellular cotton shawl away from the flat face. 'Oh look, she is going to give us a nice big yawn!'

A milky warmth came from the tiny mouth. Andrea almost felt a slight fondness. The baby was not gross, not like Quasimodo or a circus freak. Nor was she gorgeous. The nurse insisted that she was. Then Andrea saw the tongue and let out a most tactless shriek.

'Whatever is that? She has got two tips to her tongue!'

188

'Of course she has, the angel. All the better to lick ice-cream with when she is older. Twice the pleasure I bet.'

'But it is awful, disgusting.'

'Dear me, you are like your mum,' the nurse remarked sorrowfully. 'What this wee one needs is some mother's milk but she is not going to get any. Och well, at least I can give her a bit of a bottle now and again. We are good friends, us two.'

'Will you miss her when she goes?'

'Sure, I miss them all, but I don't miss them growing up.'

Andrea gave Euphemia back. She was beginning to cry again and there had been a sort of flowing upheaval beneath the nappies. The nurse took her with expertise and cooed at her while rocking gently. It was soothing. 'I will miss this one more than the others,' she said. 'Do you know why?'

Andrea shook her head. 'Why?'

'Because no one wants her.'

'I'll try,' said Andrea. It would not be easy.

Sister bustled in. She had a more pragmatic attitude and was devoid of sentimentality. Too many tragedies had sullied the moments of joy for her. She did not get involved.

'It looks as if we will just have to keep that baby for another week. The paediatrician is not happy with her breathing.'

'Is she ill?' Andrea asked.

'No, just delicate.'

'Will she die?' She hoped that she sounded suitably appalled by the notion.

'We will all die,' said Sister scornfully.

Hector hurried home, a song in his heart and a stirring excitement in his loins. What a night that had been! What a lucky fellow he was to have a wife like that, a wife who understood what he needed, one who played his game and gave him satisfaction. Legal satisfaction within the confines of what had, for many years, been a totally joyless marriage.

Since the birth of the two children, nothing much had pleased Moira and nothing she had done had satisfied his desires. He needed youth, playfulness, ingenuousness. He liked little girls. Well, Moira was not young but if she was prepared to go in for play-acting, who was he to complain? The procuring of nymphets was risky, time-consuming and expensive. Now, with a wife prepared to play the part, there would be plenty of time for business, golf and copulation. Hector didn't quite understand why almost twenty years of marriage had passed without such uxorial co-operation, but he presumed that Moira must have been fired by reading *Lolita*. Last night had been the first, he hoped, of many. Together Hector and Moira would dally and frolic into late middle age and indulge in pseudopaedophilia while drawing the retirement pension. He was a happy man as he leapt up the steps of Moray Place clutching an expensively wrapped present of baby-doll pyjamas.

'Yoo-hoo! I'm home!'

'You are very early,' was the cold reply.

'I came home to see my lovely little bride. Look, a prezzy!'

Moira accepted the box with no enthusiasm. She looked well enough but announced that she felt ill. Hector must go and get his dinner elsewhere. She had a headache.

His disappointment was great, and the urges that had been aroused would not subside with the sorry turn of events. He suggested hopefully that maybe later circumstances might improve. He tweaked her nipple and winked.

'Do not be so repulsive, Hector,' Moira replied, disgustedly brushing his hand away. 'I have had more than enough of that nonsense.'

Hector would have to find more than his dinner elsewhere.

Envy was not a vice that troubled James much. He would have liked to have been as rich as Hector but abhorred the vulgarity. He would also have relished living in Moray Place, amongst the architectural splendour and associations with a more established and eminent Edinburgh than had ever occurred near the Haymarket. But then again, a really large house would probably bring really large problems and a far more urgent obligation to entertain.

Hector MacInlay had, however, got something that James would have cherished, and that was a gallant war record. His red head had been held high as he marched fearlessly to deal death to the foe. His substantial physique had been an ornament to his regiment, and by the time he had been demobilized he had earned a DSO for doing something very brave in the Far East.

James had spent most of the war convincing the authorities that the murmur in his heart was an aberration devised by the alcoholic MO who had muttered to himself while casting about James's chest with his stethoscope. Once his health had been established and he was pronounced fit to serve, a bomb had broken both his legs during his embarkation leave and he spent the rest of his army career sorting out civilian claims against the raucous military in the Home Counties. Had he ever faced the enemy, he would have been dead scared; his was not a martial nature. His ignominious career rankled somewhat.

Once James had also envied Hector for being married to Moira. Now, when she persisted in pursuing him, he felt as he might have done had the bugle sounded the charge. He was scared. He was also horrified. The woman was a pest. Didn't she realize he had resolved to give up all infidelity and fornicating? Moira was to get behind him, for she was a temptation from the devil. It was too late, she said, James must continue seeing her. She was materialistic enough to dismiss the idea of elopement or divorce, but, nevertheless, if James left her now she would ruin his career, his family life, and reputation.

(Surely she had not heard about the house in Glasgow? Would any husband, however thick-skinned and heartless, admit to his unusual needs being met in a brothel?)

James did not have to speculate long as to why she persisted in pursuing him. He was the first to know.

Moira was pregnant.

She had made sure that the baby, when born, would be claimed by Hector, even though it would undoubtedly appear several weeks earlier and several pounds heavier than expected. James must continue to see her. She was obsessed by him, she would do anything to keep him – short of sacrificing her worldly goods. In fact, she would give those up too, even if it meant living impoverished in a butt 'n ben with the man she loved.

'No, no,' James protested, panicking. 'That cannot, that must not be.'

It would not do. Love in a Hut with water and a crust would be cinders, ashes, dust. But then, Love forgive us, this was no love. This had just been lust.

Meanwhile, Mungo MacInlay, who continued to get nowhere in Macpop or pop music, was to be dispatched to Alaska. Since he was too idle to discover much about the place, he was of the happy opinion that he would soon be cruising down the freeways of the United States. He did not realize he was bound for the very fish-packing station from whence the best Blair had returned before being sent off to London to make something of himself in the city.

In contrast, Kirsty had managed her life well. Using guile and cunning she had made certain that neither of her parents would stand in her way. She too was going south – to a crammer (the Swiss project had been abandoned). She was very happy and so was the best Blair, who was hoping to see much more of her.

When Andrea spoke to Kirsty on the phone, it was as if their summer friendship had never been. Andrea was of no further use to her. Kirsty was no longer bored or frustrated, was no longer in need of such a banal association.

Andrea, though bewildered by the sudden change, was really pleased to hear Kirsty's good news.

'How did you manage it?' she asked.

'It was easy,' was the brief reply.

'Did you ask if I take up your place in Switzerland instead of you?'

'Oh, Clootie, I'm sorry, I forgot. Anyway, it is terribly expensive and you probably wouldn't have liked it.'

'Oh well, never mind. Can I come round to see you before you go south?'

'Yes, all right, but I am very busy at the moment. Listen, give me a ring sometime. I must go, I've got to get ready.'

'What for?'

'Oh, just a party. Bye!'

'Wait, Kirsty. How can I get out of having to go back to school?'

'Just tell them.'

'How?'

'Oh I don't know. Fight your own battles. Listen, I must rush. *Ciao!*'

Magdala Crescent was like a country preparing for the onset of hostilities in a war declared but as yet not hot. Much would be demanded and much would be given but, for the moment, all was too quiet. Andrea helped Neil pack his treasures for boarding school. Procured from the second-hand shop, his uniform was miles too large. His shorts reached his shins and he had to keep his fingers straight to get any of his hand to show below the cuffs of his blazer. Ishbel had occupied her last few weeks of pregnancy with marking absolutely everything. Neil was Innes N. 428, and she had even managed to sew a nametape to his sponge. James tried to prepare his son for public school and talked to him of Civil Rights, or the lack of them, in the States, Tory party leadership, or lack of it, in the United Kingdom, and the wisdom of renouncing one's title. Neil was only interested in what really had happened at Cliveden and the Great Train Robbery, which was eclipsing everything else in the press.

With Andrea, James was embarrassed and awkward, and asked crass questions like what did she think of Cliff Richard?

Upstairs in the nurseries Janine, the nurse, procured at vast expense, waited for her charge. Nappies folded into kites were stacked neatly, bottles soaked in Milton and every crack and surface scrubbed with Dettol. Janine was Australian, single, fat and in her late fifties. Auntie Mary said one must make allowances for colonials. Janine, for her part, made none. She hated and despised everything British, she loathed children and disliked men, women and cats. It was to be hoped that she liked babies. She had no references except from the agency who had assured Mary that Janine was the best on their books. This was true. Janine was the only nurse on their books prepared to go at short notice to a handicapped or sickly baby. She was skilled at coping with infantile mortality, was a great layer out and rather enjoyed services for the burial of the young.

'If you hate this country so much why don't you go back to Australia?' Andrea asked her when she brought up her sixth pot of tea, which received her usual thanks of, 'God, can no one make a decent cup of tea in this god-forsaken country?' She was ugly as well as surly, the walleye being no help.

'Crikey, I wouldn't go back to that hellhole if it was the last place on earth.'

After that, Andrea kept quiet and out of her way. Janine, who liked to be called Nurse, called everyone else by their common noun as well, and she waited to pounce on Baby when she and Mother came home from hospital. She would take sole charge of Baby. Mother would have to go along with her routine. Big Sister would have to make herself scarce along with Big Brother, and cat must never be allowed to come anywhere near or the consequences would be dire. James found being called 'Father' rather disconcerting and Holy Roman. Nurse would probably enjoy dismembering Petunia and boiling him in a billycan.

James, sickened by his complicity, had buried his pride and bribed Mrs Orr to return. Smug and resentful, she resumed her duties and filled her basket quite openly with any items she felt she needed. Since there was no alternative, she was very sure of herself. She was, in fact, compulsory and she reminded everyone of this truth every time she battered the furniture with the Hoover and left gritty Vim in the bath.

Though it was now only August, a fire was lit for Ishbel's return. It smoked and belched into the house until a very dead

194

bird fell with a thud into the grate. Somehow the heartening blaze that had been intended was not effective. A film of soot settled on the furniture and the cards of congratulation that had been ranged along the mantelpiece appeared grubby and cheerless. Ishbel was still weak and felt exhausted despite having done nothing at all since Effie's birth. She was shattered by anguish and a deep depression. James tried to be jolly and insisted that Neil and Andrea make much fuss of her and the baby when he drove them home. The return was not triumphant. Nurse swooped and removed Effie to her realm at the top of the house to the great relief of Ishbel, who collapsed on the sofa in the sooty sitting room and stared at the late bird's pyre.

There were letters to answer and bills to pay. Milroy had forwarded the doctor's bill together with a list of expenses incurred during Andrea's stay. Mrs Lammont had always been a private patient so her granddaughter was treated the same. Three domiciliary visits did not come cheap.

It was at tea time that Andrea roused her courage and asked whether she could leave school. Surprisingly it was easy. Once she had said it it was as if her anguish about raising the subject had never existed. She crumbled a cupcake (reserved for treats) and waited for the outcry. It never came.

Ishbel and James agreed that Andrea was no academic and it would be cheaper and easier in the long run if she settled down to learn more practical skills. The sooner she could make herself useful, the sooner she could find a job, a husband, a house, a family, a secure old age and a trouble-free decline. The prospect was almost too exciting.

'Actually, I would like to go to school in Switzerland. Kirsty MacInlay was going to go there but she isn't now so there must be a place. Please, can I go?' All that came out in a rush.

'Whatever for?' Ishbel asked. 'What would you get out of that sort of caper?'

'I could learn French and flower arranging and how to talk to ambassadors and what to do with serviettes – that sort of thing.'

'What rubbish! When are you likely to meet ambassadors? We have spent thousands of pounds on getting you taught French at school, all of which appears to have been wasted. What is more, people like us do not have serviettes, we have napkins. This vulgar rubbish is what comes out of making friends with people like the MacInlays. They are nothing but upstart nouveaux riches types who made their money in fizzy drink.'

'Oh, Ishbel, that is not very kind,' James said.

'Daddy likes Mrs MacInlay,' Neil said. 'Andrea saw them at a hotel when she was on a bus trip.'

'Stop making things up, Neil!' said James.

'It is not a lie,' said Neil. 'Is it Andrea?'

'I really would like to go to Switzerland,' Andrea said.

'We'll see,' said James. 'Now then, how about more tea for us all?' He was awfully bright and keen, rubbing his hands vigorously together. 'Goodness, what a luscious brew!'

Nurse rang a handbell from the top of the stairs. The family were expected to come aloft and inspect Baby, now dressed in wholesome Viyella.

Little Effie stared at the ceiling, her slit eyes not yet focusing on her parents, who leant over the crib to gaze despondently at their child. She snuffled like a Pekinese.

'All this is your fault,' Ishbel hissed at James.

'Andrea dear, can I have a word with you?' James seldom asked his daughter to see him alone unless he had been instructed to do so by Ishbel. 'You must not upset Mummie. She is having a hard time.'

Since her return from Glasgow, James had been concerned about Andrea's health and general demeanour. She had become apathetic and lethargic. When he had collected her from Kelvingrove she had seemed to glow with excitement. The baby had delighted her, she longed to be home, she said she had missed everyone and James believed her. Now she was silent, obedient and listless. Her complexion was pale yet muddy, and though she appeared to eat she got thinner every day. There was nothing fresh about her, especially her breath, which was fetid. No friends rang or called by. After her bold request to leave school there had been no other sign of life from her. It was as if she had resolved to be obedient to some harsh rule of self-denial. Young girls in love were subject to moods, he was told by his secretary. But this was not love. There was no sign even of infatuation or idolatry, no posters hung in her room. A passion for a film or pop star did not unsettle her equanimity. According to Buster, the Brown girls talked of nothing but Peter O'Toole, and had papered the walls with him, especially on camel-back.

James and Andrea were in his study, which was all over mannishly festooned with memorabilia and snaps of his modestly sporting youth. An oar harboured dust on the wall above his desk because once, long ago, he had affected an enthusiasm for rowing. However, he had had no hand in the end of the owner of a pair of noble antlers that hung over the door. Ishbel had bought them at a sale, aiming to add class.

'Please will you be a very good girl and not make a fuss about staying here? Mummie really does need you.'

'She needs you more.'

James ignored the interjection and carried on. 'You can't go away just yet, though we might be able to manage to let you leave school and learn typing or something useful like that. We will just have to see. Maybe you could go abroad next year. Now, how about a wee present by way of consolation?'

Andrea thought. 'I would like a big, thick, pure silk headscarf with a broad border and a pattern of saddlery all over it. Like the one Mrs MacInlay was wearing when I saw her.'

'But they are terribly expensive,' James gasped.

'I know,' said Andrea. 'Mummie hasn't got one either.'

There was a silence as James thought about what was to be done.

'Dad?'

'Yes . . . sorry, I was thinking.'

'That is all right,' Andrea replied. 'I only wanted you to explain to me what it means to live off immoral earnings.'

Everyone was worried about Ishbel, who was sunk in a gloom that no one could reach, and behaved as if she alone felt the anguish of having a defective child. Mrs Gummidge in *David Copperfield* at least acknowledged that some people felt things as hard as she did. Ishbel was bent on bearing the burden alone. She made no attempt to get back into shape, and continued to slop around in maternity tents. To complete the picture of slovenliness she started to smoke again, having given up cigarettes when she had first embarked on motherhood. Now she had put that part of her life into sequestration and sat smoking all day, staring out at the tired August gardens. Her baby was well cared for and there was nothing she wanted to do.

Gradually, all friends crept away. At first, they had mustered and cooed at the baby and done their utmost to cheer Ishbel into a happier mood, but people are only capable of so much fruitless effort and now it was only Bunty who bounced in with unsolicited eggs, dahlias, gooseberries and anything else that her chaotic garden might choose to yield from its heaving turmoil.

Andrea's headmistress agreed that further education would be of little benefit, and furthermore it was unlikely that Andrea would bring credit to the school. However, despite the somewhat redundant aspect of her attendance, attend she must for the next term, or else the fees would be forfeit. Rules were rules, and by such we must live, unless of course the poor child had to be removed due to medical circumstances.

So while Neil got more excited about going away to be a boarder, Andrea resigned herself to a further term at school. She stopped eating and derived a solitary pleasure from watching the scales fall. Nurse told Ishbel that Andrea was vomiting several times a day. She was concerned in case Baby added that affliction to her catalogue of woes. Ishbel asked James what he was going to do about it.

The letter came as requested from Dr Elizabeth Robb, who apologized for its lateness but did not explain that she had just given birth and lost a premature son. She was professional; such things should not intrude. Andrea, she said, was suffering from quite a common psychologically based eating disorder. This may have been due to feelings of insecurity or lack of self-esteem. She needed to be somewhere where she was accepted for what she was and not what she felt others expected her to be. Andrea thought she was fat to the point of obesity and she would starve herself until she was so thin that her body would no longer function in the manner of a young woman. She ought to be watched and cared for, maybe away from home, maybe with other companions of her own age and she must be made to feel that she mattered and was valued for herself.

When Bunty called with some late, bug-infested raspberries, she found Ishbel in the height of rage. She was holding Elizabeth's letter as if with tongs. Her fury was directed firstly at Andrea and secondly at the doctor. How dare any child of hers suffer from a psychological complaint, and what an affront to diagnose such a disgraceful thing! How could anyone even mention a disorder of the mind to such an exemplary family? Andrea had done this on purpose. She must pull herself together. Ishbel then appealed to Bunty to keep this shameful implication to herself. As if Ishbel had not got enough to upset her.

'There is nothing wrong with being a bit off your head now and then,' Bunty said. 'Buster had a cousin who was never herself at the new moon. She managed to live quite a normal life, married, had children, hunted, all the usual things. No one minded one bit. She used to take her clothes off and run about the garden. Everything was fine till she got old and started to steal things. That was a little trying and wearing, but her family got quite used to turning out her pockets and returning the trinkets she had nicked to their rightful owners.'

'But this idiotic doctor says Andrea is psychologically disturbed. She has no business being disturbed, she doesn't come from a broken home.'

'They do have some strange ideas these days, though some of it may be quite sound. For instance, we have been told to split the girls up. Disperse the litter a bit. They do everything together, even dote on the same film star. It's time they went separate ways, otherwise they will be no good for breeding. Fiona is going to the Dough School and Marion will go there next year. They will swap about. Meanwhile Marion will spend this year abroad.'

'Where?' Comforted to know that others had relatives whose minds were sometimes awry, Ishbel seemed to be more interested now.

'She's going to a small school near Lausanne run by an English games mistress and a French woman with a degree in civilization. All the girls have to speak French and learn about art and all that. They get lots of fresh air and exercise to keep their minds off men, and do all the domestic work. That is why it is so cheap. There are absolutely no males allowed near the place. It looks good in the brochure, sort of British with mountains in the background. It doesn't fill their heads with silly ideas. They don't do conversation and curtseying to cardinals, like the place Kirsty was going to.'

Bunty seemed to read Ishbel's mind. 'I think it would be splendid if Andrea could go there too. Do let me see if there is a vacancy. It would do her the world of good to be there with other', she almost said 'normal', 'big girls. She should have people about her that are fat.'

'Like Julius Caesar?'

'Did you do that play at school too?'

'Yes,' Ishbel replied wistfully, for she had really enjoyed boarding school. 'I was Caesar's wife.'

'Above suspicion! Good for you!' Bunty was delighted to find some misery disappearing. 'I was Fourth Roman or Third Countryman – I can't remember which. We wore laundry bags.'

'Do you know why Miss MacConechy says you can leave school right away without paying for next term's fees?'

Andrea did not and cared less, so long as she never needed to put on that ghastly uniform again.

'I'll tell you why, young lady,' Ishbel said. She looked at Andrea through a veil of smoke. Her fingertips were becoming yellower every day. 'She says you can go because she wants to get rid of you. Why is that, do you think?'

'Because I am not very clever?' Andrea ventured.

'No, because you are mad!'

Ishbel had lost weight but regained no shape. She felt, and looked, like an ancient pillow whose downy stuffing had combined itself into comfortless lumps. She brooded over Neil's impending departure and was frequently found to be sniffily tearful.

Oh dear, thought James, more tears. Ishbel's ducts must be bottomless, like Loch Ness.

'He is such a wee lad, so sensitive. I can't stand the thought of him leaving his happy home.'

'Nonsense, Ishbel, you fret too much. Schools aren't what they were when we were young. There are curtains, and baths with hot water, and half-term holidays, and television on Sundays – all sorts of things unheard of before the war.'

'But boys are still the same,' Ishbel said.

'True, and a fine bunch they will be, you'll see. Look at all the first-rate fellows who have remained my friends for life.'

On reflection he could not think of one except for Smythe One, who had been killed, and Cooden Two who had gone to gaol. But Buster Brown, who had already been an Old Boy by the time James was New Bug, was a real friend, the sort that lasted whatever happened.

Ishbel bravely tried to be comforted but was not to be consoled by the thought of having Nurse and Wee Effie for additional company.

Ishbel's glare was not one of pining resignation.

'I can't afford to miss any opportunity to make money,' James added. 'We will have to be very prudent if we are going to afford all this expensive education and a nannie.' It had become obvious that Ishbel would not be devoting much time or any affection to Effie, who developed and grew after her own fashion every day in the obsessive care of Nurse.

'I think it would be kinder to the others if the baby were put in some sort of residential care. I have heard that the older children suffer greatly if a younger child who is not quite all there is given a lot of parental attention,' Ishbel said in an afflicted voice.

'But it will only be Andrea here, and she is almost grown-up, especially now she is through with school.'

'But what about the holidays?'

'Institutions have holidays too sometimes,' James replied.

'Oh God! Does no one understand the hell of motherhood?'

James had grown rather fond of little Effie and he couldn't bear the idea of any child having to be reared in a home amongst strangers, however kindly and well trained. He felt committed to seeing through the task he had so unwisely started. However, he was frightened of upsetting Ishbel's fragile composure.

'Whatever happens, we will be wanting money and so I had better see about making some. I also think that we ought to sell your mother's house.'

'What for? The rent is regular and far more than we expected. I cannot be made to suffer another loss so soon after all the other tragedies.' She looked up at her mother's portrait, which had replaced a turgid painting of a ruin without perspective, perched upon a promontory in a spell of foul weather. Effie Lammont gazed on her daughter with a quizzical detachment and an identical nose – long, thin and slightly beaked. Her eyes did not believe any of it. The bright clear colours and the profound black of her hat looked ill at ease in Edinburgh. A pearly queen as compared to a genuine monarch.

Risking much, James bravely launched into one of the subjects that had been troubling him greatly.

'I feel it might be as well to dispose of the Glasgow house. Some of the tenants appear to be rather irregular in their habits and of questionable morals.'

'Let him that is without sin cast the first stone,' Ishbel replied. 'Quite.'

James knew he was defeated. Ishbel was right about the rent, which arrived with regularity and in highly satisfactory quantities, though the manner of its acquisition was an immense worry. However, in view of his wife's delicate health, he decided that it would not be wise to disrupt the status quo. To purge his guilt, he sent a fiver to a home for fallen women. This contribution did little ease to his conscience and nothing to succour those of loose morals.

Usefulness was a virtue of the utmost importance, it could not be stressed too often by both Innes parents. They had endeavoured to be just that: though no one could find Ishbel very handy in autumn 1963, except possibly as an employer of others.

In order to become handy to the human race, Andrea, liberated from school on the grounds of insanity, was to go to Dugdale's to acquire secretarial skills. So good to fall back on, and so wonderful to have to hand should one fail to get by, as Aunt Mary remarked. She seemed to have survived without typing or shorthand, but then her double-entry book-keeping was utterly brilliant. That delight was to befall Andrea later, along with home economy. There was no call to get carried away with Cordon Bleu or floral art, Ishbel said. Any mate selecting Andrea would be getting himself a useful tool, not a priceless ornament.

'I could learn shorthand and typing in Switzerland,' Andrea remarked wistfully when her fate was announced. 'You get taught it at the school where Marion Brown is going, only they call it *sténographie et dactylographie*.'

'Pure affectation!' Ishbel snorted. 'I want to hear no more of this Swiss nonsense. I cannot lose all my children at once at a time like this.'

'Do you really need me, Mummie?'

'Naturally! You could be a great comfort to me. If you tried.'

The night before Neil went to school was grim indeed. Suddenly his *sang* was no longer *froid*. He was scared witless and cried real tears for at least half an hour. Andrea kept him locked in her room. Such lack of spine must not be seen by anyone. She knew how he felt, she spoke to him of exeats and holidays, of rugger and midnight feasts, but all he could think of was what Dalziel had told him happens to new boys or 'bugs' as they were known.

They strip you, they pee on your bed, they throw your clothes in the duck pond and they make you eat worms. These were the most benign afflictions. The rest were secret and much, much worse.

'It can't be as bad as Belsen,' Andrea said, remembering what her grandmother had said on the Broomielaw. 'You will live. You'll see.'

When James drove Neil away the next day, he did look as if he was being tumbrelled to his doom. Ishbel managed to stop sobbing for lunch, but couldn't bring herself to wave goodbye. She howled in the kitchen, an Udder Cloth inherited from her mother covering her head. Had there been ashes and hair shirts available she would have made use of them so that the whole world could spot she was grief-stricken.

Andrea held Petunia in her arms and watched at the gate till the Rover turned the bend at the top of the terrace and headed north to masculine toughness and manly team games, academic endeavour, filthy food, sensible godliness and no more Mummie.

Nurse kept a zealous watch over baby Effie. At the same time, she hinted darkly that she was a monthly nurse and would shortly have done her time. Ishbel said she would leave the hiring of a nannie to James and Auntie Mary, and would concentrate on regaining her health. They were better at these things. Ishbel had no wish to get involved, especially as everything was better managed without her interference. Evidently the drugs prescribed by the doctor to combat her depression had tranquillized her into inertia.

Andrea often played with Effie's little hands, loving the feel of the tiny grip. Her blue baby eyes still looked wild, but when her nose was not running and she wasn't spluttering, she almost appeared to smile. The slit tongue seemed less obvious now, but that smile was only wind, Nurse said. One must not expect too much from Effie yet. Or indeed, ever.

Mrs Orr said she couldn't be doing with sickly bairns. Ishbel agreed with her, for she had long nursed a horror of cripples and disfigurements, and couldn't even bring herself to be tolerant of the war wounded. On a belated honeymoon trip to Paris, *les mutilés de guerre* received scant sympathy from her, apart from her seat on the metro, and that only because she was instructed to give it up. Ishbel always Kept Left, Sounded the Horn, Washed Her Hands – and had she been a gentleman she would have Lifted the Seat. Even if someone held open the door for her in a public lavatory she still inserted a penny in the slot. She never leant out of the window and would not dream of using the communication cord improperly. She abided by the law and observed all bylaws.

15

Ishbel's exhaustion persisted. She spent most of her days staring out of the window and wondering when the leaves would fall off the trees. When they did, she hoped it would hurt. She smoked incessantly. If, as they were saying, tobacco caused cancer, then so be it. The sooner the better. All emissaries from the reaper would be warmly welcomed. Upstairs Effie throve, and became fat on formula milk.

Nurse was threatening to leave, even though Auntie Mary had failed to find her replacement. It was definite that Ishbel would not be able to cope alone. If the worst came to the worst and no capable sort was found, then Effie would have to be placed in a home, which was what Ishbel wanted anyway.

Nurse had announced that she was taking the afternoon off to go to the hairdresser. Miss Fay was to transform her into Mary Quant and bob her straggled locks, which had not seen a pair of scissors since Christmas. She had not asked Ishbel in advance, as she knew her request would be refused like the time she had asked for an hour off to visit the chiropodist, when Ishbel pleaded not to be left alone and had managed to make herself hysterical. Then the tears, snot and spit had cascaded everywhere, most unhygienically.

Effie had been fed and changed and replaced in her crib, to spend a busy afternoon gazing without focusing at some stimulating and entertaining plastic balls. With luck she would sleep till Nurse returned, but, just in case, Ishbel was provided with a bottle and instructions on how to give it. No one would have thought that Effie was Ishbel's third child and she showed no inclination to remember anything of the ways in which she had so successfully reared Andrea and Neil. A nappy, folded like a kite, was laid in readiness, but Nurse knew that Ishbel would die rather than attempt to put it on. Effie would just have to put up with being damp and smelly. After all, no one was going to call to admire Euphemia Innes. No one would wish to fondle or dandle so gross an aberration of nature.

Andrea was also out that afternoon, at the dentist's, but had returned to the house to fetch a coat. She fancied it was nippy and also she wanted to visit the dentist clad in her favourite garment, which was one of the late Effie Lammont's very dead fur coats. Andrea thought the effect was marvellous, though she looked more like a minor archduchess who had dodged the bullets at Ekaterinburg than a sumptuous starlet.

She was leaving her room when she saw Ishbel mounting the stairs towards her. She was carrying what appeared to be the baby in her arms and muttering gently. For a moment Andrea felt a pang of jealousy. Once she had been her mother's baby, who had silly rubbish whispered lovingly to her. Then she saw that the bundle was not Effie but Petunia, and Ishbel was climbing the stairs towards the baby's bedroom while issuing sotto voce instructions into the furry ear of the peeved cat, newly roused from a sweet slumber.

'Mummie, what are you doing? Can I help?'

'Andrea! What the hell are you doing here? I thought you were to go to the dentist.'

'I am just off now. It was cold, I came back for a coat. What are you doing with Petunia?'

'This wretched cat keeps on coming upstairs to the nurseries. I am frightened to death about what might happen. I was just keeping hold of it to be sure.'

'Here, give Petunia to me. I'll shut him in the kitchen on my way out, then you won't need to worry.'

She took the cat and returned him to his very favourite spot beside the Esse.

'You look ridiculous in that coat!' Ishbel shouted after her.

'So what!' Andrea shouted back.

'How dare you speak to me like that!'

But Andrea had gone before she could listen to the rest of the diatribe, which involved much talk of cruel knives piercing maternal hearts and the severing of navel cords.

Andrea read the newspapers in the dentist's waiting room as the magazines were all dolefully old and concerned motor cars.

206

The Denning Report was about to be published and scandal sheets were whipping their readership into a frenzy of curiosity.

The dentist marvelled at the corrosion of Andrea's teeth, caused by the constant acid vomit combined with large doses of PLJ which she drank to shrink her stomach.

'You are not very well, my wee girl,' he remarked kindly, and prescribed much tooth-brushing and suggested she tried fluoride tablets, though he secretly thought it was a bit late for that. 'You need building up. You are much too thin, your parents must be worried about you.'

Andrea was delighted. She bought and ate a delicious doughnut on the way home and resolved to keep it exactly where she had sent it. She was in no hurry.

Nurse had delayed her return, partly because she felt she deserved a holiday and partly because she was not at all sure about her new black helmet of hair. There are those who are doomed to have whispy strands of mixed grey on their heads and there are those who are Mary Quant. The two do not readily interchange. Miss Fay had produced a catastrophe, with which coming to terms might prove most difficult. Nurse was meandering up the Crescent wondering whether to comfort herself with an egg for her tea when Petunia shot out of the Innes front gate pursued by a screaming banshee.

Nurse caught Ishbel just before she ran into the traffic.

'Mrs Innes, Mother! Whatever is the matter?'

Ishbel recognized the apparition as her daughter's nurse.

'You devil! You fiend! How could you leave my child? My baby is dead! The cat has smothered her. The pillow is covered with the brute's fur, you can see for yourself. Oh my baby!' The screaming could probably be heard beyond the Dean Bridge.

The alleged murderer was sounding down the Haymarket at speed till he fell beneath the ponderous wheels of the laundry van and ended his life quite flat and probably without pain.

'Dad,' the van driver's son shouted, 'look what you've gone and done to yon pussy.' He bent over and picked the dead cat up by the tail, his podgy simpleton's features about to crinkle into grief.

'Och, dinna' fret, hen. It looks a scraggy kind of beastie. It is probably better off being deid. Gie it here, we'll just chuck it in yon dust cart.'

Andrea's old teddy presided in martyred majesty over her old cat's tomb in the back of the Cleansing Department's very best truck.

The following morning Auntie Mary was already there with large and detailed plans for a formidable funeral. She was greatly relieved that she had the chance to organize something so splendid. The proposed christening would, after all, considering the circumstances, have been rather awkward.

'God,' she announced breezily, 'certainly does move in a mysterious way.' Though it was quite humiliating to find that the Almighty had yet again selected such a poor specimen of His creation to be the instrument of His will. Christian history was littered with such divine quirks: consider St Lawrence the Idiot, and St Christopher. On second thoughts, perhaps St Christopher was not a good example, as there were popish plots to discredit him as fictitious, like poor old St George, but then what was one to expect from the Italians? Busy and happy, Mary chattered to herself.

The laying out of the dead was undoubtedly Nurse's forte, after which she left, saying bluntly that her business was with the living.

Ishbel clung to James. Waterfalls of tears now flowed.

'Our baby has been killed. Dear little Effie is dead. Our poor, poor wee baby.'

'I want to talk to you.' Andrea was taking a cup of tea to her bedridden mother, who was prostrated with grief.

'Not now, Andrea.'

'Yes, now.'

Ishbel looked at her daughter with her red-rimmed eyes. She had a *frisson* of foreboding, and dreaded what was to come. Andrea was too knowing.

'How did Petunia get out of the kitchen after I had locked the door?'

There was no reply. Ishbel was trembling and unable to speak.

Her nails were yellow with nicotine, grubby and encrusted with ancient chipped varnish. Andrea looked at her mother's hands.

'Did you know Ruth Ellis made sure that she kept her hair blonde till the end? I read it in a magazine.'

Ishbel gasped and made to hide her horrible hands beneath the sheets.

Andrea sighed. It would seem that her law-abiding mother had let her personal pride slip along with her hitherto immaculate principles.

'Mummie? Why won't you let me go to Switzerland?'

Still no answer, only the desperate frenzied gape of terror on a face that made no sound.

'Listen, Mummie. If I go to Switzerland I won't be able to remember exactly what I did about the door, will I? I won't be able to remember whether you were carrying the cat up or down the stairs either. Will I?'

'That was a great sadness for James and Ishbel.'

Buster and Bunty were sitting outside three weeks after the funeral, on what would probably be the last chance to appreciate the fading season. They were tough, but even so, they found the nights to be growing chilly. Leaves lay all over the paths and had quite obliterated the tennis court.

'Yes,' Buster agreed. 'A dreadful business, but a jolly good funeral, what?'

Bunty nodded. 'The best for ages. The Church of Scotland is always so accommodating when dealing with the unbaptized. Did you see that colossal wreath from the MacInlays?'

Buster agreed that the immense tribute had been well over the top. 'Neither Hector nor Moira were there,' he said, 'though recently I have noticed that Hector and James Innes are not at ease with each other.'

'Yes, aren't they strange?' Bunty replied. 'They are like two nervous dogs sniffing each other with their hackles up before a fight. I suppose Moira felt that, being pregnant, it might be tactless of her to go to a baby's funeral.'

'Hector is frightfully pleased with himself about that,' Buster said.

'I wonder whether Moira is delighted too.'

'Well, old girl,' Buster said, patting Bunty's knee, 'judging by the size of her latest gin order, I would say she is in two minds about it.'

'I am so glad I got all that child-bearing out of the way before middle age. Some women go barking mad when they get over forty.'

'You haven't, my love.'

'No,' Bunty laughed. 'I was born barking. Incidentally, I had another letter from Marion today.'

'Still happy, I hope?'

'Of course. She says that Andrea is doing well too – at least she was last Friday. They are only allowed to speak English on Fridays. It makes up for having to eat something called poison du lac.'

'Andrea seems a nice enough child, but not very jolly.'

'Well, it was tough losing her cat like that.'

'And her baby sister.'

'True. It was probably a good idea to send her away before the funeral, all desperately distressing.'

Bunty took a gulp of gin, having fished an extremely tardy drunken wasp out of her glass. 'Marion says La Maison Jaune is not too bad except for the veal sausages. She says they taste, smell and look like white rubber, but then she and Andrea both dote on the *tarte au fromage*. The headmistresses are a bit quaint. They share a bed. The girls are only allowed to bath once a week, which is a typical piece of continental grubbiness, but they have to hang their mattresses over the balcony daily. Last week a pig was killed just beneath their window.'

'Well, it is meant to be a finishing school,' Buster observed. 'Would you like another drink? Whatever is up with the dogs? Has someone rung the bell?'

Fiona, who grew stouter with every cookery lesson at the Dough School, was the only Brown child at home, as Angus had gone off to do Oxbridge entrance.

'Dad,' she shouted, from the dining room window, 'there are some foreign men at the door.'

'Tell them we are not at home,' Bunty said imperiously. 'These mormons are getting beyond a joke.'

'They want to see Mr Brown. They are talking foreign. I think it is Spanish.'

Buster's heart leapt, struck by an absurd notion. Surely it could not be news of Dolores after all these years? He hoped not. The memory of the thighs was to be cherished, not destroyed by cruel reality and the flabby flesh of age. Still less did he want any young person from abroad coming all this way to seek employment, recognition and to call him Dad, or *Padre*.

Mother and daughter sat beneath the elderly copper beech and ate the day's lesson, a fair-sized bombe, while the rooks carried on their perpetual feud. Daylight and pudding were both at an end when Buster returned.

Fiona remarked, 'Those men were awfully cross and kept on waving a picture of a woman and a baby at me, and talking about somebody called Hermana Juanita. I thought I recognized the mother in the picture.' She wiped some cream from her skirt with a fallen leaf. 'I know! It was that Spanish maid who used to work for the MacInlays, the one that was sacked. What did they want with you, Dad?'

'They didn't want anything with me,' Buster replied. 'Wrong Mr Brown.'

'My mother always said I was marrying an awfully common name,' Bunty said. 'I must go and cook the supper, that pud has made me peckish.'

Buster gazed into the autumnal sunset.

'They are looking for Wee Angus.'

211

Epilogue

Lac Léman, November 1963

Andrea and Marion were amongst the few girls at La Maison Jaune with complete and original sets of parents, so when Andrea received James's letter telling her that he and Ishbel had decided to live apart for a while, she resolved to tell no one. After all, it would seem to be of little importance to anyone but herself, and she had learnt not to bore others with her personal troubles. Anyway, she was not too sure how troublesome this event would turn out to be.

From her mother, she had received no word, though she had written several letters addressed to both her parents. From now onwards she would have to write to them individually. Then maybe, she hoped fervently, Ishbel would write to her. Andrea, despite all that had been, did not wish to be estranged from her mother.

A *jour de fête* had been announced. These occurred on an arbitrary basis and were prone to coincide with an unpleasantness between the headmistresses. The entire school would be given bread, chocolate and something strange from the *charcuterie* and told to take *une jolie promenade*.

The lakeside hotels were already closing and they presented their dead shuttered faces to that spectacular view so often reproduced on chocolate boxes and jigsaws. The rich, sick and lonely who were stretching their latter days in luxurious and tedious retirement sat huddled on terraces in case the autumn should bite and hasten them to another shore. The extreme cleanliness of Switzerland would imbue them with hygiene and endear them to their god. They had hair that, if left to itself, would be white with years, unlike that of the poor prisoner of Chillon. The school had been taken to visit that château and to gaze upon the very spot where the wretched fellow had been incarcerated.

Andrea had found the place strangely compelling, like the bottle dungeon at St Andrews. The lake was calm as glass, quivering occasionally because of the slight breeze and the sluggish ways of the resident fish. The Dents du Midi were discernible in outline only, against the sky, which was already changing to evening pink. A tiny island on which grew a solitary tree was the only punctuation mark in the flat plane of water.

'Queen Victoria planted that tree,' said Andrea.

'She never! Who said?' Marion liked to collect facts.

'Thierry told me.'

'Is that the boy who gave you those carnations?'

'No, that's Luc.'

'Well then, is it that one with the motor bike?'

'Guy the Grotty? Not likely,' Andrea replied.

Marion was quiet for a while, wondering whether Thierry was the walking dream whose father was the chef de gare, and whether everybody who looked like Françoise Hardy got to get flowers.

'What are you crying about, Andrea?'

'I'm not crying. It is a beautiful view though, isn't it?'

'Yes, I suppose so. Here, can I swap my chocolate for your sausage? Or can we club together and buy a *gâteau vert*?'

As Andrea searched her pocket for francs, she felt her father's letter. She took it out and tore it into tiny pieces and threw them onto the water where the ink smudged and the paper mingled with the floating fallen leaves.

The girls had funds enough for two green cakes and a dose of Claud François on the juke box singing '*Chaque jour c'est la même chose*'.

That day in Dallas world affairs were receiving quite a jolt.

'What are you going to do next year, Andrea?'

'More growing up, I suppose.'

213